OIL STRIKE

John Wingate

OIL STRIKE

Published by Sapere Books.

20 Windermere Drive, Leeds, England, LS17 7UZ,
United Kingdom

saperebooks.com

ISBN: 978-1-80055-573-0

FOREWORD

It was the Innochervie disaster that finally alerted the Energy Squad, as the nation's Oil Security Force became known. The tensions between the Western democracies and the Russian-sponsored Middle East oil bloc were at a dangerous level. If the enemy had not shown its hand so soon...

Who knows? The final, appalling disaster might have been even worse. God knows, it was terrible enough...

Excerpt from Alan Brodie's official report to the Director of Naval Intelligence.

1

'Read that, Mr Brodie.'

Alan Brodie reached across the desk for the crumpled sheets of paper which the man in the grey suit was pushing towards him. The tally on the door — 'Captain C. R. Otway, RN, Directorate of Naval Intelligence' — had been the only clue to the middle-aged man's identity, and Alan Brodie had been sent down from Ullapool by International Oil to report at ten on this Friday morning to Room 301, Ministry of Defence, in Whitehall. Hubbard, the senior petroleum engineer at head office, had explained nothing: 'I don't know what it's about,' he had said briskly, 'but be there on time. You don't keep the Navy waiting.'

Brodie felt the shrewd eyes watching him. He was about to ask the question that had been worrying him for the past 12 hours, but the captain forestalled his query: 'I'll tell you why we've sent for you, once you've read that,' the officer said quietly, tapping together the tips of his splayed fingers.

The handwriting was in pencil — barely legible, and written in haste. There were several sheets, each ruled in small, criss-crossed squares. The left-hand edges were jagged, as if ripped from a loose-leaved notebook.

I'm about to be murdered... The stark words were scrawled diagonally across the page. Immune now to the embarrassment of the other man's gaze, Brodie read on:

They've followed me all the way from the airport. Sure of it now — in a cab behind. No time. Wrote the other pages during flight — AF 512 from Orly. Trying to make police station. (Another cab's passed — is sitting on our outer wing — they're closing in.) For God's sake, whoever finds this take it to DNI (Navy), MOD IMMEDIATELY — please. I'll be dead before I can fin...

A zigzag scrawl across the bottom of the page — then no more. Glancing across at Otway, Brodie carefully placed the first sheet on the desk.

The other pages were more legible, but obviously written in haste during the flight:

He did it so neatly and quickly that no one except me, who was directly behind him, could have noticed. He barged the queue so brazenly that 1 was nonplussed as I was swept onwards by the press of the crowd — and he's joined us too easily after all the other security checks... A small man, about 5' 2". Dark. Sallow-faced Frenchman, probably (could be a Corsican). Dark blue suit, well-cut. Dapper little guy, sleek black hair, longish. He hasn't looked to the left or right since he gate-crashed the queue. (Amateurs always look guilty, peering round to see if anyone's caught them out.) He merged at once with the jostling crowd queueing to board the aircraft...

The 'elephant trunk' by which we boarded the plane had several corners in it before connecting to the Mercure's door. The trunk was divided into two, down its length, and the guy had nipped in from the left-hand side, at the entry end, by dodging under the partition rail. The stewardess at the security barrier had misdirected us down the wrong division of the trunk, so we all had to about turn and walk to the other half of the trunk for the after door in the plane. The queue began to compress again as we neared the entry door, clutching our boarding passes... If he's a hijacker, I thought, the boarding procedure will show him up, unless he's got hold of a pass. When we reached the stewardess at the door, he was next ahead of me. I waited to see whether he'd got a boarding pass, but I had the 'twitch' and was ready for anything. His turn came at the door. The stewardess paused, her hand outstretched for his pass. He murmured something. The girl's eyes flickered, that was all. No one would have noticed — not unless they'd been watching, as 1 was. It was all so smooth... I followed, and now I'm sitting two seats behind him, on the aisle side.

What is he? Airline security agent — and armed against hijackers? If he is, how can the stewardess be in on the game? More likely he's a hijacker who has fooled the girl... The engines are revving up and we're taxiing out towards the runway. What the hell should I do? I'll look bloody ridiculous, accusing a fellow passenger. I'll stick to watching him. If anything should happen during this flight, if anyone finds this, my notes might help the enquiry...

And on the next page, in large, heavy writing:

Anti-climax — nothing happened! The guy turned at the bottom of the exit gangway and took a quick photo of us descending. He must have been Security. Throughout the flight he spoke to nobody — strange business, the whole thing...

Six sides of the paper were covered. Brodie handed back the sheets across the desk. 'Where did you find these? And why bring me all the way from Ullapool to read them?'

'The police found the corpse at the back of Goodge Street.' The captain was speaking unemotionally. 'They'd slit his throat and hacked off his head. They found the rest of the body stuffed upside down into a dustbin, with the legs hanging out.'

Brodie pictured the sleazy, dark alleys off Tottenham Court Road. They must have cornered their quarry, killed him and left him among the rat-infested garbage.

'The police found his wallet and diary untouched. His murderers did their stuff and quit. It was a paid-up killing.' Otway slid a black and white photograph across the mahogany top. It was from the Metropolitan Police records and, like all official pictures, seemed unnatural. The face jolted Alan Brodie: in semi-profile, the man bore a distinct resemblance to himself — older, perhaps, and the face more lined. A string of reference numbers was printed across the foot of the photograph. 'We know him,' Otway said. 'He's worked for us for years. A good agent. His name was Allan Brody — two "l"s and a "y".'

'Behave naturally, Mr Brodie,' Captain Otway had said when ushering him out of Room 301, 'as if nothing has happened to alter your life.'

Alan Brodie felt the resentment building up inside him as he settled back into his plane seat. He had plenty of time now in which to subdue the turmoil of his thoughts.

As if nothing had happened to alter your life... The man was a nutter — and now he, Alan, was trapped by the Official Secrets Act. And not only that, as Otway pointed out: he now had specific duties to carry out for the MOD, under the authority it wielded through the Naval Discipline Act. He'd been a fool to join the RNR — and just when life had begun to run smoothly...

'Keep your eyes open and report anything suspicious to me, Brodie. You're in a difficult position.'

'What d'you mean?'

'As you must have guessed, we're up against immense forces: the power of limitless money. In unscrupulous hands, this weapon can destroy or subvert anyone, at any time. We're on to an organization the like of which we've never met before...'

Otway's words were still fresh in Alan's mind. The precision of the captain's summary had been made more impressive by the calm matter-of-factness with which he had spoken: 'So far, we know that a faceless organization of Middle East powers has been set up to fight the Western democracies in everything short of hot war. There's no need to spell out who's behind the organization ... but we're almost certain they've set up a group to plan fresh atrocities when the situation so demands. Ruthlessness and violence are their weapons — and with limitless funds they can afford the best equipment. This force is called their Action Division. We reckon we know who commands it.' Otway had turned to gaze out of the window at the traffic streaming along the embankment. The Thames swirled gently downstream. Pigeons were fluttering amongst the thinning leaves of the plane trees. 'It's an ugly world.' He turned suddenly. 'You'd better watch out. If their money is used to assassinate at will, you don't think they'll risk any mistakes, do you?'

'How d'you mean?'

'They've got agents everywhere — and certainly in the Ullapool area. They'll know by now that there's another Allan Brody. They might have rubbed out the wrong man...'

Alan's eyes strayed to his window in the BAC One-Eleven. The green fields of Oxfordshire were gliding beneath him, far below. Puffs of white cloud sailed by, and a thousand feet lower to the westward a silver bullet slipped past — another jet, on opposite course... An hour now to Edinburgh and there he'd be picked up by International's helicopter which made the daily circuit between Ullapool and the capital.

It was difficult to believe that there was another world, monstrous and evil, prepared to destroy anyone who should obstruct its policy ... and that these sinister forces were now impinging on his own life.

'Would you like a drink, sir?' a soft voice asked. The Caledonian stewardess was smiling down at him, her tartan glengarry perched upon soft, blonde hair.

'Scotch and water, please.'

Oil man, she thought. Two out of three were in oil these days — a regular bus-run the service was becoming. And now that Ullapool, on the west coast, was suffering the fate of Aberdeen, there was twice as much work for the airlines. She emptied the miniature and held out the glass. He smiled at her as he took it. His sandy hair and eyebrows, freckled forehead and blue eyes, probably meant he was from the east coast, she reckoned — he seemed about 28, a good-looker in a rugged way. Ambitious and stubborn probably, with that tight mouth — she could get to know him, if it was not for her impossible way of life. Six foot plus, probably, when he was on his feet ... and broad-shouldered — definitely a go-getter...

'Thanks — *Slainte-a-va*... Here's to Scotland — and to her oil.'

She laughed and passed on down the aisle.

'Drink, sir?' He heard her voice repeating the invitation, behind him now, as she continued ministering to her passengers. She had a good figure under that unflattering uniform. He grinned to himself. Thank God he was still fancy free — there was little talent in Innochervie, except for that Macgregor girl. Sheena, they called her, though in Gaelic the name was Sine. A pity she was already booked.

The One-Eleven had reached its ceiling now. The foothills of the Lake District were sliding into view, their slopes red with autumn bracken. Incredible, the contrast of this beautiful scenery and the peace of country life with — he shut his eyes to try and extinguish the nightmare images that flashed before them. After showing him the photograph of the murdered

Brody, Otway had moved to another floor in the rabbit warren that was MOD. He had locked the door and then projected slides of the Brody dossier. Even now, Alan could hear that cool, dispassionate voice listing the details of the agent's career, posing the queries of the murdered man's identity, of why he was liquidated.

Allan Brody, American naval architect and designer — a top man in the US oil world. What was he doing after leaving the sheiks in the Gulf? Why was he reported to be in Gdynia, in Hamburg, and then in Rotterdam? 'Ships were his world,' Otway had said. 'He discovered something and was on his way to tell us...' Otway was unlikely to leak more than was necessary to an oilman, a young scientist still attending his RNR annual drills. It was a strange coincidence that there were two Alan Brodies in the oil world, even if their names were spelt differently. The opposition *must* have been after the dead man... Why should they need to eliminate himself, Alan Brodie, a run-of-the-mill physics graduate? Admittedly, he was a useful unit in International Oil: he'd become a grade 1 professional diver (learnt in the Navy) and he was in on the research team which was pioneering the largest and most advanced steel production platform yet to be built, *Sulisker One*. But that didn't make him a target for the enemy in this oil war — or did it? 'They will leave nothing to chance,' Otway had said, 'if they think they've boobed.'

Since the West's military threat to move in on the Middle East oilfields, the international temperature had soared. Now that Britain was becoming independent of Middle East oil, and particularly since International were exploring the potentially rich *Sulisker* field, tension was near breaking point.

'Fasten your seatbelts, please. We're making our approach and we'll be landing shortly at Edinburgh. Captain Munro and his crew hope that you have enjoyed the trip...'

Alan Brodie felt the jolt as the jets eased their power; then sensed the loss of height as the One-Eleven began its descent. There was the grey city, tucked into Arthur's Seat. The land of his fathers, but what a different country now, with its wealth and new-found political power.

Alan was not looking forward to meeting the senior petroleum engineer again — Hubbard was an awkward man with whom he never felt at ease. He was nearing retirement and felt jealous of his younger assistant. The north-western fields would be exploited by the new generation, the up-and-coming men whom Alan Brodie represented. Hubbard would be furious if Alan tried to explain his MOD visit without divulging Otway's confidences.

As Alan passed through the exit barrier, he automatically glanced at the messages board. At the head of the list, marked 'urgent', was his name. The phone boxes were all occupied and it was ten minutes before he could get through to Ullapool.

Hubbard rang off impatiently. He was having to cut short his Sunday golf. He'd be waiting in his office, which he'd opened up specially.

The helicopter unloaded its sole passenger onto Ullapool's new heliport at the edge of the town. The natives had fiercely resisted the advent of the choppers which inevitably were disturbing the centre of the port, but the taxi companies were thriving. Hubbard was staring out of his window at International's house flag, clasped hands on a blue ground, which was flapping in the wind alongside the St Andrew's cross. He turned impatiently as Alan entered.

'Dunno what you've been up to, Brodie, but you couldn't have been away at a worse moment...' The senior petroleum engineer was scowling resentfully.

'What's up?'

Hubbard was clearly too involved in his own problems to fuss about the London visit. '*Explorer*'s going through the last stage more quickly than they thought. They want you up there right away.'

'Strike?' Alan felt his pulse quicken. After all these months of doubt, after that tremendous gamble with millions of pounds sterling, the geologists could be right after all — and International were going to be the first there...

'Why are you looking so pleased? You know damn well they've raised our hopes before.' Then Hubbard added grudgingly, 'But the core samples are good.'

Alan turned to go. 'Any hopes of transport?'

'No. Choppers are fully committed and the weather's fouling up. Charter someone at Innochervie.'

Alan turned on his heel. Thank God for that — action at last. If there was no other way to reach the rig, he'd bum a lift in a supply boat.

2

Alan had forgotten Hubbard's boorishness by the time the chopper had lifted him across Loch Assynt. With the rotors flashing above them in the sunlight, Wester Ross became a fairyland on this clear autumn day. Ben More soared to the eastward and then the lochs began to sparkle beneath them. The vivid colours made even a hard-bitten oilman glance twice. Western Scotland stretched out before them, with North Minch close on their port hand, where the white line of the Atlantic swell curled lazily against the jagged coastline. The leaden greens of late summer were giving way to the rust and ochre of autumn. Then, to port and about ten miles distant, he recognized the landmarks of Innochervie.

He had always liked this sleepy little fishing port — at least, what was left of it, after the final governmental decision resulting upon the second Enquiry. Even now, with the vast complex of the West Coast Construction Company and Cul Mor Services swallowing up the northern shore of Innoch Loch and Glendhu Bay, he felt he was arriving home, after leaving the hideous mess that Ullapool now was.

When, two years ago, the exploration companies had been optimistic that there was oil on the continental shelf to the north-westward, the government had at last learned that red tape had to be eliminated if Britain was to benefit from the oil bonanza. Too many platform contracts had been lost to the Norwegians and French because of strangulation by Whitehall bureaucracy. Even the civil servants had woken up. The pendulum had swung too viciously, too fast, in Alan's opinion, towards what passed for progress. A motorway to Ullapool, new docks, vast servicing areas spreading like a cancer along the shores of Loch Broom, all these had metamorphosed the little fishing port into an ugly, modern industrial town. Aberdeen was vast enough to absorb the new oil industry, but Ullapool was being swamped. Alan had been glad to leave the place, and now, looking down again, he could see the arterial roads clawing their way across the slopes of the mountains, then dipping into valleys and surging across flying bridges over the moors to Innochervie. Nothing could withstand the rapid onrush of the motorways. It was not surprising that the local community was split down the middle: conservationists versus progressives. Alan could sympathize with the conservationists, in spite of his job as International's yard overseer on *Sulisker One*. 'Progress' was destroying Innochervie's ancient way of life. Whether the changes could be termed 'progress' was a debatable question.

'Hold tight,' the pilot bawled above the noise of the rotor blades. 'Going in.' The chopper, piloted by the 'cowboy' of the private helicopter hire company, swooped across the crests of the seaward hills. The sapphire sea-loch opened up before them and there lay the diminutive port, nestling under the hills and protected from the westward by its crescent-shaped peninsula. The old crofts were sprinkled sparsely across the hillsides. Alan could see the white boxes which were the buildings for the construction workers; the inner fishing harbour with its new co-operative fish dock; and the monstrous rearing-towers, pointing like crimson missiles into the sky. All these landmarks were familiar to him now. West Coast's yard, with the gigantic scale of its steel structure, did not seem too incongruous when set against those forbidding mountains and the hills which plunged sheer into Loch

17

Innoch. The chopper swooped, stood on its nose and bumped to the ground.

'Thanks, Jim.'

'Okay, Alan. See you...'

The pilot was off again, his helicopter twirling into the sky as soon as Brodie was clear of its rotor. The battered Ford Escort was waiting for him and, five minutes later, he was threading his way past lorries meeting the trawlers' morning catch. Alan strode up the steps of West Coast's administrative block, in which International hired an office overlooking the 50-acre complex of *Sulisker One*'s construction. He flung open his office door and dropped his bag in the corner. Stuffing his hands in his pockets, he stared through the window at the colossus for whose progress he was responsible to International. He was critically absorbing the progress made during his absence when the sun vanished and a rain squall spattered against the glass. He glanced at the clock on the wall: a quarter to ten — he'd got enough time for a quick look round before nipping down to the harbour for a lift off to *Explorer*. He grabbed his hard-hat and raincoat from the hook on the back of the door, shoved on his boots and hurried out into the rain. Before him, across the mud, the steel monsters reared up gaunt and red against the lowering clouds sweeping in across Innoch Head.

As he squelched his way through the morass, his thoughts returned again and again to the 'weather window', that short period next year, between June and mid-August, when *Sulisker One* must be in position for sinking onto the seabed. The human element was the deciding factor, and the welders held the key. They could make or break the project, and by the way things were going they seemed intent on destroying it. There was unrest in the yard, and no one knew for certain the source of the subversion. Everyone pointed at the communists, but now, after his meeting with Captain Otway, Alan was having second thoughts.

The main stumbling block was communication. Not only did management have a physical problem of rapidly contacting others by phone or by walkie-talkie, but it was also difficult to inculcate new ideas and leadership. In this sprawling complex, with more than 800 men dispersed throughout the yard, inside and outside those huge jackets, it seemed impossible for management to convince the manual workers that the man at the top was as deeply involved as the lowest paid member of the workforce.

The nearest of the four jacket legs, each 480 feet long and 24 feet in diameter, lay horizontally in its semi-circular crutches. The lower half had been jacked up and welded together since he'd been away. Working to a tolerance of an eighth of an inch, with these masses of immense proportions, involved brilliant engineering, particularly when sections arrived from a number of countries. Parts of this jacket had been constructed in Holland, Belgium and France — and now all the sections had been assembled and welded together. The fourth leg was almost completed. The yard had just finished the deck truss of the sea platform — and that comprised over 3000 tons of steelwork.

'Is this the fourth leg, mate?'

Alan turned. A GPO engineer, wearing his yellow hard hat, was huddled in his oilskins, his head turned from the driving rain as he shouted into the wind. He was in a hurry on this Sunday morning and sounded bloody-minded. A trench digger was standing by, its engine ticking over, while the driver, waiting for orders, grinned sardonically at the irritable telephone engineer.

'It's too big to miss — it's opposite us, over there.' Alan pointed to the gigantic cylinders lying horizontally beneath their rearing-towers.

'Thanks, mate. It's an 'orrible day, but the bastards'll only let us in here on Sundays.' The man trudged towards the yellow van that was waiting for him. It skidded off and disappeared in the direction of one of the rearing-towers. Communications at last. Until now, an ex-Army landline had been used to connect the job manager's site office to the admin block. The wire was constantly being cut, so permanent telephone communications had recently been ordered. The GPO worked surprisingly quickly these days.

Alan plodded through the mud, past the jackets and around the seven rearing-towers, each of them 15 feet higher than St Paul's cathedral. The jacket would slide, via the cradles which were already constructed, onto the ways. The huge steel edifice would then be floated out into the bay.

He glanced at his watch, which was misting up in this damp — 10.35. He'd better get a move on or he'd miss Iain Macgregor, who usually sailed on Sunday mornings. Brodie clamped the raincoat about him as the rain slashed into his face. In the distance he glimpsed the oilskinned telephone engineers setting up their U-shaped shelter. The yellow digger was bogging down as it trundled along the perimeter line. Poor sods, having to work on a Sunday in this weather — at least someone had a sense of urgency.

He hurried back to his office, his morale low as he contemplated again the chance of installing the platform on site in time. Getting it out there would be hazardous in itself — the 70 miles to Sulisker from Innochervie was an exposed passage for such an unwieldy tow. He grabbed his bag and sou'wester and battled out against the wind. He was soaking wet already, so he might as well walk to the fish dock. With luck, he'd catch *Wanklyn*. Macgregor was a thruster and proud of his new supply ship. He'd picked up the job through merit and, probably, because of his support in the village for the 'pros'. There was little logic in Cul Mor Services appointing to their expensive new vessels local skippers whose hearts were not in their jobs. The fish dock, nestling under the lee of the green-turfed promontory, came into view. The trawlers, moored together in their trots, took up the length of the quay. Their crews were swilling down after the morning's landings and the orange buoys, slung vertically in the rigging, were glistening in the rain.

The three supply boats kept themselves aloof, at the far end of the jetty. There was overt war in the village now — the 'antis' versus the 'pros'. One hell of a tragedy, Alan thought, when conservationists, if only they would compromise a trifle, could produce a working agreement with the oil industry, for the benefit of the whole community in the port.

'Morning.' Instinctively he uttered a welcome as a gaunt figure strode past him from out of the rain, a woman at its side. Alan recognized the Macgregor parents, a native family now divided by the schism of fundamental loyalties. The husband was a violent 'anti': a fisherman of the old school, he was convinced that the oilmen would wreck the fishing grounds. All his life he'd fished off Rona and the decision of the final tribunal had embittered him to near insanity. Alan had listened to his tirade at one of the many meetings. Donald Macgregor was a fighter. There was no response from the couple as they swept by, huddled against the wet. Alan felt the chill of rejection. *Sod 'em*, he thought. *Nothing will ever satisfy them.*

'Hi, Alan.' The greeting forced him to peer upwards from beneath his sou'wester. It was the Macgregor daughter, Sheena. In her shapeless oilskins, it was difficult to recognize her, but the oval of her face, glistening in the rain, was cheering in these foul conditions. They'd met at the local dance which West Coast had organized in an attempt at uniting the village. The evening had been a disaster, the 'foreigners' making off with the local talent. Alan had met Sheena there, his only contact so far with the world of women since he'd been on the west coast. Her mother and father had been sitting on chairs at the edge of the floor in the village hall. Mrs Macgregor's disapproval of her daughter's behaviour was only too evident by the shocked contempt which had smouldered from behind her steel-rimmed spectacles.

'Morning, Miss Macgregor,' Alan shouted. 'Off to kirk?'

'Aye, Mr Brodie. You coming with us?'

Alan smiled. Her voice was music, the accent of Wester Ross, but he was in a hurry, off to Sulisker. He could think of better ways of observing Sunday than by listening to the Reverend James Maclaren taunting his subjugated flock.

'I'm looking for your brother,' Alan said. 'I'm hoping he'll give me a lift out to the rig.'

'You'll catch him if you get a move on,' she sang out. 'See you. I must catch up with my Dad.' She hastened after the two figures disappearing in the rain. The dismal sound of the kirk's bell floated down on the wind.

The Sabbath took precedence for three-quarters of the Macgregor family. Iain, the go-getter, was the outcast, but Alan felt sympathy for the daughter whose loyalties must have been sorely stretched. Sheena acted as agent and secretary for her brother. If she finished her paperwork, she would put to sea with him and take her watch with the best of them.

'Poor kid,' Alan spoke to himself. 'Stuck between the devil and the deep blue sea. At heart, I'll bet, she's on her brother's side, but she daren't show it.'

A ship's hooter blared from the far quay. He glimpsed a seaman singling up at *Wanklyn*'s stern. Alan broke into a run, waved his arms and yelled above the wind.

3

'We will now sing hymn number…'

Donald Macgregor's mind wandered when he regarded that sanctimonious humbug, Lewin Scathlin, walking to the steps below the pulpit to lead the hymn singing. Half the village knew he spent Monday evenings, when his wife was at bible class, with Dolly Tusker, the 60-year-old widow who ran the post office-cum-village stores.

'Wake up, Dad. It's 397.'

Sheena, his beloved daughter, was nudging his elbow and pointing to her open hymn book. Charles Wesley's hymn it was, his words embarrassingly appropriate for Innochervie at this moment:

'Help us to help each other, Lord,
Each other's cross to bear,
Let each his friendly aid afford
And feel his brother's care.'

And that hypocrite up there, pale-faced and aesthetic in his rimless glasses as he led the singing — what a travesty, when Innochervie was split asunder…

'Up into Thee, our living hand,
Let us in all things grow…'

The words were beyond Donald's comprehension. The Reverend James Maclaren was scowling down at them from his podium, his black figure menacing as he brooded upon the sinners below.

Donald's memories of the first Enquiry were vague, but he could never forget the second. Enough time had now elapsed for opposing opinions in Innochervie to crystallize. Over eighteen months had slipped by since Maclaren had convened the first conservationist meeting in the village hall. Dougal Gordon, the intelligent but meek headmaster of the infants' school at Begga Brig, was elected chairman of the Save Innochervie Association. The Reverend James Maclaren, as befitted his dignity, was invited to become president but, to put fire in the belly of the 'antis', Sim McIver was unanimously dubbed secretary of the association. Sim, in his early thirties, was the estate ranger, and lived by himself on Hoyea, the islet at the entrance to Loch Madach. He was the laird's head keeper and responsible for the deer and the fishing. He was part of the bleak countryside and there was no one in the district who knew this wild region better.

McIver lived for his native Wester Ross, which was why the Scottish Nationalists had battened on to him. In his croft in Hoyea, accessible on foot only at low tide, Sim had become a recluse, keeping his own counsel until the port was threatened by the oilmen. After the decision of the second Enquiry had stunned Innochervie, the red sails of Sim's yawl could often be seen dipping across Hoyea Bay as he sailed towards the landing on the north shore of Madach Point. He would be about his business of rallying the crofters and fishermen to resist the impending invasion of their homeland. But they all realized now that he had started too late. Even the redoubtable Sheila Burns, eldest of the three sisters running the Errabeg Hotel on the crest of the hill, admitted as much. She was Sim's organizational right hand and a capable, formidable woman. Too little resistance, not organized in time...

Donald now sat down. Scathlin was returning to his pew, his duty done as the hymn ended.

'...but, brethren, it is not too late...' The minister's rhetoric was the more forbidding as he intoned in broad Glaswegian:

'…it is not too late to repent of our failings in attending the house of God. Let us ask for the forgiveness of God for not attending the bible study meeting held in the house of our sister, Mrs Macintosh, last Monday. May they be forgiven and may their omissions be put right in the week to come…'

Donald Macgregor winced in his pew. The damning flood poured from the lips of the forbidding figure leaning across the rail of the podium. His red face was staring down at them, reproach and disappointment in the unnaturally large eyes peering from behind the thick lenses. He'd ramble on for a full half hour yet.

Macgregor was uneasy. The pattern of his settled life had been disturbed by the oil boom. The swift mobilization of the forces of so-called progress had swept all before it. He thought of motorways curling through the glens from Ullapool; the flying bridge that now spanned Kylesku; the roar of the juggernauts as they lumbered with their loads of steel and concrete through the mountains and along the loch shores, befouling the clean, sweet air of Wester Ross; last, and worst of all for him, the rape of Innochervie which had been his family's home since the Vikings drove the Celts westward and across the North Channel.

Like so many of the men of the Western Isles, Donald had served as a T-124 man throughout World War II. As a young fisherman, the life in an armed trawler of the Royal Navy had come naturally to him. He'd received a flesh wound at Dunkirk when bringing off the troops, but apart from offshore patrols in the Channel for two years, he had done nothing very significant during that period. He had longed to return home to his native Wester Ross, the Isles and Innochervie. To be plunging into the seas and heading for Sulisker Bank was his continuous dream. But that was years ago — and Donald sighed so deeply that his Sheena, his black-eyed witch of a daughter, dug her elbow into his waist. 'Shush, Dad.'

The formidable Maclaren was in spate now. Donald tried to ease the discomfort of his pinewood pew: this was one of the rare moments during the week which he had to himself. He'd married Cornyn Moragh five years after the war, as soon as he could support himself by his fishing. She'd been 28, he 31. The Moraghs, Cornyn's family, came from down the glen and were staunch Free Church, so that Cornyn, after the arrival of the children, was soon running her family with a strictness alien to Donald. He knew he would be in trouble when he returned home this morning, for she was incensed at having to cook dinner for Iain before he sailed.

The lines softened in Donald's rugged face as he glanced down at his last-born. What happiness this dark-haired, slim girl had given him. She was a true Macgregor: easy-going, eager for life, a dreamer, like himself — unlike Iain, four years older, who was ambitious and determined. Taking after his mother, Iain still fought fiercely with his sister, but they were too fond of each other ever to 'part brass rags', as they used to say in the Navy.

'...and when the day of judgement comes, my brothers, what shall we say then...?'

Ridiculous fool — what did he know of the stuff of life? What did Maclaren know of the agonized longings in men and women, of despair, of joy, or even of loving his neighbour? What experience had he had of the winds and the seas? He'd never been out with the fishermen, not once in his sanctimonious life. The fish dock was as far as he ever reached. He was happier skirmishing against his real foe, his Presbyterian opposite numbers. Maclaren's beliefs were a travesty of Jesus's teaching, Donald was beginning to realize, as he watched the serpent eyes mesmerizing their captive congregation — but why in the name of God had these tribulations hit Innochervie and, more relevantly, split wide his own family?

Cornyn and Iain had immediately taken up the sword on behalf of the development of the port. 'Let 'em come,' Iain had said after the second enquiry in September, a year and a half ago. 'There'll be work for the school-leavers. The village will live again, instead of dying on its feet as it is now.'

'Aye, Father, the bairn's right,' his wife had spoken up. 'There's no future for us if the young ones have to leave home for places such as Glasgow. You'll know as I do, man, they never come back and the city's just a sewer. There'll be work enough here and in Ullapool, if they find the oil out there...' She had nodded her neat greying head towards the seaway that ran to the northwards, to Sulisker, Iceland and the Arctic. The women of Innochervie always referred to their enemy as 'out there'. It was that grey, restless ocean eternally beating upon the rocks of Innoch Head and Seal that ate into the souls of the womenfolk — the sea that for generations had claimed the allegiance of Innochervie men, the call of which they could no more resist than the attraction of women. And it was the sea that now was posing a fundamental problem for Donald Macgregor.

When West Coast Construction had finally arrived and taken over Glengrudie Bay to build its gigantic steel production platform, the men of Innochervie were forced to decide where their future lay — they could either continue fishing with their inshore boats, or throw in their lot with future development, as their Iain had done. But the lad was ambitious and meant to make something of his life. He'd only recently married, so he had not yet much to lose. If ever he was slung out of his present job as skipper of *Wanklyn*, Iain was convinced that the arrival of the new industry which was devouring Ullapool and Innochervie was a godsend, and the only way to save this remote region of Scotland — but, from what, Donald wondered?

At first, Donald had been attracted neither to one side nor the other. He preferred to be left alone with his fishing, to drink his dram and to dream his dreams. Then they had arrived, the oilmen from across the borders. They swarmed first into Ullapool but soon overflowed to Innochervie. At the beginning there was just a trickle of Sassenachs: the English were at least the recognizable foe. Traditionally, they were all out for what they could exploit in Scotland, but this was nothing new for the natives. But the real shock was caused by the speed of the foreigners' influx — the nasal twang of the Americans, the incomprehensible Dutch, the chatter of the Balkan people, the harsh syllables of the Spanish and Portuguese, the numerous languages of the Middle Easterners, the lilt of the Irish and the musical fluency of the French. To house this invasion, those dual-purpose prefabricated excrescences had been thrown up. Though they would become holiday homes if the oil industry failed, to Donald they were suppurating wounds fouling his beloved hills. It was not that he disliked humanity. But he was bitterly resentful because his own croft had been compulsorily purchased, at a good price, admittedly, to make way for those lines of temporary houses. Money was no compensation for the loss of a home in which Macgregors had lived for over a 100 years.

He and Cornyn could never adjust to living cheek to jowl with their neighbours. Although, in contrast to his croft, the houses were equipped with all the modern conveniences and the rents were absurdly high for the local people, a ransom that only the oilmen could pay. The people of Innochervie could do without the artificial comforts of modern living. The grievance so bitterly felt by the people of Innochervie was that they had been offered no choice. For centuries, solitude was the weft of their existence. The granite crofts had huddled together for mutual protection, but each dwelling, each croft, was a separate family entity. Nowadays, if a man did not choose to live in some kind of socialist commune he was branded an outcast and, by inference, dubbed a snob. He was sick to the back teeth with this new society. He yearned for the past which he could understand, when a man either worked or starved, tried to lead a moral life or was damned ... but still enjoyed a genuine liberty.

'We shall now sing hymn number 479, brothers,' the minister announced.

'Commit thou all they griefs
And ways into His hands,
Take His sure truths and tender care
Who heaven and earth commands.
Who points the clouds their course,
Whom winds and seas obey.'

Lewin Scathlin was taking up his place again beneath the judgement seat. The lenses of his spectacles gleamed as he peered in the gloom at the hymn book extended firmly before him. The flat treble of Mother Gordon, poor Dougal's formidable aunt, broke into song before Lewin could strike his tuning fork. The conflict had begun. Neither would compromise with the other for the remainder of the hymn — Mother Gordon usually won, being half a bar ahead. Scathlin always seethed at the indignity, but he never surrendered.

'And I shan't give up my *Seamew.*'

'Shush, Dad.'

He was muttering to himself as he heard Sheena's clear soprano rise beside him. Her thoughts were far away, he'd bet, with Sim, that red-haired scoundrel — but he, Donald Macgregor, would finish adapting *Seamew*, whatever else might happen. He could see her now, propped up on her shores on the sea-washed turf at the water's edge of the inlet in the lee of Seal.

He had bought the wooden hull in 1962 for fifty quid. Angus was relieved to be rid of her. She had been built some time before the First World War. Her original fastenings had been of iron nails dipped in pitch, and when these became sick in the 1950s, Angus had refastened her throughout with galvanized ones. Donald had bought her because, secretly, he could not bear to see her broken up — after all, he could always use her as a store. With the heavy demand for auxiliary vessels as stand-by boats for the oil rigs, he was busily refitting her. He could fleece the oil tycoons — or he might even use her himself, if the fishing was not killed. Among the gaunt poles, from the heads of which the nets of Innochervie's fishing fleet once hung, *Seamew* lay in solitary state, rugged, ugly, but once more purposeful. Her broad bottom was shining with black pitch; more and more of the new pitch-pine boards grew daily pink with primer, as Donald built up her bows for the seas she would encounter off the Butt. Sim had scrounged him some seasoned oak, so Donald had cut back the rot at the heads of *Seamew*'s deck frames. Then he scarfed lengths of Sim's timber to them, so that *Seamew*, with her heightened freeboard for'd, was almost ready for sea. With her Gardner and its massive flywheel, *Seamew* would be as reliable as most, but distinctly slower. She was no oil painting, but after he'd slapped on some of that emerald green enamel and spent a few bob on gold-leafing her name, carved on each bow, he could be proud of her when he launched her on the next equinoctials… Suddenly Sheena was nudging him and he followed her glance to the northern aisle.

Sheena heard Sim McIver first, barging against the creaking door of the porch. She could see that he was drunk, his flaming hair wild and bedraggled from the rain. Sim staggered up the aisle, glared at the Reverend James Maclaren who was about to bless his flock, and collapsed into the pew ahead of Mother Gordon. He leaned forward, slung his arms across the pew front and bowed his huge head. Sheena could see his lips working but, even in the shocked silence, no sound came from him.

The minister, for the first time in his sixty-two years, was nonplussed — and Sheena saw the smirk on her father's face. In the long silence that followed, only the slashing of the squall against the clear glass windows reminded his congregation that they were earthbound mortals. What had caused their black sheep to return to grace? Poor Sim must be in real trouble.

'Let us thank God that he has seen fit to bring repentance unto sinners,' Maclaren boomed. The podgy hand was raised in blessing and then, as Sheena bowed her head, she heard men's cheers floating up from the fish dock. As soon as it was decent to do so, she started to follow her father with the hurriedly departing congregation. The door creaked. The noise of laughing, shouting men filled the emptying kirk and, in an instant, everyone was chattering in the porch. Sheena stood back and waited until the last parishioner had pushed his way past her. She crossed the aisle and silently eased herself into the pew beside Sim. Slipping her arm about his heaving shoulders, she pulled him gently against her tweed coat.

4

Sunday, 10 October, 5.10 a.m. John Tregonnel stretched his tired frame: next December he would be forty-one, and that was old for an oilman. He watched Joe Wadham, his senior tool pusher of the second shift. With slick competence acquired from four years' experience, he was operating the drilling controls for the final stretch to the possible pay zone. Tregonnel barely heard the roar of the machinery, the clatter of the chain, the familiar cacophony that was part of life on board a semi-submersible rig. He had enjoyed five hours' sleep, the first lie-in he'd had for over a fortnight. When nearing the final breakthrough, all his skill and knowledge were required to watch over these final yards of drilling. He'd known many Sundays like this, when even the forces of nature seemed to decide to ease up for this one day in the week. The sea was a calm, undulating expanse of steely grey. A flock of fulmar flapped across the shaft of light reflecting from the leaden clouds, while the sun climbed from below the horizon.

'How's it going?' he yelled across the working deck.

'Great. What are our chances today, d'you reckon, John?'

Tregonnel shook his head, a sardonic smile on his face — he was too old a hand to commit himself. 'One in seven chance of success — you know that, Joe.'

'We've used five of 'em — I've a feeling in my water we'll strike this time.'

John Tregonnel moved over to the rail running along the side of the platform. Fifty feet below him the sea rose and fell peacefully against the vast legs of *Explorer*. Sixty feet below the surface, the submerged ballast tanks supported the semi-submersible. By flooding or pumping on them, in the same way as a submarine's trim and buoyancy were controlled, the semi-submersible could be raised or lowered in the water.

International had contracted Flanagans to explore the Sulisker field and to find the oil, so this was an important day for Tregonnel, the contractor's head tool pusher. He was responsible to them for the efficient and safe operation of *Explorer*, their semi-submersible which had seen better days. He also had to decide when to summon International's big boys, always difficult to assess because of the accommodation problems posed by this gently heaving monster. Petroleum engineers felt queasy if there was movement: *Explorer* shifted only about four or five degrees in heavy weather, though she might be heaving considerably. These were the conditions last week, and twice he'd been forced to operate the button to disconnect the ball joint — the heave was exceeding the limits of the trombone joint. The whole string then hung free on the Rucker system, so everything was safe — but he was relieved that he had not shouted for the scientists last week. He crossed to the other side to watch the shift working around the rotary table.

Hour after hour, night after day, for five months now since *Explorer* had begun drilling Sulisker, the shifts had been working flat out. They had been lucky: only 30 per cent downtime during these hurricane-force gales at the end of April. God, but it could blow up here — the lows came swinging in from the Atlantic, one after the other, in endless succession. The depressions seemed to pass north-west of Iceland but a few, worse than the others, would split and come belting across Sulisker. He couldn't forget that last terrible storm — no one knew what force the wind had reached, because the anemometer had carried away. He'd been worried when numbers three and four anchor cables parted, because *Explorer* began yawing on her axis and dragging. Thank God the wind was south-westerly, or the seas would have piled her up on North Rona if the storm had veered to the northward. But the Butt of Lewis never seemed far away — only 28 miles due south.

He left the rail, the incessant racket of the draw-works engines too much for his nerves. He'd snatch a few minutes of quiet before the day caught up with him. He strolled to the chopper deck and felt the breeze on his face where the updraught swept across the lip of the pad.

He'd been out here long enough. He'd told head office he'd stay on for another ten days, because he felt sure he'd be through the crust any day now. He wanted to be here for three reasons: he reckoned they might drill through at any moment; he was having trouble with this shift; and Margaret was down in Padstow with her old Mum, so there was little point in his taking leave if his wife was away from home.

The sun, just appearing over the eastern horizon, was already starting to warm up the new day, even in this latitude. International was the first company to explore this area and, from log readings during the last three weeks, their geologists hoped they could be right with their first hunch. 'Let 'em get on with it in the North Sea,' the MD had said, 'and leave the west coast to us. The continental shelf is large enough.'

Explorer's position had been fixed by satellite navigation to within 25 yards. The supply ship had laid out in a star pattern her eight anchors, which were then buoyed with flashing red lights for night use. Then it was up to him, John Tregonnel — but he wished now that he had not signed on with Flanagans. Not only was *Explorer* obsolete by modern standards, but International's management were accepting Flanagans' practice of cutting corners and turning a blind eye to government safety regulations and standards. Tregonnel had stood up, as far as he could, to the North-Western drilling superintendent, but his bread and butter depended upon obeying orders. Someone at the top must have deceived the UK Offshore Committee and the Department of Energy, who set the standards, because these practices would not have been permitted in the North Sea. That was why Flanagans paid *Explorer*'s head tool pusher £10,000 a year — to do what he was told.

His main worry was the abysmal quality of the gang in the first shift. Pisces, the Anglo-Dutch giant, could afford to pay British Airways to lift out by helicopter the weekly shift who worked a one-week-on, one-week-off routine. This expense was beyond International, who could relieve their shift only once every fortnight by contacting a helicopter company which had recently set up in Ullapool.

Meldrum, tool pusher of the first shift, was a good man, but he was certainly lumbered with a poor lot under him. There was hardly a reliable hand among his 35 men — they needed continuous supervision, so much so that Tregonnel had been forced to order Meldrum below to catch up on sleep because he was clapped out — and in this job you couldn't afford mistakes. Flanagans did not pay enough, and the east coast was attracting the better roustabouts. So, thanks to the contractors, he was forced to accept the dregs of the industry. If only Flanagans would subcontract for their hands to the Continental Shelf Drilling Company, *Explorer* would be efficiently operated. Instead of having to accept this cosmopolitan mess of Portuguese, Belgians, Yugoslavs, Moroccans, Spaniards and reject Americans, John could then enjoy the luxury of competent men, trained by CSDC, who specialized in providing efficient manpower for drilling rigs.

He spat over the side. He was looking forward to the second shift returning on Thursday.

A tool pusher must know what he was doing out here, when handling £10,000,000 worth of gear. First, a hole had to be drilled in the seabed which, at Sulisker, was at a depth of 380 feet. In this sandy, gravelly bottom, the large bit had run into no trouble. At 150 feet down in the crust, they shored and cemented the line of steel piping around the 36-inch diameter hole. The base plate was clapped on, from which the wires ran back up to the rig, so that he could connect up the marine riser. Then they had fitted the massive 40-ton blow-out preventer and the master-gate, with its battery of self-actuating, remotely controlled valves. If the well went wild, the preventer was their main safeguard, and it could shut down the well instantaneously from the drilling control console. By closing around the annulus inside the well, the preventer could control these immense geopressures until the well could be brought back under control. Tregonnel was always alert for the first indications of a blow-out — a sudden quickening of the drilling, reduction of pressures, bubbles in the mud — all these were warnings. A blow-out could destroy the rig and all on board it in a sudden, blazing inferno … and thoughts about how to cope with this catastrophe were always at the back of Tregonnel's mind. Only good drilling practice could control these problems by ensuring that they never arose.

From 150 feet onwards, down to their present depth of 12,000 feet below the ocean floor, had been tough and needed dogged perseverance. Bit after bit had been changed and the entire drill string had to be pulled from the well, broken down into 90-foot lengths and stacked in the derrick. Changing the bit was the easy part. Now everything had to return down the well — 90-foot length by 90-foot length ('tripping', it was called) — before drilling could begin.

From the top of the preventer, the giant marine riser ran back to a point under the rotary table on the derrick floor. All the drilling operations took place inside this larger pipe which was held in tension against the rise and fall of the sea by the Rucker system.

John squinted at the derrick head above him. From the crown block supporting the weight of the entire drill string, the massive wires hung down to carry the complex of travelling block, swivel, kelly and mud hose. International were gamblers enough to accept Flanagans' proposal to start production with *Explorer*, instead of operating with a traditional production platform. It would be an economical solution for International, but hazardous. It was rumoured that a North Sea company had got away with it, but it was not worth the risk in the long run. The real problems were the weather and the hazard of fire from spillages. Head tool pushers accepted the risks — blowouts were rare, but if *Explorer* suffered such a disaster while in production, and the rig was not properly moored, what then? He switched off his imagination, appalled at the nightmare which could so easily become reality.

The oil industry was ultra-conservative. It was dealing with elemental forces, so it moved forward only step by tried step. The American, Drake, struck oil at 69-and-a-half feet and that was the beginning of the modern oil-rush, but as far back as 4,000 BC, John thought it was, bitumen had been used by the Persians. The material had been used in building the tower of Babel; by Noah when he fashioned his ark; and, according to the Bible, in weaving Moses' basket which was daubed with slime and pitch.

Ridiculous, Tregonnel mused, to realize that now nations would risk destroying their own planet in their search for this elemental stuff. Strange, when you considered what it was — the substance was believed to be derived from minute marine organisms pressurized since prehistoric times by sedimentary rock. The weight of these rock layers had squeezed out the precious raw material from the source rock, and the oil then escaped along any route it could find — normally through porous rocks which sometimes led to the surface. He had been told that probably more of the world's oil had been lost by natural escape through the crust than still remained underground today.

Since Drake's Pennsylvanian strike, mud had been used to control the pressures, to cool and lubricate the bit. From the mud tank, the viscous fluid was pumped up through the drilling mud hose to the kelly, and down through the drill string. Spurting out eventually through the apertures in the revolving bit, the mud washed away the drill cuttings and cooled the bit, at the same time supporting the walls of the well. The consistency of the mud was altered as necessary to suit the changing conditions. Normally it was the petroleum engineer's job, but John had accepted the responsibility. He knew when to vary the mud's character — he could cope. He had even used ping-pong balls and cellulose flakes at times.

Driven upwards by the pump on the platform and by the force of gravity, the mud circulated up the outside of the drill string before returning to the rig through the marine riser. The chippings that reached the surface were sieved by the chattering, vibrating screen just below him, and the fragments were analysed by the geologists. A vital function of the mud was to control pressure in the well and so prevent a blow-out

— if high pressures were met, the weight of the mud was increased so that the pressures were blanketed and controlled.

'Chow, boss.'

Tregonnel turned round. A grinning galley boy, an eighteen-year-old from Thailand, was holding out a mug of strong tea.

'Thanks.'

One thing was good about this rig — Flanagans had hired an excellent catering firm. The work in this brisk air induced hunger. Good food and plenty of it made a contented rig — he'd always been insistent about this. But he did not feel like work this morning — he was tired and the anxiety of working to the safety limits was getting him down. Even if they struck oil, no one would know for weeks whether the field would be large enough to exploit: a new rig, perhaps, and the laying of miles of underwater pipeline cost millions.

'I'm through,' Joe was yelling. 'We're bloody well through!'

He sensed the excitement in the tool pusher's shout — so they'd negotiated the difficult rock, and now it was only a few short feet, maybe, to the pay zone — he felt a kick in his stomach at the realization. 'I'm coming up, Joe.'

As he clambered to the control platform, he was reminded of the immensity of their task. The earth's crust was some 21 miles thick. *Explorer* was drilling into about two miles of it. It was like sticking pins into an elephant. He'd set Joe right, then wash up in the accommodation space. With their own fresh water, a couple of films a week, and video-tape television, there was little more that could be done for men's contentment out here — except women.

At eight o'clock, John Tregonnel decided he would resume the controls himself. Denis Patterson, the head scientist from Ullapool, had approached him to murmur that there was certainly a possibility. But what experienced petroleum engineer would ever stick out his neck?

'Alan Brodie's on his way, Denis,' Tregonnel said. 'Should give you a break.'

'Maybe.' The dour Yorkshireman retired again to his minute lab at the back of the bunk space.

The head tool pusher was concentrating on his job, the coloured knobs of the control levers only inches away from the flick of his fingers. It was upon him that the final responsibility of a possible strike depended. A few more yards, maybe... The drilling floor was now the centre of Tregonnel's world. There, in a frenzy of anticipation, the drillers and the roustabouts were slapping on another 30 feet of pipe. The chains were slammed home, the section clamped. *Pity the shift doesn't always work so well,* John thought. *We'd have been through days ago.* He shoved the control lever across. The travelling block creaked, the swivel squealed and the interminable drilling began again. He glimpsed Patterson crouched above the microscope, intent on identifying the drillings. To the geologist's right was the chromatograph, set to record the minutest trace of hydrocarbon — he swore beneath his breath, more to give vent to his feelings than to any specific frustrations: the scientists should soon be able to tell one way or the other. Was the grind of the last five months another wasted slice out of his life, or would there be a strike? Was this just an isolated showing of gas, or could it be the real thing?

The eternal question milled through his mind — some big decisions would soon have to be made, and the earlier Alan Brodie could be up here the better. John had suggested to head office that he should stop drilling to test the formation while waiting for Brodie to arrive, but his drilling superintendent had ordered him to continue coring, using only the core bit. The testing equipment had been flown out by chopper, and the logging experts, during the last few days, had been unable to dampen their enthusiasm. Even the petroleum engineers were beginning to grin. The eighteenth core definitely showed gas, and only then had he been ordered to stop drilling.

Tregonnel felt a strange tranquillity this Sunday morning. Perhaps it was the calm after the storm, but there had not been many fields which he had drilled where he had felt so certain of success. Sulisker had, from the first, been a bastard; but the rewards, if International's gamble was successful, would be colossal. First in this area, and with an option of three more concessions if they found oil, International had taken a calculated risk when other companies had lost their nerve. Sulisker could make or break International — and that meant those who worked for them, too. But things were looking good and the logs were continuing to throw up optimistic evidence — the hydrocarbons were plentiful and only yesterday the final obstacle was surmounted when the geophysicists reported that the reservoir rock had good porosity. The gas should flow — if it was there.

Last week, he'd finished running the seven-inch casing down to the target depth, and yesterday the driller and his crew of roughnecks had finished the cementing. Meldrum had run the production tubing and packers, and the complicated set of valves and controls. The Christmas tree was fitted, so that downhole pressures could be controlled during the production test. Roderiques, of Offshore Logging Services, was ready to perforate the casing. If there really was gas, it was trapped there, ready for the flare boom people, once the packer — the tough rubber sealing — had been sent down and fitted. They were working on this operation now, while he'd made sure the mud was ready and that there was enough of it. The gas pressures had to be held in check by the Christmas tree while they tested the flow rate during flaring.

The disadvantage of flaring was that the whole world knew when the rig had struck oil. This well was confidential, so coring was taking place in secret. The drilling floor would be cleared while he, Denis and two petroleum engineers packed up the core in its wooden box to send back to head office. If International wanted secrecy, the company could achieve it — but of course there were always rumours... Out here, if he flared on this bright morning, there was a chance that it would not be seen from the Butt — and there were no rival choppers coming out today.

The head tool pusher flared *Explorer* at 11.07 on Sunday the tenth. The geologists from head office had authorized the production test after studying the logs and core sample. The Christmas tree on the rig had been fitted. The flare booms had been connected. The production tubing and packing had been run. The casing had been perforated. Now they were using the Christmas tree to control the well pressures. Tregonnel was on top of his job, quietly giving orders, his eyes everywhere at this crucial stage, while the scientists measured the flow rate. Would the well be worth exploiting? That was the vital question.

'Okay, John,' Patterson said quietly as he emerged from the radio room. 'We reckon it's all right. Start to release the pressures, please.' The crunch had come.

'Ease back on the mud, Joe,' Tregonnel ordered.

The background racket of the generator increased in pitch, as the load on the mud pump diminished. John Tregonnel was watching the gauges: very gently now — once the mud pressures were less than those of the gas trapped below, then... He had never felt so tense. He could feel around him the knots of keyed-up roustabouts. Some watched the gauges, others stared upwards at the pilot light flickering 150 feet above the sea. The geologist waited too, his thoughts 12,000 feet below the rig where the gas should at any moment start surging into the well holes. But the head tool pusher concentrated on nothing but his pressures.

At 11.07, there was a sudden shock in the air above them. Mud and seawater spurted out and then a crimson flame roared from the flare booms.

'STRIKE...! S-T-R-I-K-E!'

The cheering from the men on the derrick floor was drowned by the roar of the flames. The contact production test engineer was concentrating on his readings and his controls. Tregonnel heard nothing. It would not be his fault if this strike went wild.

5

The captain of *N779* stifled a yawn as he leaned back against the for'd control room bulkhead to regard his newly trained team. Now 32, Kapitan Petrov Krassin was one of the three most senior submarine COs in the modern Soviet navy. He was nearing the peak of his operational career in submarines, a fact he realized only too well when he had been appointed to this nuclear-powered 6000-ton unit of the newly formed northern fleet. Though old by modern standards, *N779* was still a formidable weapon, but her main role, he had been briskly informed, was to work up the COs who had recently graduated from the submarine commanding officers' course held at the new base of Novaya Zemlya. *N779* was also to train the high proportion of young seamen in her ship's company, so this patrol had been no pushover. Potential crews were pouring from the training schools now that the expansion programme was gathering momentum.

Krassin watched his First Lieutenant overseeing the watch. An efficient officer, Lieutenant Ilyin had the makings of a good CO — controlled, decisive, a swift thinker. He could soon be recommended for command. Krassin wished he could feel so sure of his protégé, Lieutenant Andrei Lanov, whom he had been endeavouring to knock into shape since the boat sailed from Kronstad seven weeks ago.

'More rise on the fore-planes.'

The monotonous routine continued day after day. The officer of the watch, young Molonek, was issuing his orders to the petty officer sitting in the control seat. The man eased back on the combined control column, and Krassin felt the immediate response as the boat took on her bow-up angle. The hum of the motors and the purr from the fans were an accompaniment to this way of life that was now part of Krassin's existence. But he was concerned at Lanov's lack of progress — an adverse report did not reflect credit on the people who were trying to train him. Lanov had come to him with a question mark against his name.

Though he'd scraped through his 'perisher', as the command course was nicknamed, the Kapitan of the attack teacher had criticized his apparent lack of imagination and initiative at times. So he'd been appointed to *N779* to be smartened up. Krassin was notorious in the northern squadrons for his ruthless efficiency, a reputation of which he was well aware.

'Ten minutes to four, sir.'

'Thanks, Number One.'

At last the clock had moved round to the time of departure from this dismal billet. There were few ships passing this way on which he could carry out simulated attacks to improve Lanov's techniques. For eleven days, *N779* had been prowling around this Sulisker rig, probing the British defences and waiting for something to happen. Yesterday their patience had been rewarded when the drilling rig had flared. A stream of orange flame now danced from the flare booms — and at last a reaction of sorts had been produced in their VIP passenger.

Krassin was certain that the presence on board of Faqus, the mysterious character now about to be shaken from his slumber, had had an inhibiting effect on Lanov and the ship's company in general. The silent stranger had spent much of his time at the periscope observing, making notes, thinking. Krassin had picked him up at night at the rendezvous off Rockall from an unidentified submarine (one of the *N*s, he was certain). Only then was the Commanding Officer of *N779* to open the sealed envelope which had been burning a hole in the Kapitan's safe since leaving the base.

The Commanding Officer of N779 is to offer every facility to Kommandant L. Faqus, who will be transferred from a friendly submarine during the night of 28/29 September, in rendezvous position 090 — Rockall 10 miles. The requirements of this officer are to be given priority over all other objectives of your patrol.

'Shake the Kommandant.'

The pale-faced young seaman who kept the working log hurried aft towards the officers' sleeping quarters. Petrov Krassin, even after rubbing shoulders for eleven days with the uninvited guest, felt a peculiar twinge of apprehension at the prospect of confronting him again in a few minutes. Faqus was the most formidable character that Krassin had ever had the misfortune to encounter.

'Pump 450 gallons from K to Z.'

Petrov Krassin turned to watch the trim engineer checking the illuminated lights as he operated his trimming controls. The captain of *N779* felt satisfied with the progress he'd achieved in training his team.

'May I take a look, please, Kapitan?'

Krassin turned swiftly. Faqus had slid into the control room within half a minute of being shaken. He slept in his clothes and was awake at the slightest disturbance. This huge man, nearly seven feet tall, moved like a shadow.

'It's still dark, sir,' Krassin said, as he snapped down the handles of the periscope, 'but there's enough moon to see.' He swung the stick round, lining up on the flares flaming in the breeze that had freshened with the dawn.

'You're on, sir.' The captain stood back to allow the passenger to peer through the eyepieces.

'Don't dip her now,' Krassin ordered quietly, '60 feet.'

Kranek was doing his best, but with his lack of trimming experience he could easily lose a foot or two and blind the observer at the periscope: Faqus would note the fact. Krassin watched the crouching giant now grasping the handles of the stick. Clad in the olive-green tracksuit which he had affected throughout his time on board, Faqus stood motionless, his massive shoulders hunched as he forced his forehead into the rubber-padded facepiece. His cranium glistened in the artificial light — he was bald on top, though the sides of his head sprouted gingery hair sprinkled with grey. It was impossible to gauge his age, with that smooth skin; his face was unlined by normal standards — but he was probably in his early fifties. The slit of a mouth and the nerve pulsing in his jaw were the only hints that this repulsive creature was alive and human. Beneath the eyepieces, his heavy jowl was showing the shadow of an early morning beard, but apart from this lapse he was, as always, master of himself, a man of silent, suppressed power... Since the first moment of his embarkation, he had talked to no one other than Krassin.

'Kapitan Krassin, would you be so good as to...? Kapitan, perhaps you would ask your officers...? Kapitan, please...' Only smooth requests — sibilant, courteous, never raising his voice. This reptilian manner and appearance made Krassin's flesh creep. The handles snapped shut. 'I've finished with the rig, Kapitan. Take me south now, if you please.' The cold, dark eyes bore into Krassin, evaluating, summing him up.

'To the storage buoy, sir?'

'Yes, Kapitan.' Nodding, he turned to make his way aft towards the wardroom. 'I wish to eat now, Kapitan. Please be off the buoy by dawn. Be so good as to inform me when we are five miles distant.' He had turned his back — but still every syllable was distinct, though he had not raised his voice.

'Course for the buoy, sir, one-seven-eight,' the navigating officer volunteered.

'How far off land?'

'Three miles off Cellar Head; two point five off Tiumpan.'

'Water?'

'Least depth, 200 feet, sir.'

'That'll do. Take her down to 90 feet, Number One.' He was glad that his First Lieutenant was on the trim.

'Speed to arrive at twilight, Pilot?'

'Eighteen knots, sir. Morning twilight at 0548.'

So they were on their way at last. Good riddance to a bloody awful eleven days, a patrol wrecked by that inhuman pig who had, by his mysterious forcefulness, stamped upon all of them his ruthless personality. Petrov Krassin felt the boat dipping beneath his feet, watched carefully the pointers swinging across the depth gauge as she swooped to her new depth. These nuclears were true submersibles.

'312 radar mast down, sir … wireless mast down, both periscopes housed … one-seven-o revolutions…'

'Very good.'

He'd enjoy half an hour for coffee with his officers off-watch; time for a shave too and a brush-up after breakfast, before his ETA at the exposed weather storage buoy, *Sula*, as the oilmen called that floating production unit off Stornoway. The patrol orders told him that *Sula* was moored and ready to receive its load from the pipeline as soon as the oil began flowing from Sulisker.

And now Faqus needed to inspect this new buoy. He'd study it for days on end, taking endless notes, trigger-happy on the periscope camera. What the hell was the guy up to? It was irritating not being in on the picture. The man was not Russian and most certainly not an Arab either. More probably, from his bone structure and the inflection of his passable Russian, he was of German origin — eastern Bavarian, perhaps, part Czech, part Austrian? But you didn't pry with Kommandant L. Faqus: he was totally self-sufficient.

The captain of *N779* cast his eyes over the gauges before leaving the control room: 'Call me when you cross the 50-fathom line, pilot. I want a good visual fix of the Butt, so I'll come to periscope depth. There's too much fog in this bloody place.'

Krassin felt in a better humour. He could trust his senior lieutenants but he wished he could say the same of Lanov, pleasant enough character though he was. If only there could be a few tankers milling around *Sula*, so that Lanov could carry out a dummy attack — he was in need of unsimulated attack experience to give him confidence.

'Kapitan in the control room.' Petrov had barely sipped his coffee before the inevitable call summoned him.

'What is it?'

'HE, sir, bearing 195°. Probable tanker.'

The sonar officer stood by his plot, that vertical slab of transparent polythene illuminated from behind by a luminous filament. Concentric circles spread outwards in a web, the centre representing the submarine's position.

'She's here, sir.' The officer's finger stabbed at the bright spot, three circles from the centre. 'Her course, one-three-o. Range four point two miles: speed 20 knots. I think she's decreasing, sir — her bearing is drawing slowly ahead.'

Probably a tanker bound down the Minches for the Irish Channel and Heysham. But why was she easing down? 'Any other contacts?'

'No, sir. All round sweep completed and area clear.'

'Slow.'

The captain watched the log, as the boat's slight trembling swiftly decreased, while the speed came off her... Eight knots.

'Periscope depth.'

Kranek was managing well, in firm control, checking here, easing there, but Number One had silently arrived again to stand behind the junior officer's shoulder. *N779* swooped upwards, silently, at a 15° bow-up angle — 180 ... 120 ... 100 feet and levelling off as the bubble in the inclinometer drifted to the centre of the fluorescent tube.

'Sixty feet.'

Krassin opened the periscope handles and clamped his eyes to the lenses. No one had yet invented a technique to ensure that a submarine coming up from deep would not stick her periscope through the bottom of a stopped ship.

'312 radar, all-round sweep completed, sir. All clear, except for contact 185°, four point two miles.'

He swung the periscope to the bearing. It was still very dark, but across the sheen of breaking wavelets he glimpsed the smudge of an indistinct silhouette.

'I think that's her, Number One. Am I on bearing?'

'Yes sir, 184°.'

He slapped up the handles. Down hissed the glistening tube, a complex of lenses, sextant, rangefinder, camera, desiccators.

'I'll let her pass ahead. Visibility's shutting down. She's a bit too close.'

The fog would explain the tanker's decrease in speed. *N779* would be crossing the 50-fathom line at any moment. He'd alter course outside for safety. He'd be clear of the inshore shipping lane, and could stay deep at speed to be at the buoy in time for his ETA.

'Take her down: 90 feet.'

The navigating officer was crouched over his table, his dividers flicking at the chart.

'Twenty-two knots, sir, for same ETA of 0548.'

The monotonous process was repeated. He would stay in the control room now, since he'd be coming up from deep again in 40 minutes.

The silver flush of dawn was stealing across the base of the night clouds when finally *N779* came to periscope depth off Tiumpan Road. Petrov Krassin marvelled — an emotion he kept strictly to himself — at the splendour of each new day. Today was no exception. Already the stratocumulus was washed crimson by the sun mounting steadily from below the horizon. The sea was still a leaden grey, a succession of white slashes through the periscope lens denoting a moderate sea. A fleck of spray smeared the glass momentarily.

'There she is ... the tanker.'

A ship of about 70,000 tons was some miles ahead, forging southwards with a bone in her teeth... Petrov continued his sweep and — there it was, spot-on for bearing, the first sign of the huge cylindrical buoy: that pale finger rearing from the horizon must be the jib-head of the crane mounted on one side of the helicopter platform. In ten minutes, he'd see better.

'Ask Lieutenant Lanov to report to me.' If this tanker rounded up towards *Sula*, she might cross *N779*'s bows and the submarine would then be in a good position for a dummy attack. The exercise would break the monotony, before Faqus monopolized the periscope.

Sula was coming up now — another tanker was swinging in the tidal stream to the moorings of the buoy. She was a medium-sized ship, no more than 80,000 tons, who was obviously exercising the new procedures: a smart vessel, one of International's by her colouring.

'Distance off the buoy?'

'Three point two miles.'

'Sir, you sent for me?' Lanov was behind him, anxious to please.

'Yes, Lanov. We could be lucky. If that other tanker to the south-west of us rounds up, we might get a crack at her. Take the attack periscope.'

'Thanks.'

The 27-year-old lieutenant flicked his fingers, and the steel tube slid upwards from its periscope well. He was a smaller man, broad and squat, with unusually fair hair for a native of the Ukraine.

'Is that *Sula*, sir, the storage buoy you were talking about?'

'Yes … capable of storing 40,000 tons of oil. Our intelligence people know that the British have struck oil at Sulisker. One of their most enterprising oil companies is exploiting the field as rapidly as they know how. They have been taking tremendous risks.'

Lanov seemed happy at the periscope, calmly estimating his angle on the bow, as he asked, 'They'll be filling the storage buoy, then, sir?'

'As soon as they can. The oil company is obviously sure of the field's potential, because they are using the rig as a production unit until their platform is ready. They've gambled on the future, and have revolutionized procedures.'

The captain was at the periscope and checking Lanov's computations. All was well so far, so Krassin continued, 'They hope to have their Sulisker — Butt of Lewis pipeline almost finished by next summer, ready for the platform when it is settled on site. The company has taken risks, because it has had cash flow problems, apparently. Our people reckon the British wanted a quicker return on their capital, so they first completed their pipeline from Stranraer to the storage buoy.'

'It looks as if the initiative has paid off.' The silky monotone behind him came from Faqus. The man missed nothing.

Krassin ignored the interruption. 'Mind if I carry out a mock attack on that tanker, sir? It'll give Lieutenant Lanov some practice.'

'Carry on, Kapitan.'

'The tanker's rounding up, sir,' Lanov said. 'Altering towards…'

Krassin flipped his periscope handle to high power. There she was: three miles off and steering towards. Her upperworks were rose-red in the sunrise and a bow-wave creamed at her bottle-nosed bow.

'Diving Stations,' he snapped. 'You have the ship, Lieutenant Lanov. Start the attack!'

6

The supply vessel, *Wanklyn VC*, did not slip from the Innochervie jetty until 2 a.m. on the morning of Monday, 11 October. Bound for Sulisker, she had let go her lines on Sunday morning but, as she cleared the Point of Langa, she was recalled by the base in Glendhu Bay. '*Explorer*'s re-wound motor is ready,' the stoical manager of Cul Mor Services had called over the RT. 'Drop it off for us, Iain, after your *Sula* delivery.'

The lads had been 'chokka' and the most frustrated had been International's drilling engineer, Alan Brodie. But, with *Wanklyn* lunging through the swell walloping in from the north-westward, Macgregor was content that their plans had been delayed. It was not often that his sister could accompany him on a trip, and he needed her administrative help. Running a supply vessel of this size created mountains of paperwork. Sheena was his partner in their enterprise and she proved handier than most men. She had nipped on board after kirk yesterday, clad in trousers and red anorak, all set to carry out the inventory for the annual stocktaking. The 200-foot *Wanklyn VC* demanded efficient running, internally and externally. Sheena had saved him thousands.

Iain stared aft in the darkness, to the illuminated working deck heaving in the trough of the seas. A fine ship she was, with her twin red funnels prettily athwartships, at the after end of the bridge. Her high bows and hull were painted orange, the best colour for low visibility. This scheme set off the white gunwales and the bridge which, raking fashionably forward, dripped from the condensation of the dawn. The red duster flapped lazily from the buff tripod-mast stepped snugly on the upper wheelhouse deck. Her working deck was spacious, clear of obstruction and well protected. *Wanklyn* was all that a modern oil rig supply ship should be.

He was proud of his new vessel, his first command as skipper in one of Cul Mor Services' fleet. He yawned and the noise jerked Bill, one of the best deckies, into alertness.

'Mug of tea, skip?'

'Not now, thanks. I'll get my head down before we fetch up. Course 240°, Bill. Nothing in sight. Give me a shout when you see *Sula*.' He moved to the companionway, took his weight on the rails and slid down to his cabin below. The steady thump of the twin diesels was a reassuring accompaniment as he shut the door behind him. He doused the light and threw himself on to his bunk. In seconds, he was asleep.

Sheena Macgregor had been called at five by the cook, One-Slice-Jack. A stalwart character, he was the oldest man in the ship and treated her as he would his granddaughter. If anyone on board had dared any nonsense with her, Jack would have split open their skulls with his meat-axe. From the first, she always pulled her weight and had therefore been accepted by the mate and the bos'n. From then on, there had been no problem: she had enjoyed the constant chiakking. She was one of them, and a working partner with her brother.

She washed, ran a comb through her hair and slithered down to the galley, warm and comforting with its bright lights, where she brewed a mug of cocoa. She clasped the thick china between her mittened fingers and stumbled back up the ladder to the break in the working deck by the winches. She enjoyed watching the dawn, in the shelter there, at the rail. She dipped her head below the deckhead beam and stepped out into the darkness.

'Sheena — what are you doing here?' Alan Brodie was at the rail.

'I've plenty to do today. This'll be the only peace I'll get,' she said.

She leaned on the gunwale, her arms stretched along the cold steel. She felt the wind in her hair, the bite of winter in her cheeks. She smiled up at him. She'd become interested in him since the village dance and she had often wondered... She liked his easy, self-reliant manner. He needed no encouragement from others, this man — he seemed to know where he was going.

'D'you often help your brother?'

'Aye, when I can.'

The seas slopped against the side. The exhaust from the twin funnels thudded overhead.

'Tell me about yourself. Why haven't you left Innochervie?'

His voice bred confidence — on impulse, she began to tell him of their life at Innochervie: of her childhood in the forgotten fishing port; of the peace and the unbroken tradition of this simple way of life; of having to board away from home during the week, at a school near Inverness, and how homesick she had been. Then she talked of her successes, but how she had given up the idea of the city, because she preferred the uncomplicated and decent life of her village.

'And then we came,' he said quietly, 'to ruin it all. Cigarette?'

'No, thanks. Given it up.'

She reached for his hand, where it gripped the rail. He seemed so steady there, rock-like in their topsy-turvy world which was now Innochervie. His fingers were warm as he entwined them in hers.

'Although you're in the other camp, d'you understand our feelings?'

'I do.' His other hand closed around hers. They leaned on the rail, silent, watching the silver streaks of dawn. She could feel the warmth of his body through his duffel coat, as he leaned against her.

'D'you feel lonely sometimes, away from the south?'

'A bit.'

His arms were about her and, alone in the dawn, they kissed. She hadn't meant to respond and she pushed him away, surprised by the intensity of her feelings.

'I've not made many friends up here,' he said.

She moved away towards the bridge ladder.

'Sheena,' he called softly. 'Sheena, come back.'

She paused and turned towards him. His face was pale, strained in the first light.

'Shall we meet again, Sheena?'

'Maybe we could arrange that, Mr Brodie.'

She turned and scuttled up the ladder to the doorway in the verandah at the after end of the bridge.

Already the Red Duster was visible, flapping its shredded fly against the lightening horizon. A Molly bird shrieked, gliding downwind as it narrowly missed the funnel.

The October sun was above the horizon when Iain Macgregor returned to the bridge. He peered through the central window at the EWSB terminal emerging from the murk on his port bow.

'Bring her round to southward, Bill,' he ordered. 'We'll pass astern of the moored tanker. I'll try to get under the crane.'

'Okay, skip.'

Bill was a reliable hand who knew his job. Pity he had so much trouble with his missus.

'Course 230°.'

Iain nodded. *Wanklyn* was well on time. They'd have breakfast in comfort, while the EWSB's hands hoisted out the cable. A relaxed half hour would make a break, while Sheena discussed the inventory. The terminal was coming up clearly now, a colossal orange mushroom gyrating in the tidal stream. So they'd given it a name, had they? *Sula*, emblazoned in large red letters, after the rocks of Sula Sgeir, close to Sulisker. Swinging to the EWSB's extended mooring, that 80,000-ton tanker, in contrast, seemed a toy boat.

This huge storage barrel, 100 feet in diameter, was like a giant fishing float. Nine anchors held it in position to ensure minimal movement of the flexible oil hose connected to the bottom of the cylinder. From the sea emerged a broader stalk, protected by vertical fenders. In this tideway, a supply boat could moor only down-wind and down-tide, so he would take *Wanklyn* around that tanker's stem. He could read her name now — *Pamir Barque*, one of International's coastal tankers.

'Come up under her stern, Bill — but watch her swing.'

'Aye, aye, skip.'

The red jib-head of *Sula's* crane lurched rhythmically across the cloud, as the huge float gyrated gently in the swirling tideway. In the toadstool top of this vast cylinder, 36 men worked in three watches. The accommodation and office deck was immediately below the chopper pad. Under the living quarters were the computer rooms and the electronic gear. And the bottom level contained the pumping compartments and machinery spaces.

Iain wondered how soon the oil would be flowing in quantity from Sulisker. The frustrating and subversive strikes at West

Coast were holding up the production platform, *Sulisker One*, but this buoy was ready: the underwater pipeline had been laid to Eye and connected up through Stornoway to Callicvol Bay, two miles south-east of the Butt.

'Morning, brother.'

Iain wondered about his sister. Sheena's relationship with Sim McIver had always been platonic, he was sure: Sim was a strange one, a recluse, prickly, holding the world at arm's length. He knew his wild moors and rivers, but Iain had never been happy when Sheena had insisted on visiting the gillie who was living by himself on Hoyea. 'He's only a friend. He wouldn't harm anyone,' she'd said.

Iain felt her eyes on him where he stood by the autopilot. He knew she was itching to take the weight of the watch from his shoulders. He turned and smiled at her.

'Can I?' she asked, her black eyebrows arched.

'Okay,' he said. 'Take over from Bill, but mind where you're going. I'm rounding up under that moored-up tanker's stem. I'll cross ahead of the big 'un: she's in a hurry, by the looks of her. Why's she got those tugs escorting her?'

Sheena curled up in the bridge chair, her long legs tucked beneath her. 'They'll probably practise picking up the connecting hoses,' she said, 'once *Pamir Barque* has slipped.'

Iain pushed open the wheelhouse door and moved on to the verandah deck. He'd make the most of this chill sunlight while waiting for these monsters to clear the area. The wind had an edge to it now, so he slipped into the lee on the starboard side. He shoved his hands into the pockets of his donkey jacket and fished out a cigar. A dawn like this, with a calm sea and a light breeze, did him good — the demands of the day would crowd in upon him soon enough.

The slab side of *Pamir Barque* was painted a raucous orange: her name, in brazen contemporary lettering, emblazoned the white upperworks of her bridge structure. And International's unimaginative 'clasped hands' badge was splayed across her blue funnels. Sheena was bringing *Wanklyn* round nicely, Iain's little ship heeling to the turn. The tanker's transom, ugly and square, reared above them — and then the supply boat was lunging into the grey water beyond.

Wanklyn's skipper leaned on the rail, his chin in his hands, as he watched those two giants. The other tanker was larger, her black hull setting off her finer lines. She was less than a mile off now, her two tugs fussing ahead of her, white hillocks foaming at their blunt, fender-festooned bows. They were altering up and beginning to turn, the toots of their sirens drifting across the water. They began to heel in the silvery sea now streaked by catspaws from the morning breeze. Idly, his eyes followed the fantastic shapes writhing in ceaseless patterns on the surface — what was that, there, ten degrees on his port bow? An aluminium broomstick, flicking through the water. Then he saw the feather, the plume of spray and the slick of bubbles.

'Periscope!' he heard himself yelling, half turning towards the wheelhouse. His hand shot outwards, pointing at the sinister intruder. That *was* a periscope — and beneath that flashing lens someone was watching him.

'Hard a-starboard, Sheena,' he yelled as he clawed his way to the wheelhouse door, 'or we'll ram the bloody thing.'

Another plume emerged, smaller, but close to the first. Then they slid beneath the surface, less than half a cable from *Wanklyn*'s fore-foot.

'Hold on!' he yelled into the wheelhouse. 'She'll tear the arse off us.'

Sheena was standing there, cool, her hands flicking the autopilot, though her face was drained of colour. Skipper Macgregor lunged for the emergency alarm button. The klaxon howled, jerking men from their berths.

He leaned across and shoved the pitch control to 'stop'. If *Wanklyn* could ease down in time, her stern would lift... Mesmerized by the slick of bubbles, he watched them disappearing beneath the flare. He gripped the rail and flexed his knees, waiting for the shock.

7

'Start the attack.'

The control room team were already scrambling silently to their stations as Lanov repeated his captain's order. Andrei Lanov, eyes glued to the eyepiece, was aware that the familiar drill was taking place behind his arched back. The attack computer was being linked automatically to the firing mechanism in the tube space: the tubes were being 'blown up'. The fish being brought to the ready — and the action state of each torpedo would be blinking in the monitor behind him. If this was for real, two mammoth tankers would be blazing infernos within the next few minutes.

'Don't dip her, Number One.'

He could hear the Old Man at the other periscope. It was reassuring to know that he was there, for Lanov did not yet feel confident of flinging about a boat of this size. He was still nervous of her, perhaps because of the trimming problems he'd experienced in conventionals.

'Get a move on, Lanov. The computer can't work unless you feed it.'

That was better — he could judge the angle on the bow more precisely now — a gap was opening up between the funnel and the port island on her bridge wing.

'I'm fifteen degrees on her port bow. Bearing *that* … range *that*…' He pressed the button of the rangefinder.

'Good,' he heard Krassin murmur behind him. 'Not far out. Get off track.'

He snapped the handles shut. He'd left the periscope up too long.

'Course for 120° track?' he blurted over his shoulder. 'Up periscope. What's my director angle?' He'd gain time during the turn.

He grabbed the handles sliding upwards past him. The lens, swamped with light, blurred, then cleared. He dared not speed up or the stick would show.

'Two tugs,' he said. 'One on either bow. Bearing *that* ... and *that...*'

'Red two-o. Green one-five, sir.'

'Course for 120 track,' the computer operator called, '345°. Your DA, red one-three.'

'Starboard ten, steer 345°.'

'Steer 345°, sir.' The helmsman's voice was calm, reassuring.

'Down periscope.'

He'd have to speed up or he'd miss his DA.

'Ten knots,' he ordered. 'Starboard 15.'

For an instant his eye caught the captain watching him. He dare not raise the stick now or the 'feather' would show. Suicide, in wartime.

'For exercise, for exercise, for exercise,' he repeated, 'stand by, numbers one, two, three and four torpedoes. Limited salvo.' Peacetime drill. Someone had once fired live torpedoes during a dummy attack.

His orders were repeated. Red lights glowed in the monitor.

'One, two, three and four torpedoes ready, sir.'

'You've been blind for too long, Lanov,' Krassin said. 'Over 90 seconds since your last look.'

Lanov nodded. 'How far to go for my DA?'

'Fifty-eight degrees, sir.'

'Take a look,' Krassin ordered. 'Almost two minutes now.'

'I'll miss my DA if I slow down, sir.'

'It's your attack.' Krassin was like that. Cool, rarely interfering.

'Twenty degrees to go, sir.'

'HE green one-four-o, sir.' Lanov barely heard the sonar officer's announcement.

'Diesels, at speed.'

The report was superfluous: the scuffle overhead of the propeller noises was overwhelming.

'Fifteen degrees to go, sir.'

'Slow.' Lanov counted to ten, watched the pointer of the log creeping backwards while the boat lost way... 7 knots ... 6.5 ... 6 ... 5.8...

'Up periscope. Put me on my DA.'

He glimpsed the captain bent double, crawling on his knees as he snatched at the handles of the all-round periscope.

'Keep her down, Number One,' Krassin rapped. 'Don't break surface.'

Lanov uncoiled himself as the stick slid upwards between his hands.

'Course, sir, three-four-five.'

'Stand by.' Was that his own voice giving that confident order? Sounded strange — here it came, the sudden shaft of light, the brightness...

'Put me on my DA.'

Someone behind him was yanking at the handles.

'On, sir.'

The blur of the lens ... the agonizing wait for the glass to clear...

What the hell was that? An orange slab of steel, a plunging stem slashing the water, a flurry of foam at her fore-foot, as the trawler rode down upon them. On the bridge rail, a seaman was pointing frenziedly. His head was thrown back and he was yelling.

'Emergency, change of depth! 300 feet,' Lanov shouted, slamming shut the periscope handles.

The klaxon blared. He saw the anger on the captain's face.

'I'll take her.'

Krassin's orders rapped like pistol shots: 'Stop. Shut main vents. Both planes hard-a-dive. Keep her stern down, Number One.'

Lanov stood back. This was the end. That trawler had not been there the last time he'd looked. She must have been hidden behind the moored tanker. The bloody thing was turning under full rudder at full speed. If she struck N779's pressure hull, she'd slice them open. The pointer on the gauge seemed stuck. Number One was flooding as fast as he could, but *why wouldn't the bastard move?* Why didn't these nuclears have an emergency Q tank like the conventional? At any moment now, the deluge, the roar of the water exploding through the gashed pressure hull... She was beginning to sink bodily, sweeping downwards. He forced open his eyes to focus on the gauge — 63 ... 69 ... 75 feet.

'All watertight doors shut, sir.' Number One, calm, unemotional.

Silence — no one moved.

A shock, a crash, a juddering shook the hull. The lights flickered, then blacked out. A rending jolt overhead was followed by water splashing through the lower gland of the after periscope. N779 was laid over to port, as if some giant hand was pressing her down.

'Blow main ballast.'

The captain's order rang through the control room. The HP air screamed along the lines. The boat catapulted to the vertical, steadied, began to check her downward swoop.

'Reverse the planes. Half ahead.'

Fractured aft? Flooding? Lanov felt a curious detachment — this disaster was of his own making, his fault.

'A hundred feet, sir. I've got her.' Number One again, unflappable.

'Coming up, sir — 90 ... 75 feet...'

The submarine was swooping upwards. If only they could reach the surface... She might wallow there long enough for them to bale out.

8

It was the screech of rending metal that jerked Alan Brodie from his dreams of Sheena. The ship shivered, listed heavily to port and then, above the pandemonium, he heard the blaring of the klaxon… He rolled from his upper bunk, saw that the lower berth was empty, and grabbed a couple of orange lifejackets from the corner cupboard. Time to grab warm clothes? Fire — or drowning? The door slammed backwards against the unnatural roll and, still in his vest and pants, he was flung outside, clear of the cabin.

He heard the hiss of water exploding under pressure, the cries of men trapped in their berths, the thudding of fists upon the jammed doors … and then he felt the ship settling beneath his feet as her stem began to sink. He hauled himself along the passage, where the water was already swirling across the tiled deck from the crew's heads and shower compartment. Had Macgregor put *Wanklyn* aground? Collision probably, the worst of disasters. No time to escape. He had to reach the midship ladder if he was to make the upper deck. He clawed upwards against the slippery deck of the passageway.

As he clambered past the engine-room, a blast of hot air forced him to turn. The door was cracked open and through it he glimpsed a section of the chief's ashen face. He was trapped by the weight of the safety door which he could not open against the rising water and the force of gravity.

Brodie was beyond rational thought, as he barged against the door. He did not feel the pain as the sole of his right foot was sliced by the treads on the deck… He slithered in the blood, then felt the door inching open. He flung himself at the door but it would not budge. The fingers of a hand slipped through the aperture, the knuckles streaming blood where they forced their way through the crack. The door flew suddenly inwards. The roar from the diesels, the gob of steam, the deluge of icy water as Alan dragged the choking man into the passageway...

'Take hold of me, chief...'

Alan half lifted the crazed man, a dead weight, towards the upper-deck ladder which had torn adrift from its fastenings. He grabbed with his free hand at the slippery rail. He could fight no more — the water was swirling up beneath his knees and the chief was gasping, half-submerged in the deluge...

He saw the chink of light where the after screen door was slamming against the roll. With the chief, he could never make it. He hung on, trying to gain a foothold, rung after rung — then suddenly he was catapulted upwards as the ship pitched for her final plunge. Together they slumped across the combing of the after screen door, the wind knocked from Alan's lungs as he lay gasping for air, unable to move for pain and exhaustion.

He heard the cry of a woman's voice. They were being dragged across the deck, while someone was encircling his neck with a lifejacket. They collapsed across the rail as the seas surged up to meet them. Then his fingers, pulped and bleeding, clasped the lifelines hanging from the rubber inflatable jerking crazily alongside.

'Hold on, Alan — *don't let go!*' Iain was bellowing above the gobs of air exploding in the water. 'Hang on, while we get the chief inboard.'

So they had a chance? They had escaped the sinking ship but he cared no more as groping hands tore at his jacket. Obscenities dented his consciousness and then he was rolling across the side of the inflatable to flop, fighting for breath, onto the slatted bottom boards. A voluptuous numbness was overwhelming the pain, and destroying his will to fight. *Hold on*, they told him, *hold on*... How easy to let go, to slip away — and he dimly knew his feebleness must be the oncoming of exposure. God, survival had been so near... He gasped for air as a sea hit them, the icy deluge smothering them all.

'For God's sake, don't give up, Alan!'

That must be Sheena's voice — he felt her hands slapping his face, tearing at his vest. She was swathing him in the sodden sweater she'd peeled off herself. She lay across him, passing him her lifegiving warmth... Gradually he began to breathe more easily, and then the rigours of his trembling body eased. She lifted him, her arms beneath his shoulders, to a sitting position against the rounded side of the raft...

He'd fully regained his senses, sensitive now to the pain. The chief lay, an inert mass, alongside him. The skipper, sprawled across him, was giving him the kiss of life. Above the gunwale, Alan saw the black side of a hove-to tanker; a tug was passing across her bows.

Less than a cable distant, a whorl of water suddenly heaved. A whale-like apparition surged upwards, breaking the surface of the sea. The black hull gleamed in the pale sunlight, as cascades of water streamed from the free-flood holes. From the summit of its crumpled fin, a battery of masts and periscopes drooped like lilies over the lip, a shambles of twisted wreckage in the swirling maelstrom.

Alan never knew how long the submarine wallowed there. Her fin leaned crazily forward; her after-end reared high above their heads, her mammoth propeller still churning and glinting in the sunshine.

N779: her pendant numbers showed plainly, painted across the side of her fin — then she subsided, with only a frothing swirl to prove the reality of her sudden appearance.

'D'you see that?'

Brodie was uncertain of his reeling senses, but then Sheena was nodding in confirmation as she stared at the void. She was shivering violently, where she knelt in the bottom of the raft.

'Oh, thank God.' She was crying now, her body wracked by sobbing as the snarl of approaching outboards drowned the confusion of the seas.

'Boat's coming.' Iain flung his jacket around her, as the orange lifeboat swept alongside.

'You're all right,' a Yorkshire voice was yelling. 'Watch out for the swirl when we hit the cables — the tide's running fast. Make fast quick.'

Alan felt the jerk on the inflatable as the painter snatched. The lifeboat threshed as she went astern and then crashed, half-swamped, alongside the landing stage of the gyrating *Sula* buoy.

9

'L.' Faqus, or 'Al' as he was known in Europe, had always been able to stand back and evaluate himself dispassionately. At this instant, with the submarine hurtling downwards out of control, he acknowledged to himself that, for the first time in his 54 years, he was terrified. He had killed, he had mutilated, he had tortured men and women. Never once had he suffered a pang of abhorrence or remorse. He never wasted time in self-recrimination; he was paid to ensure that these necessary functions were executed. Even as a youngster, adrift in concentration camps after the war, he'd felt no horror at what he'd witnessed. Clinical murder by both Russians and Germans of thousands of inmates was part of his childhood. A job to be done, that was all — and that was one reason why he'd risen so quickly to the command of ACLA, the Attack Commando of the Liberation Army.

If the General Staff decided that the objective had to be achieved swiftly, violent military action was often the sole solution. The more ruthless the operation, the better. If psychological shocks could jerk the Western world from its lethargy, the more resolutely would capitalism take practical steps to right injustice in the Middle East.

ACLA was busy these days and Faqus had his hands full. He was thankful that he'd finished reconnoitring the Sulisker complex: Operation Scimitar should be a pushover.

'180 ... 240 ... 270 feet, sir...'

From his starboard for'd corner in the control room, Faqus watched the luminous pointer sweeping around the depth-gauge. In the glow of the emergency lighting, he could watch the chaos swirling around him.

The captain stood in the centre of the control room. The First Lieutenant had taken over the trim. Orders crackled through the boat — were repeated, carried out, checked. Gradually, as the submarine picked up speed, the terrifying bow-down angle came off her.

'Make your reports.'

'After ends intact, sir.'

'No water in the engine room.'

'Pump space dry...'

The reports streamed back via the loudspeaker system to the darkened control room.

'300 feet... I've got her, sir,' the First Lieutenant reported finally.

'Slow,' Krassin ordered. 'Four knots.'

Faqus licked his lips, the sweat dripping from the tip of his nose, salty to his taste. He closed his eyes to blot out the horror in his imagination. He knew now the meaning of hysteria, as an uncontrollable desire to shout began to overtake him. He just *had* to escape this constricting tomb. Terror was, for him, a novel experience.

'Fore ends watertight...'

'Tube space dry, sir.'

The captain hesitated while his eyes swept across the gauges: checking the monitors and dials; glancing at the gyro repeater, at the log...

'Open up watertight doors,' he ordered, the sting now absent from his commands. 'D'you hear there? This is the Kapitan speaking...'

Faqus leaned forward. Krassin was playing it cool ... a mercy he was in command, and not Lanov. Faqus sighed deeply. No one had noticed his abject fear, though his face must be ashen. The young sonar operator, less than a pace to Faqus's left, was certainly pale, but the man still managed to trace with a steady hand the plot on the Perspex board.

'We were rammed by an unseen trawler: she must have been out on the far side of the moored-up tanker.' The captain was matter-of-fact, keeping his men in the picture as he talked to them over the intercom. 'She's wiped off both periscopes and our 385 radar. We'll investigate later, when I have a chance to surface. If we can raise the 191 mast, at least we'll have something to navigate with.' He paused, searching for words.

'We seem to be watertight. We're 45 feet off the bottom and I'm coming up to 450 feet. I'll stay there, until we are clear of the area. We'll return to Archangel, passing clear of the Faroes. I'm breaking off patrol now. We'll be blind, so we're in the hands of the sonar team.' He paused, then added quietly: 'Keep silent. Remain at diving stations. Make no mistakes and I'll get you out of this.' The loudspeaker snicked off.

Faqus wiped his sweating brow. His fingers were trembling and he wanted desperately to reach the heads before he disgraced himself. Stomach turned to water... He knew now what the expression meant.

'Excuse me, please, Kapitan.' He pushed his way past Krassin who, hands on hips and feet astride, was watching the trim. Faqus slipped past the sonar operator and hurried from the control room.

10

John Tregonnel watched *Storm Petrel*, no first-timer at Sulisker, pitching in the seas 60 feet below him. Wind was against tide and an unpleasant sea was spewing up against the legs of *Explorer*. Even this experienced skipper had his work cut out coming alongside beneath the crane.

Storm Petrel was loaded to the gunwales with diesel drums for the generators and with the piping that Tregonnel had requisitioned after he had been ordered by head office to use *Explorer* as a production platform. Even if the rules were being bent a trifle, this Sulisker concession was so remote that no one bothered them. The Navy's Offshore Patrol Ships were fully stretched in the North Sea, coping with the nosing Russian trawlers testing British defences.

Kit Meldrum was down on *Explorer*'s working deck, where he was standing by the supply boat's lines. He was charge-hand of the roustabouts, but this shift was about the worst that Tregonnel had known. He'd sack the lot, if the personnel manager in Ullapool could promise replacements — but these days even roustabouts were rare.

'For Gawd's sake, catch the bloody thing!' Meldrum shouted.

Another heaving line curved through the air to plop across *Storm Petrel*'s pitching fo'c'sle head. A man grabbed it, hauled in, hand over hand, until he had slapped the eye over the bollard. Then he waved the warp away. Kit flung a bight over the capstan drum; the pawls clanked and the wire began to come home. The crane was ready and they'd be sending the diesel up first.

Tregonnel respected these supply boat skippers and their crews. In all weathers, throughout the year, they kept the rigs going with everything from food to diesel, from spares to re-conditioned machinery.

When *Wanklyn* had sunk a few weeks ago, Cul Mor had lost their replacement hydraulic pump and motor destined for *Explorer* but, within three days, they'd sent out another, complete with its re-wound motor. Not a bad effort, even though the pump was running hotter than its predecessor.

The loss of *Wanklyn* had shocked the West Coast. There had been only five survivors: the chief had died on arrival in hospital, but Brodie had been lucky. Tregonnel had missed Alan's visit, particularly when instead they'd sent out Brodie's boss, that morose fellow Hubbard.

There seemed to be more noise than usual down on the working deck. Irritated, Tregonnel moved over to the rail, as the first lift of drums began to swing upwards from *Storm Petrel's* deck. The crane driver was certainly trying to beat the gun.

John could see only too clearly that an emergency was rapidly developing. The mate in *Storm Petrel* was yelling, but his words were unintelligible. He was crossing his forearms, signalling to those on the rig to secure the warp and to stop heaving... The wire was bar taut and, even from where John stood, he could hear it strumming as it snatched with the strain.

'*Vast heaving...*' Tom was shouting angrily at the winch operator who, his hands full with a riding turn, was unable to free the bight.

'You stupid bugger. Let the fucking thing go.'

Kit was stumbling across the greasy deck to grab the steel-shod wooden bar available for just such emergencies.

John Tregonnel watched the supply boat plunging in the seas. Unable to move ahead because of the rig's leg that would stave in her bows, her skipper seemed powerless while the tidal stream swept his ship across the steel structure: her bow thrusters must have packed in. A horizontal strut nipped the boat just below her rubbing strake. She bounced off, crashed again, the shock catapulting her against the roll. The pile of pipes shifted, snapping the securing chains as if they were pack-thread.

John heard the yells, saw the first rows of pipe skedaddling across the deck. Row after row slithered to the rail, jerked, several tumbling into the waves. The sea boiled and, as the remaining lengths crashed from side to side in the well of the working deck, so *Storm Petrel* rolled with the shifting weight.

'Stand clear!'

As the hands on *Explorer*'s deck scuttled for shelter, the wire parted. With a crack it curled backwards, end for end, whipping and lashing in uncontrolled fury. Forced by the tide swishing against the cross-struts of the rig, *Storm Petrel*'s side was taking a pounding as she gathered sternway.

'Under below!'

The warning shout spun Tregonnel on his heel. The crane driver, disconcerted by the crack of the parting wire, had been careless in that split second. He'd traversed his jib too fast and the hoist of diesel drums had swung wide. The net was caught in the lattice of the derrick. The second drum was already slithering through the torn mesh to follow the first which had crashed to the steel deck of the derrick floor. The drum had split and the stench of the fuel reached Tregonnel's nostrils as the second drum crashed. He watched the stuff spreading across the plates and deluging over the edge into the machinery space below. Mercifully, the shift had seen the danger and scuttled clear in time. Tregonnel swore: all this incompetence was caused by too much noise and because of the idiots he was forced to accept for this work. Kit Meldrum was tired out and his shift were beginning to resent his driving.

'Watch it!' Tregonnel yelled up to the crane cabin. 'Bloody lucky you haven't killed someone.' The driver turned his back. He continued gingerly to extricate the net. The load had jammed in the mesh, so no more drums could fall. Tregonnel breathed again. Diesel was reasonably safe in comparison with the other nastiness that could spill... He felt a tap on his shoulder, and turned round to see the shift engineer standing by him.

'That hydraulic pump's running hot,' the engineer reported. 'I've got to stop it: I'll put the secondary on the line, if the trouble's serious.'

John nodded. He'd had his fill today, but he understood the difficulties of the engineers — *they* seldom let him down.

'If you have to. We've had enough downtime this month.' He followed the engineer to the edge of the ladder and watched him as he shut down the hydraulics and began to unbutton the inspection plates on the pump. The machine and its motor must be hot, because he was working gingerly and keeping his fingers clear of the metal. There would be a loss of power, but the delay wouldn't be long — and the Christmas Tree could always be operated by hand in emergency.

A sheet of flame spurted suddenly upwards from the electric motor driving the pump. Tregonnel saw the engineer leaping backwards, shielding his face from the heat. The spanner he was using dropped with a clatter to the deck. Tregonnel saw the flames licking towards the diesel fuel which was still swilling idly across the moving deck.

'*Fire!*' Tregonnel yelled, as he leaped towards the alarm push. He started to jump down the ladder for the extinguishers, but the engineer had recovered his balance and reached them first. He was wrenching at the crimson cylinders as the hands rushed across to help.

'Okay —' Tregonnel yelled. 'You deal with the fire. I'll see to the BOP.' He dashed back to the control panel to close down the stack. He stabbed at the controls to shut the rams.

Now that the flare had automatically closed off, only the wind and the shouting down below disturbed the sudden silence. The foam from the extinguishers swiftly smothered the flame and doused the smoke. Tregonnel breathed again: a blow-out at this stage in his career would be too bloody much. Closing down the Christmas Tree had shut off the flare and the rams within the BOP stack had functioned normally. He had lost some downtime, but fire on a rig was the one hazard with which he could take no risks. The shift was hosing down now and clearing up the mess, while the engineer waited for the metal of the pump and motor to cool before continuing with his inspection.

Tregonnel returned to the control panel — all seemed to be well, but he felt a strange unease now. Too much was going wrong. Though *Storm Petrel* was still unloading beneath the crane, several pipes had ditched overboard. They could have fallen on to the BOP stack.

'Ask Jake to come and see me,' he yelled down to the working deck. 'Get the diving bell ready.'

Jake O'Keefe was one of the most reliable divers on the coast and it was fortunate that he was carrying out his routine inspection on *Explorer* this week. Tregonnel would feel better once he knew that the BOP stack had not been damaged. He wished he could shake off this feeling of uncertainty —

something was wrong and he could not explain the cause of his anxiety. He'd once experienced the drama of a well running wild when he was a young roustabout. He'd never forgotten the incident... If there was a bad spill from *Explorer* now, the conservation mob on the west coast would clobber International. The bird colonies and the wildlife would be smothered and the coasts of Sutherland and Wester Ross would be fouled for years to come. And after such a disaster, the head tool-pusher would not last long.

The engineer was climbing up the ladder. He was holding something in his cupped hands and moving gingerly on the slimy plates. As he approached, Tregonnel noted the concern on the man's grease-streaked face, while he held out his cupped left hand. He looked around him swiftly to check that they were alone.

'Take a look at this, John,' he said softly. Tregonnel touched the blackened substance, two or three ounces of it, held in the engineer's hand.

'Sand?'

The man nodded.

'Where d'you find it?'

'In the bearings — pump and motor.'

The engineer had lowered his voice, so that Tregonnel could barely hear him against the breeze and the shouting of the shift below.

'Must have been planted ashore, John,' he continued. 'No one could have got away with it here.'

'Is there much of it?'

'Just right. He knew what he was doing — the bastard.' The engineer was bitter. He'd had his work cut out recently keeping the machinery going.

'Keep this to yourself,' Tregonnel ordered. 'Collect all of it that you can. Shove it in a plastic bag and bring it back to me.'

'What are you going to do with it?'

Tregonnel was gazing across to the eastward, to the summits of Ben Foinaven tipping through the misty horizon.

'Send it to Security at head office,' he said quietly. 'This is sabotage.'

11

Alan Brodie knocked back the last of his coffee. He always enjoyed his leisurely Saturday breakfast in the dining room of Innochervie's only hotel, the Errabeg. He needed to unwind after the shock of his *Wanklyn* experience, and this break at the end of the week gave him time to think. There was much on his mind at the moment, after he had stumbled upon last week's incident on *Explorer*.

Yesterday, Friday 29 October, he had returned to his office to finish the paperwork after making his final tour of the week around the *Sulisker One* jacket. The frames had been successfully reared and buttoned together. The ways were ready. Now the cranesmen and riggers were making their final preparations for the launch on Monday, in only two days' time. The Scottish element had wanted nothing more than a quiet, family affair, but the board, with Sir Anthony Anstruthers as its chairman, had insisted upon a traditional launch with due pomp. So it was to be all bull, with the Englishman's idea of how the Scots would love it. The organization was driving the manager of West Coast incoherent, but he'd managed to rake up the Fort William pipe and drum band. If only Anstruthers would launch secretly, as had two of the other companies. If anything went wrong in a public ceremony, it would be wretched publicity for International. But the board would not listen, preferring to invite VIPs from far and wide, rather than the locals. Alan would be thankful when Monday was behind him — and so would the Security people, after the recent sabotage on *Explorer*.

It was only luck that had brought the incident to Alan's notice, when he'd been clearing his in-tray yesterday evening. Checking on his defect list, he'd been surprised at the demand from *Explorer* for yet another replacement pump and motor — and when he'd asked the evasive Hubbard about it, the secret had been leaked. As soon as Alan had realized that the police had been informed, he had taken no further action, because Otway's division at MOD was automatically linked to police matters connected with internal security affecting the Services — but the whole affair had left an unease in the minds of those concerned with the success of this enormous *Sulisker One* project.

Alan sat back and watched the inshore boats busy about their morning's work in the little port half a mile away, down the hill and nestling beneath the shoulder of the promontory. There was one advantage of working for International Oil: the company looked after its people. The pay was good, health cover excellent, and accommodation expenses were generous. International had paid Alan's hotel expenses since he had set up his office in Innochervie. The calamity for the village was that prices had soared and no one, including the salmon fishermen who came from some way away, could afford to stay here now — except the oilmen.

The Errabeg stood below the crest of the hill, at the head of Loch Madach, a mile to the northward of the Seal promontory. In its commanding position overlooking Hoyea Bay and Seal, the hotel was sheltered from the north and east and, on a clear day, the Butt of Lewis was visible 40 miles across the restless waters of North Minch.

Passing through the hall on his way upstairs to his room, number 17, he was accosted by the manageress from her crescent-shaped office. From this observation post, she missed nothing. In her fifties, Sheila Burns had served in the WRNS and she ran her hotel efficiently. She wore the kilt always, was proud of her ancestry and, paradoxically, of her Oxford accent. Her greying hair and thickening waistline were deceptive — she was an energetic woman, enthusiastic in all that she did.

'Your sandwiches are ready, Mr Brodie,' she said. 'Will you be taking tea or coffee?'

He had forgotten about the food. He itched to be off, for Sheena would be waiting at 10.30, outside the chandler's store.

'Don't bother about coffee, Miss Burns. I'll just take my sandwiches … and a couple of bottles of beer?'

He could see that she was appraising him, amused contempt in her shrewd grey eyes. He was an oil man and, though bringing wealth to her hotel, he was part of the forces destroying the way of life on the west coast. As Sim McIver's secretary, and responsible for the organization of the Save Innochervie Association, she could show no quarter to the enemy. But guests at the hotel were somewhat different. Brodie and she respected each other, despite the age difference and the guerrilla warfare between them — the whole village knew that Sim and Sheila Burns were organizing a demonstration for Monday, launching day.

'You shall have your beer, Mr Brodie.'

'I'm a bit late…'

'We will not keep you waiting.' She pressed the buzzer at the side of her desk. 'By the time you've got your things together, we'll be ready for you.'

He smiled feebly. By now, all Innochervie would have enjoyed the embellishment of the recent goings-on, in spite of the tragedy of *Wanklyn*. It had been difficult enough to snatch a few moments with Sheena, without the whole community knowing. She'd phoned him at his office, the day he was back from hospital, but she'd been secretive. He sensed her anxiety. 'I *must* talk with you.' It had been a bad line and she'd spoken softly.

'What about?'

'There's no time to lose. When can we meet, Alan?'

They'd fixed a date and time, but she'd hung up without a farewell.

'Thanks, Miss Burns. I'll be down directly.'

He was glad to reach his room. Time had dragged this morning, even though, before breakfast, he had walked round *Sulisker One* for his final inspection. The eyes of the engineering world were on this mammoth project. A platform of such immensity had never been launched before. In the final analysis, whatever the designers had calculated, it was only the practical performance which could prove whether the feat was feasible. He'd rendered his report to Hubbard. There was nothing more that Alan could do but wait for Monday. At last, he was off to meet the girl of whom he was growing fond.

As he slipped into corduroy jeans, he found himself whistling the Skye Boat Song, an unusual exercise for him. Smiling, he pulled on a sweater and reached for his anorak. He grabbed his haversack from the cupboard, laced up the walking boots he'd bought in Fort William, and picked up his stick from the corner. Before leaving his disordered room, he glanced through the window: a green field, blotched with brown patches of reed and marsh grass, sloped down to Hoyea Bay. That pasture supported the three brown and white cows which were now chewing contentedly by the stone wall. Miss Burns, with her two sisters, knew what they were at: the hotel was never short of milk during the winter. He slammed the door of number 17 behind him and hurried along the corridor to the staircase.

'Been waiting long?'

'Just got here,' Sheena said. 'Will it rain?'

He glanced up at the scud flying across Seal. Down here, the chandlery was in the lee, but across the tops there would be wind.

'I've got my woollies on.' She laughed, pulling her red, belted raincoat more tightly around her.

He slung the haversack across his back and set off at a fast pace along the pebble beach on the north shore. He heard her scuffling behind him until, after ten minutes, they reached the cove where *Seamew* was propped on her shores, her new fo'c'sle head glistening with a fresh coat of emerald green.

'I love the smell of paint.' Sheena reached for his hand when she came up to him. 'When I was a girl, Dad used to work the boats.'

'Iain's helping now?'

She undid the green scarf she'd tied about her head. Her black hair streamed in the wind. 'Does them both good. Brings them together a bit, while Iain waits for another boat.' She pressed his arm. 'Come on — it's a fair way to Innoch Head and we haven't much time.'

She turned away to gaze across Hoyea Bay where the grey seas raced. It was low water and the yellow strands connecting Hoyea to the mouth of Loch Madach were visible where the surf broke. Freeing her hand, she stuffed the scarf into the pocket of her coat and tucked her trousers into her rubber boots. She ran off, following the sheep tracks as she climbed towards the highest peak of the promontory. Scrambling through the fading bracken and over the heather, sure-footed across the lichen-covered boulders, she was challenging Alan to keep up, but he preferred following her.

She was calling down, laughing at him from the summit, her cheeks flushed from the exertion and the biting wind. He was gasping for breath when he reached her, but she took his arm and nestled into the hollow of his shoulder.

'Wish it could always be like this,' she murmured. 'It's the real world up here.'

He put his other arm round her, but they could not stay up here long in this cold. It was nearly noon already; at three they would have to start back if they were to return before dark.

'Where shall we go, Sheena?'

She shook her head and smiled. 'It's up to you — but there's shelter down there by the Head.'

She was off again, skeltering down the long incline stretching towards Innoch Head. She waited for him at the bottom, where the sea-washed turf merged with the heather. She took his hand again as they strode in silence towards the rocky point thrusting into North Minch. The cliff fell sheer into the sea where the waves were breaking upon the rocks.

'Find somewhere out of the wind, Sheena. I'll take a look over there, nearer the lighthouse.'

They separated, Sheena exploring the northern shore while he searched the western tip of the headland. Somewhere dry and out of the wind — that was all they needed. After ten minutes, he gave up. The ground was sodden, and whenever he found a possible nook, it was open to the blustery wind. He retraced his steps to see whether she had succeeded, but he could not find her. He was about to double back, when a pebble plopped at his feet.

'Hi!'

She was tucked into a small cave, down by the rocks. As he ran towards her across the turf and scrambled the last few yards over the slippery granite, a shaft of sunlight pierced the clouds.

'It's dry here and out of the wind,' she called. She had taken off her raincoat and was leaning against the slab of rock, her hands behind her back.

He went up to her and pulled her roughly into his arms.

Suddenly she jerked upright. 'Look! Look there, Alan ... a wee seal.' Her hand still around his, she pointed towards a bewhiskered head popping through the surface of the sea. The seal seemed to be laughing at them, but then he dipped, his ochre outline just visible, as he cruised towards the sheltered cove. They struggled to their feet and ran to the edge of the rock. Surging with the swell, the seas were thundering into the gullies below them.

'There he is!'

Alan spotted him, further out this time — but the seal was now aware of the two intruders.

'Our little seal,' Sheena whispered. 'Isn't he beautiful?'

The brown head with its stiff whiskers disappeared without a ripple. The pale shadow vanished into its element.

He pointed towards a red dot plunging amongst the white horses at Hoyea Bay, uncertain of his eyesight.

'That's *Katriona*,' she cried, 'Sim's yawl. He shouldn't be out in this.'

They watched the small boat running under her red jib before the wind and yawing dangerously. The seas which were breaking upon the causeway under her lee seemed too close.

'Suppose he can't cross any other way,' Alan said. 'He must have good reason to leave his croft today.'

'We can watch him, but still keep warm, d'you think?' She tossed her dark hair and laughed. She led him back to the shelter of their cave, where they sat closely again, his arms about her. Her mood had changed. 'Alan?'

'Yes?'

'He's the reason why I asked to see you.' She hesitated, then went on, 'You see, I'm a bit scared.'

He felt the prick of jealousy. 'What's he done to you?' He spoke softly, but in the wind she did not hear him. 'What's he done to you?' he repeated.

'That's not it.' She laughed shortly. 'Sim's been a companion to me all these years, ever since we were bairns. He loves me, but differently from you.'

'How so?'

'We're friends, Alan. He loves me, but, can you understand…' She was gazing wistfully at the red sails bobbing in the confused waters. The yawl would soon be rounding Madach Point, in the lee of which Sim would moor her in the sheltered cove. 'He thinks a lot of me. He'd never harm me.'

'Why then?'

'He's in real trouble — up to his neck in it, I'm sure. He's desperate, Alan.' She sighed and laid her head against his chest. She took his hands and entwined his fingers with her own. He waited for her to continue.

'You know he runs the Save Innochervie faction? He's been drinking more heavily than usual, so I picked a good day to catch him at Hoyea. I wanted to help him, because he listens to me sometimes. I hadn't seen him for a while and his appearance shook me. Sim was a frightened man, Alan — *really* scared. I've never seen him like that before. All sorts of other failings, yes, but never terror.'

She paused to watch the yawl hardening her sheets, as Sim prepared for the close-haul.

'In his cottage, he loosened up — enough to put the fear of God into me too. That's when I decided to come to you, Alan.' She glanced up at him. 'I can trust you — you do understand that?'

He tightened his arm around her. 'Go on, if you want to.'

'The Nationalists soon latched on to him. They've used him ever since, for their own ends. But they hadn't any money, so there wasn't much that he could do, other than hold meetings and march up and down with their banners. Sim's a man of action. He was about to chuck it all up — the big boys were too much, both for him and Innochervie — when money suddenly began pouring in from somewhere. The sky was the limit, so long as progress on *Sulisker One* and the development of the port could be interrupted. Anything Sim wanted, he got. Of course, amongst his needs was the whisky.'

'The drink wouldn't buy Sim's soul — not a character like him, Sheena. He couldn't operate if he was permanently slewed.'

'He's managed pretty well so far — unlimited booze was the start of it. Next, they tried fear. You remember the murder in June, among the welders in West Coast?'

'When they found the bashed-up body — Jakins, the non-union man?'

She nodded. 'They killed him because he was on to something. Sim is certain Jakins had rumbled them. And then, in July…' She hesitated, waiting for *Katriona* to round up into the cove. Her jib began shivering as she luffed up. 'One night in July,' she went on, her clasp tightening between his fingers, 'a man called at Hoyea. A foreigner, Sim was certain. There were five others with him, strong-arm men. Their Volkswagen van was loaded with gear. Sim wouldn't tell me what, but they offered him 10,000 quid in cash, as future payment — "a sort of blackmail", Sim said.'

She was speaking softly. She glanced about her, even in their solitude, peering at the cliffs and across the heather to the hill. 'First, they threatened him. Then they beat him up, horribly, and kicked him in the balls. But Sim still wouldn't take the money. They were about to leave, when the big foreigner turned at the doorway. This is what Sim told me; these are his words he used, because I just could not forget them: "The Macgregor girl's a nice bird, isn't she, Sim? Good-looker, isn't she? Right shape, too?"' The colour had drained from her cheeks. She was hesitating, but she forced herself to continue. She spoke so low that he could barely understand her. 'The brute said, at the end, "Pity to mutilate her for you, Sim, wouldn't it? Wouldn't take much doing, not with a razor, would it?" They left then, silently, in the night.'

The mewing of the terns, dipping in the air currents below the cliff-tops, was the only sound above the surge of the seas. Her fingers were clutching at the back of his hand, her nails drawing blood. She sat there motionless, her head tilted back, her eyes closed. 'Can you understand, now, why Sim has had to go along with them? Why he's scared, why I'm frightened?'

'The police. Why doesn't he go to them?'

She laughed shortly. 'The Innochervie fuzz? And Ullapool? They've got their hands full with all the drunks. There's an oil boom, remember?'

'If he'd gone to them,' Alan conceded, 'I wouldn't give much chance for him — or for you.' He wanted to tell her of the other Brody; of the role that he, Alan, was having to play up here for Otway and his lot — and why hadn't MOD contacted him yet?

But Sheena was running on, unburdening her fears: 'There's an organization, Sim says, working amongst West Coast's labour force. He used to think that the upset was the usual communist-caused trouble, but he's certain now that it's organized from outside — by something big... Sim wouldn't tell me any more, except that he was very overworked just now. I left him then. I am sure he was feeling better, having told me. He made me promise that if anything was to happen to him, I was to come to you.'

'Me?'

'He said that they know you are not what you appear to be. Knowing me hasn't helped and you're on their list. They'll get you when they're good and ready — if there's no chance of using you, and when the time is right for them.'

'What did he mean by that?'

She shook her head. 'I suppose, as International's overseer here, watching *Sulisker One*, you know what's going on.'

Alan felt the strands closing about him. He was entangled in this invisible, sinister web, through no choice of his own, because a man had been murdered in a London back alley... Up here, in this wild country, the nightmare was unreal, too fantastic. And yet...? Launching day was on Monday. Sim was busy and so was Sheila Burns.

'Alan.' She had jumped up and was hurrying to the cliff edge. She stood motionless, staring across the bay at the yawl now rolling at her mooring. 'Down by the landing — *there*, Alan, look.'

A Volkswagen van was drawn up at the end of the cliff track. A cluster of men was advancing towards the solitary figure stumbling across the beach.

She ran back to him and threw her arms around his waist, binding him tightly. They watched the dark figures hustling

Sim towards the truck. Then they pushed him through the side door. The vehicle reversed, turned, and disappeared behind the headland.

Alan looked down at her where she leaned against his chest. She stared back at him, fear in her smouldering, black pupils. He bent down and kissed her on the lips. Gently he prised her from him, as he bent to collect her raincoat and the untouched sandwiches.

'What are we going to do?' she whispered.

'Back to the hotel. To my room. It's cold and it's getting late.' He stretched out his hands to her, to lead her home, back across the turf and up to the summit of Seal. 'Have a sandwich, girl,' he said. 'Good for morale. You'll be needing your strength.' He tossed her a squashed triangle of brown bread. She laughed, munching as she scrambled after him.

12

They lost track of time. From somewhere, a gong was sounding, echoing from the hall below.

'I'd better go, Alan. I'll slip out when you reach the dining room.'

He raised himself on one elbow to look down at her. With mock sternness, he said, 'Miss Macgregor, if you don't eat with me tonight, that's your lot.'

'Dad will be worrying.' She was wriggling away from him, trying to reach the edge of the mattress. 'The neighbours have a phone.'

He pushed her from the bed. 'Hurry, or the soup'll be cold. They never wait.'

In the dining-room, Alan felt that all eyes were upon them, for there were not many evenings when he had not been alone here. They felt like a couple of truant schoolchildren, but Sheena's telephone call to her father had eased some of the tension in her mind. Alan had sensed her anxiety — she was twenty-one, but an understanding daughter who made allowances for her traditional upbringing. It was this heritage that the influx of wealth was destroying.

'Sheena?'

She took his hand beneath the table.

'I meant what I said.'

'About marrying?'

'Yes. But you ought to move away from here for a bit.'

Her eyes were upon the tablecloth, following the outline of a sailing boat she was tracing with her fingernail. Her hands were small against his own. 'D'you think I'll leave you now, with all this going on?' Her voice was low and difficult to hear. The middle-aged waitress, a worthy grandmother from the village, was dishing out the rice pudding when Alan sighted the manageress bearing down upon them from the far side of the dining-room.

'Stand by for squalls.'

She withdrew her hand before Sheila Burns reached the table.

'Good evening, Miss Macgregor. There's a telephone call for Mr Brodie.'

Sheena forced a smile. Miss Burns's face was grim. Alan rose from the table.

'Will you take it in the kiosk? Or you can use my office if you wish.'

'Thanks. But I'll use the phone box.'

The bitch, thought Sheena, watching the woman following Alan from the room. *She's still got a decent figure and is neatly dressed. It's not just the village strife that's bugging her. She needs a man.*

'It was Iain.'

She heard Alan's voice, but had not seen him approaching through the double doors at the end of the room.

'Iain. He's worried about…'

Suddenly she was alert, the whirlwind fears swirling about her. 'Sim?'

'He sent a message via the shop. Dolly Tusker phoned it through to Iain's house.'

He was taking his place beside her: the room had suddenly become silent. 'Get on with your pud,' he whispered.

They continued with their meal, the chink of cutlery upon china the only sound. Then, gradually defeated, the other guests broke into monosyllabic conversation, and a murmur of self-conscious Scottish droning permeated the room.

'Sim wants to see you,' he said quietly.

'When?' The colour had drained from her face.

'Tomorrow at low water. As soon as we can cross the causeway.'

'I'm frightened, Alan,' she whispered.

He placed his hand upon hers, for all the world to see. 'Don't worry. We're both going — he's asked for me too.' He pushed back his chair. 'Come on. It's time I took you home.'

Sunday broke, a rough, blustery day with bright patches of blue sky and driving clouds sweeping their shadows across the hills. The gulls were shrieking and wheeling down by the cliffs, a distant accompaniment to the thunder of waves pounding upon the pebble-beach. Alan and Sheena scrambled down the cliff path to the causeway.

'Another two hours,' she said, 'before we can cross to Hoyea.'

'First we'll have our beer and sandwiches.'

'Shall we see our little seal?'

The afternoon was over before they knew it. Too soon, the white surf receded from the rocky ridge. A strand of shingle began to show as darkness fell.

'We can cross now,' she said, peering from the hollow of his shoulder. She jumped up, pulled him to his feet and led him by her accustomed route along the causeway. Hopping from rock to rock between the pools, and judging the intervals between the splashing breakers, she managed to reach the islet without drenching them both.

'Did you bring your torch?'

He tapped the pocket of his anorak. It was dark now and he could feel the solitude of the island pressing upon him.

'You told Iain when to expect us back? My brother worries too much about me.'

'Sim seemed very agitated and was insistent that Iain told no one else.' Alan went ahead, following the path that wound through the rocks and up the cliff face towards the summit of the islet. It was a black night and, with autumn drawing in fast, there was a dankness in the air.

'Careful, Alan,' Sheena called from behind him. 'The path drops now, down to the glen where the cottage is.'

'I won't use the torch. Take hold of my anorak.'

He, too, was feeling a tension he could not explain. The stones were slippery and he eased his pace to prevent them scuffling down the side of the rocky hill. A persistent doubt was niggling at the back of his mind — had they been shadowed since leaving Innochervie? Were they being watched? Was Sim's telephone call made under duress, a trap to lure Sheena and him over here? He felt sure, from her silence, that she must be sharing the same anxieties.

He was picking his footsteps carefully now, trying to minimize the noise. It was very dark but here, down in the glen, they were out of the wind.

'You'll see the croft at any moment,' she whispered. 'Sim can watch this path from the kitchen.'

When Alan left the gulley, the wind hit him. It was battering against the rocks and he hesitated, unsure of his direction.

'There,' Sheena said, 'to your right. You can just see his light.'

A yellow pinpoint was flickering in the darkness. It was difficult to judge the distance but, from the pounding of the surf upon the beach, the croft could not be far above high water mark. Alan's hand tightened around Sheena's as they advanced slowly towards the light.

A lonely tree was bending to the wind, the branches dancing before the light in the window. He could see the loom of Sim's croft, a low-lying cottage, tucked beneath the outcrop of rock that gave shelter from the gales. If Sim enjoyed this solitude, Alan mused, he was welcome to it. Sheena's hand suddenly tightened its grip. He stopped abruptly.

'Something's wrong, Alan,' she said softly, against the clamour of the wind.

'How d'you know?'

'He normally draws his curtains.'

Alan hesitated. 'Stay in the lee, Sheena. Yell if you need me.'

He pushed her behind the shelter of an outcrop of rock. She was calm, but he felt the pressure of her fingers as he left her. He yanked out his torch. As he approached the front door, the shingle of the path crunched beneath his feet. Something was banging in the outhouses at the back of the cottage. The light, a dull yellow, from a glass rectangle in the upper half of the doorway, was flickering — then Alan heard the generator thudding from somewhere at the back. As he approached the massive front door a black Labrador bounded towards him, barking furiously, its hackles raised. Alan held out his hand for the dog to scent and suddenly the animal was around his legs, sniffing, reassured. Its tail began to wag and as Alan spoke to it, it leapt up, its front paws at his waist, and began to whine. The dog was matted with mud. There was something wrong, he was sure, or Sim would have opened up for the dog by now. Alan banged upon the door with the butt of his torch.

As he waited, he could hear the wind battering against the rocks and whistling about the chimney. He beat again upon the woodwork, but the Labrador was taking no interest as it trotted to the outhouses at the back. Sim probably kept his front door locked against the wind, and used only his back door, through the yard. Alan followed the dog. At the rear, another light from a small window threw a pool of yellow into the back yard which was enclosed by a low brick wall. Several of the outhouses were carved out of the rock. Above the rounded roofs, the low cloud was sweeping across the rising moon. Alan pushed open the gate and hammered on the back door. He sensed the panic mounting in him and he rapped again swiftly.

He tried the handle … pushed… The door was locked. Behind him, the dog was whining in one of the sheds while the shadows danced crazily across the yard from the light escaping through the ill-fitting curtains. He crouched to the level of the window-sill to peer through the cracks.

By craning his neck, he could just see across the coconut matting on the kitchen floor. On the draining board of the sink a motley collection of unwashed crockery was stacked. The living-room door was half-open, an upturned chair lying across the sill. His eyes traversed the beam of light swaying in the shadows from this main room, the source originating probably from some swinging central lamp.

The stone floor of the kitchen was strewn with fallen objects — several books, a smashed saucer, another chair and a broken whisky bottle, the trickle of the spirit still dark upon the flags. The foot of a table-leg was protruding from behind the edge of the living-room door.

His gaze shifted to the vertical slit of light from this doorway: swaying in the draught about 18 inches above the floor, two boots were visible, with trouser-ends tucked into them. The legs were masked by the edge of the half-opened door. His mouth was dry as his torch smashed the panes of the kitchen window in front of him. The glass tinkled onto the stone yard and the Labrador started barking. Alan wrenched off his anorak and slung it across the jagged glass in the window-frame. As he levered his body through, Sheena called him from the front of the cottage.

'Stay where you are, Sheena,' he yelled out into the night.

He fell to the kitchen floor, to the crash of the remaining crockery from the sink. He hauled himself to his feet and dragged together the curtains of the kitchen window. Torch at the ready, he advanced slowly towards the living-room and kicked open the door. He gasped with horror as he stared at the corpse hanging from the iron hook in a wooden beam of the ceiling. Sim's bearded face was purple, his tongue black in his contorted mouth, protruding eyes staring sightlessly towards the kitchen door, hands stiff in *rigor mortis*. The table from which he had jumped was in disarray, a glass lying on its side, a collection of cigarette ends sprinkled across the table-top where he had upset the ashtray. But it was those sightless blue eyes, protruding from their sockets as they stared towards him, that shook Alan most…

Sheena … she must be shielded from this horror. He slammed shut the door of the living-room as he watched the handle of the front door jerking up and down.

'Go round the back. Wait outside, Sheena.' He was trembling as he searched for a knife in the dresser drawer. His instincts impelled him to cut down the stiffened corpse, but then caution held him back. He must use the telephone in the corner to fetch the police. He picked up the instrument but the line was dead. He wrenched open the living-room door and threw up into the sink. Sheena was calling at the window.

'Alan. Quickly.'

He wanted to puke again, the sweat wet on his forehead. He slammed the living-room door shut behind him, swept back the kitchen curtains and clambered out through the window. Looking up at him with sad eyes the Labrador stood in the yard, its tail between its legs. Sheena crouched beside the dog, consoling it.

'You're as white as a sheet. For God's sake, Alan, tell me what's happened.'

'Sim's dead.'

Though she smothered her face in her hands, she had known it all along.

'It looks as though he's taken his own life,' he said, his words drowned by the clatter of the ill-fitting doors of the outhouses. 'Don't go inside.'

'The telephone wires have been cut,' she said, under control now. 'He wouldn't have done that himself, would he?'

Alan did not answer as she pulled him towards the furthest of the three outhouses. She flung open the door and switched on the flickering light.

'In there, Alan.'

The glow illuminated the shed, encrusted with cobwebs and years of dust. On the floor were two stacks of boxes — one was labelled in red 'Danger: Explosives', the other 'Detonators'. From the rusting hooks on the wall hung a row of yellow oilskin jackets and trousers. Above them, each neatly perched on its own hook, were six yellow hard hats. On each safety helmet was stencilled in black the unmistakable emblem of the GPO.

13

Alan had half dragged Sheena down to the eastern shore of Hoyea. By the light of his failing torch, he could see the white surf of the incoming tide already swirling across the highest slabs of rock on the causeway. Slithering and falling in the darkness, they finally floundered, soaked to the skin and their fingers bleeding, upon the beach at the southern tip of the entrance to Loch Madach. The new moon was rising behind Ben Grudie, which stood black and gaunt against the silver cirrus streaking the night sky.

'Can you go on?'

'Yes. I'm warmer now.' The trembling of her body had ceased, but her teeth were still chattering.

'We must tell the police.'

'Take the loch track,' she said. 'We could go up to the hotel and use the phone.'

'No. Once we've reached the village road, we'll go straight to the police station. We don't want the world knowing yet.'

He took her arm and together they scrambled down the gravel track skirting the southern shore of Loch Madach. A nightjar screeched from the slopes to their right, and he felt Sheena's fright as a sheep scuttled away, invisible in the clumps of heather. Twenty minutes later, ten minutes past ten by his watch, they were striding down the hill of the metalled road, towards the glimmering lights of Innochervie.

'What are you going to tell them?' Sheena asked. He caught the unfamiliar note of indecision. 'D'you really think that Sim cut the phone wires himself?'

'Yes.'

'He took his life. You think that?'

Sim was dear to her, a friend to whom loyalty was due. But from the moment that Alan had been able to think rationally, one question persisted. Where had he seen those GPO hard hats before, and why were most of the explosives boxes empty when he tested their weight? If Sim had been inextricably involved in some atrocious plot, he might be so weighted down by guilt that, with the maudlin effects of whisky, he *could* take his own life, rather than face up to the enormity of his actions.

'Sheena — he committed suicide. Sure of it.'

She removed her arm. She walked down the hill, apart from him now, silent as they neared civilization. 'Take me home,' she said softly. 'I'll be safe with Dad while you're in your huddle with the law.'

Innochervie had been faintly amused by its acquisition of a modern police station. The onset of crime had brought the inevitable retaliation of the forces of law and order. The village now boasted an Inspector's house and a row of four freshly-painted police cottages: one for the sergeant and three for the constables, the murder of the welder having prompted this decision. By the porch light of the detached house, Peter glanced at his watch — half past ten and already late for Innochervie. He could save time by knocking up the senior officer. The door opened, and a tall, moustached man, about 45, wearing a blue cardigan, was staring down at him in suspicion.

'Are you the Inspector?'

'Yes. Inspector Brague. What's the trouble?'

'Can you spare me a moment? It's very serious.'

The Inspector stood back. The warmth, light and the normality represented comfort beyond measure for the soaked figure from out of the night.

'My wife will fix you a cup of tea. How'd you get in that state?'

For the first time since he'd blundered in upon the obscenity of Sim's death, Alan was beginning to feel cold and the first effects of shock. He found it impossible to control the trembling of his limbs as he told his story. The Inspector, whose shrewd but disillusioned eyes never wavered from Alan's face, listened in silence as he jotted down times and details. Alan emphasized his own doubts and suspicions and, when he had finished his statement, a woman brought in a tray of tea and scones, freshly buttered and spread with honey.

'You're holding something back, Mr Brodie.'

Alan calmly met the blue eyes staring steadily at him from the weather-beaten, lined face. The man was not to be fooled. Alan waited until his wife had left the room. 'I've got to make a report — London.'

The Inspector's eyes searched his face. 'Whitehall?'

'Ministry of Defence.'

Brague pushed the phone across the table. His eyes were alert and cautious now. 'So it's you,' was all he said. 'Headquarters wouldn't tell me who it was.' He smiled apologetically. 'I've tried to cover the West Coast yard and Cul Mor Services, but I'm always short of men. So it's you.' And he whistled beneath his breath. 'You can dial straight through to London.' He rose from his chair and left the room, closing the door behind him.

Otway had told Alan to go through the exchange for the Duty Officer. He could hear the signal already ringing at MOD.

'Ministry of Defence.'

'This is an urgent call from Scotland. DNI's Duty Officer, please.'

'Who, sir?'

'Duty Officer.'

'Hold on, please.' The phone clicked and eventually a crisp voice came on the line: 'Your name?'

'Alan Brodie.'

'Who d'you want to speak to?'

'Captain Otway of DNI. Urgent.'

'DNI? Hold on.'

The line clicked again, then went dead. Someone else spoke up: 'DNI Duty Officer here. Are you Lieutenant Brodie, RNR?'

'Yes. I must speak to Captain Otway.'

'I know about your assignment, Brodie. We've been expecting you. What's the trouble?'

Alan paused. Otway had said that no phone was safe… 'A man's been murdered.'

'Yes?'

'The death is connected with tomorrow's ceremony. Certain of it.'

'Yes?'

'This is bloody urgent. I've got to speak to Captain Otway. Can't you give me his private number?'

'We're not authorized to do that. Ex-directory.'

'But I *must* talk to him — can't you understand?' Alan could feel the anger mounting inside him, but the more infuriated he became the less chance there was of reaching Otway.

'Sorry, Brodie. Those are my orders.'

'There's no time…' Alan shouted into the mouthpiece. 'They're launching tomorrow.'

'I'll inform Captain Otway.'

'At once?'

'Immediately. Have you a telephone number?'

'My hotel: Innochervie 327. I'll be back there in half an hour.'

'Right. I'll try to reach the captain.'

The phone went dead. Alan slowly replaced the receiver. It was already quarter past eleven. The Errabeg would soon be locking its doors, but tonight Sheila Bums might be up late, making clandestine preparations for their protest tomorrow. She wouldn't appreciate a late telephone call from London, but there was no option — events were moving too swiftly. The ceremony was due to start at 10.30, less than 12 hours from now. He rose from his chair and knocked on the door.

'Get through?'

'They're ringing me back at the hotel. Thanks for your help.'

'I've done nothing — but sign your statement, please.' The policeman handed Alan the buff form. 'I'll be going over to Hoyea after the launch.' He paused, then looked up at Alan.

'So you think it's suicide?'

Alan felt the feebleness of his own inadequacy. The forces of evil were crowding in and no one seemed to be combatting them.

'Inspector…' Alan was finding it impossible to convey the desperate anxiety that he felt. 'Tomorrow's an important day for Scotland. There will be many people here, including VIPs. I'm certain Sim McIver's death is connected with tomorrow. For God's sake, can't you recommend the authorities to delay the launch for a day or two — until you have enough time and men to police the area properly?'

'You're joking, Mr Brodie.' The Inspector was irritated. 'You don't imagine the authorities can cancel tomorrow's preparations, do you? There's too much at stake. The top engineers from all over are already here, scattered around Ullapool, Fort William and Glasgow.'

'How much security have you laid on?'

The Inspector hesitated, before looking Alan straight in the eye. 'Enough for the lunatic fringe, Mr Brodie. But I haven't sufficient plain clothes coverage for professional sabotage.'

'That's what worries me, Inspector. I'm certain Sim's death is connected with tomorrow's ceremony. He wouldn't have taken his own life because of a demonstration by the Save Innochervie faction.'

'It's the drink. McIver's been hitting it hard lately. I've had him in cells twice during the last month. You're insinuating he could have been murdered, aren't you?'

Alan knew that the Inspector was leaving the mystery open. He was waiting for Alan to fill in the details.

'I must get back for MOD's call. Thanks for the tea and your kindness.'

The wind was howling outside, battering against the houses. As Alan climbed back up the hill, he could see the floodlights silhouetting the cranes and the steel monster waiting in its cradles. There was a light burning in the hotel where Sheila Burns was still working in her office. The door was unlocked, and, as he pushed it open, he heard the faint ringing of a telephone.

'That'll be for me.'

'It's very late, Mr Brodie.'

He ignored the reproach, slammed shut the door of the kiosk and lifted the phone. The decisive voice at the other end could be none other than Otway's.

'Who's that?'

'Alan Brodie.'

'You wanted me?'

'Yes, sir. Is the line secure?'

'No — but you'll have to risk it, if it's so urgent.'

Alan gave his account of the last 48 hours in the barest outline. The events seemed so lame now, as he tried to describe them dispassionately. 'I've heard nothing from you, Captain Otway, since the submarine collision, but I'm putting on record that I think McIver's death is connected with tomorrow's launch. There's a lot going on up here, but it's all beneath the surface and impossible to pinpoint. People are frightened.'

'What d'you mean?'

'McIver was threatened a few days ago. So was his girl, and now I'm also on their list.'

'Who are "they", Brodie?'

'I wish I knew. But I think they're some underground organization run from abroad. There are a lot of foreigners up here.'

'Be more specific.'

'Subversion and violence by communists, Marxists, and the lunatic fringe.'

'Who's behind it?'

'McIver wouldn't say. He was afraid for his life.'

Alan could just hear Otway at the other end. They were both talking as quietly as they could, both acutely aware of the lack of security.

'Couldn't MOD call off tomorrow's "do", sir, until the police have the security buttoned up? Too many incidents point to disruption tomorrow.'

'Impossible. We've arranged top-security. We'd be pleased to see what's in the wind.'

'How do you mean?'

'Come up to see me on Wednesday. Things are moving fast.'

'Morning or afternoon?'

'Morning.'

'Sorry to bother you so late.'

'That's all right. But, Brodie...'

'Yes?'

'Don't worry too much about tomorrow. Get some sleep. The area's properly covered.'

The alarm woke him at six but, in spite of his short night, Alan was in good form when he drove into West Coast's yard. Dawn was breaking behind Ben Grudie, and the latticed steelwork of the platform was stark against the lightening sky. After so many months of hard work and frustration, it was difficult to realize that, once the cranes had finished fussing around her, *Sulisker One* would be slipping down the ways in less than four hours' time.

So many battles — environmental, political, bureaucratic and economic — had been fought. Now the goal was almost reached — the launch with its alien ceremonial, the flotation into the loch, and the tow to Sulisker — that was all that remained now.

Alan began his final inspection before the launching ceremony. Already, overalled men were ambling desultorily around the ways, checking the cradles, manning the cranes, sprucing up the spectators' arena. Because of the prolonged disagreement over whom to invite and the manner of the ceremony, no one would admit the fact, but this *was* a proud day for West Coast. No one had so far built such an enormous steel structure, let alone attempted the 'controlled launch' to settle it on site — and only this practical attempt would show whether the designers were right. If they were wrong, their error would be expensive — over £100,000,000. Alan stood back for a moment to survey the supine monster.

Like a huge wedge, the colossus lay on its side, its vast flotation legs cocooned in their red cradles. The huge buoyancy spheres gleamed from the dew that had condensed on their steel circumferences. And looming overall, one on each side, the gigantic cranes stood poised on their tracks. Each crane stood 380 feet high. With their main beam and fly jib, they reached 400 feet. Alan could see the orange-coated crane drivers climbing towards their control cabins.

'Morning, Alan.'

Sam Campbell, the site manager, was carrying out his last rounds. He had aged visibly during these last 18 months. Alan had not envied him his job. Endeavouring to maintain schedules and datelines in these difficult days was more important to International than cost. Catching the weather window was what mattered.

'All well, Sam?'

Campbell grunted. 'Be glad when it's over. Can't stand bull, particularly the English version … and spending a week's work on this!' He glanced upwards and snorted. The site manager continued on his way, checking the details, missing nothing. Alan followed him to the far side of the platform. A breeze was blowing from the north-east and it was cold in this sector where the rearing towers stood gaunt and useless now: 4000 tons of final steelwork had been used in their construction and over 8000 tons of temporary — and soon they would be demolished, their task completed. Their huge pulley blocks swayed gently in the breeze, and the wires of the tackles sang where they hung idly. The Met. Office people had predicted two days of reasonable weather, which was just as well with a launch of such awkwardness in an exposed quarter of the yard. He glanced back for the last time upon the scene he would probably never again witness.

The spectators' area had been roped off in a semi-circle, the scaffolding of the stands rising in tiers behind the half-moon arena in front of the slipway. Two flagpoles, one with the St Andrew's cross, the other with the Union Jack, stood at each corner of the arena which had been covered with yellow sand and shingle for the band. Heavy rollers had flattened the semi-circle, but heaven help the counter-marching pipers if rain turned the area into a quagmire. Strings of bunting were festooned about *Sulisker One*: to one side, and facing the top end of the platform, the launching stand had been rigged, complete with champagne bottle impedimenta. The rostrum gleamed white with its fresh coat of paint.

Though it was only 8.30, the first of the guests were trickling into the stands — probably the minority, the local contingent. The sun was peeping above the low-lying hills, so it looked as if nothing could postpone the launching now. At £16,000 a day deadtime, waiting could be an expensive business — and once the piledriving operation on site had been completed, they could all breathe again. The steel platform deck and the modules would be towed out and built on top. Over 30 wells would fan out from *Sulisker One* and three more platforms might eventually be built to develop the whole field.

Sam Campbell was not the only executive who felt jumpy. Alan, too, felt uneasy. He'd be relieved when the launch was over. The horror of yesterday was still too vivid, and he'd be glad when Sheena arrived. He'd try to fix a seat next to his in the official enclosure, but she'd probably stick with her father who had been invited in his capacity as *Seamew*'s skipper. Alan glanced towards the Ullapool road which cut into the hills of

Ben Grudie — a line of traffic was crawling towards Innochervie, and some of the cars were parking in the heather-bound tracks outside the village. The sunlight was flashing on their windscreens and he could hear the distant sound of revving engines. Innochervie would be in the news today.

14

Donald Macgregor had lost count of the times he had turned over. Ever since the dog next door had barked, at 3.30 this Monday morning, he had been unable to find again the solace of sleep. He lay awake, flat on his back in the double bed, staring through the pale rectangle that was the night sky above the Saddle on the far side of the loch. The hours were passing slowly, with so much on his mind. It could not be far off five — the neighbours next door would be at it soon. Regular as an alarm clock, they were, at 5.20 every morning: the rhythm of their bedhead tapping against the flimsy dividing wall of the modern semi-detached was a torment to both Comyn and himself, but for different reasons.

Though officially he and his wife slept together, they belonged to different worlds, each to his and her side of the bed, never touching each other now — she, because she had no need to, he, because he had no desire. They were two strangers, each in their loneliness, neither brave enough to snap the final cord of physical parting.

There they went, their magnificent neighbours next door... The happiness the Hudsons shared together was reflected in the laughing eyes of the buxom wife, married to Charlie Hudson some 19 years ago. They rarely missed this prelude to their day, but the rhythmic knocking and the squeaking springs were a condemnation to both Donald and Comyn. He could sense her now, pulling the bedclothes around her head to shut out the sounds. 'Disgusting,' she'd said. 'Can't they think of anything else?' But to Donald, the Hudsons' orchestration lifted his spirit, awakened the past. He could see his Rosie now, stretched out for him in her June bed in the ling behind Ben Grudie. No one had ever loved him as she had — Sheena was the proof. They had moved south for a time and no one had guessed when the Macgregors returned to Innochervie with their new baby. They reared the child as their own, although Comyn had never forgiven Donald and had always resented Sheena.

The tempo next door was reaching its climax — then suddenly the silence of the early dawn. The yellow glow from the light that the Hudsons had just switched on was reflected against the telegraph pole at the end of their garden. Another day had begun.

What a bloody business was this oil invasion. Not only had its advent been the final straw between Comyn and himself, but the ripples were now spreading between Sheena and him, prising father and daughter apart to destroy the love they'd shared so intensely.

He'd never seen Sheena so upset as when she'd returned last night, shivering as she stumbled through the doorway. Her clothes were soaked, her hair a tangled mess. She'd crouched in front of the parlour fire, silent until her mother had gone upstairs. Then she'd poured out her heart to him, telling him of Sim's tragedy. Donald had felt sure she was holding something back… He sighed again and turned, his back towards his snoring wife.

What would the police find when they went to pick up the body? He hoped there was nothing to incriminate Sheena, who had so often crossed to Hoyea to see him. In many ways, Donald was happier with her friendship for that oil man, Alan Brodie. He seemed a more normal individual and, by the change that had come over Sheena, they were very much in love. 'He wants to marry me, Dad,' she'd told him when she'd come in late after supper on Saturday. Comyn had played up, as expected, but he'd been sharp with her, before putting his arm around Sheena's shoulder.

'Let her be, woman,' he'd growled. 'Brodie's all right.'

'He's not for our Sheena,' she'd snapped. 'He's not one of us, and you know it, Macgregor.' She'd flounced out to the yard, the discussion firmly concluded. Alan Brodie was an up-and-coming young man and would make Sheena happy. Sim was dead — Donald felt sad at the loss of a friend, of a man who was standing up for the traditional life of the crofters and who would have fought the oil invasion to the end. But why should he be murdered? Sheena had not answered the question, but had intimated that she would not be attending the ceremony today. Who would be leading the demonstration now? Sheila, or Dougal Gordon, the headmaster?

Donald stretched and yawned. First light was breaking now over the hill line of the Saddle and the red warning lights on top of the TV mast were difficult to see. He rolled silently from the bed. He'd make the tea, early though it was. The antis were gathering at half past eight, at Stonecroft Farm. He must not be late, now that Sim was dead.

Sheila Burns felt the tension mounting inside herself. Though the local constabulary had recognized the antis full well, she and all the demonstrators, over 60 of them, including Dougal and the minister, James Maclaren, had been permitted through the gates of West Coast. They had been allowed to find seats in the crescent-shaped stadium rigged up in front of the jacket. Sheila looked round in astonishment at this squandering of money — there must already be several hundred people here.

'Lovely day, Miss Burns.'

She recognized the voice of Inspector Brague. She smiled. There had always been a bond between them. Brague was a fair man whose job it was to keep the peace — but his Scottish heart was in the right place.

'Perfect day for the ceremony, Inspector.'

He chuckled, rubbing his gloved hand with anticipation. 'Ceremonial demo, Miss Burns?'

She laughed as he stood back for her to enter Row H, where a seat had been reserved for her. She sat down, relieved to rest. She had slept little last night, after hearing of Sim's tragedy.

'You ought to have stopped this launching, Inspector,' she said. 'It's not decent, after what happened last night.'

'Impossible, Miss Burns,' Brague said. 'We're so busy, I can't even cross to Hoyea until the evening tide.'

She watched his dark blue figure merge with the crowd now milling through the gangways. Someone was waving to her from the other side. Dougal Gordon was ready, then — there also was Donald Macgregor, but his daughter was not with him. The majority of the Save Innochervie army seemed to be here, but where was the minister, James Maclaren? Her pulse beat faster as her moment drew nearer. They'd be watching her, taking their cue from her when she thought fit. The band, imported from Fort William, was already assembling. The English board of directors had at least enough gumption to hire a Scottish band. Their march past, to the skirling of the pipes, would make the morning a pleasure, even though they had been hired at a cut-price fee.

Sheila Burns felt resentment smouldering inside her as she regarded the steel platform confronting her. At least International had shown a little imagination. The bottle of champagne would be broken by Miss Anita Charlton, the programme stated, the first female secretary to have been engaged for the *Sulisker One* project. A formidable task, Sheila thought, for some chit of an English girl.

The clock across the way was showing 10.28, so they'd soon be off now. At that moment the band produced a drum roll, and then the first strains of the National Anthem floated towards the hills of Ben Grudie. The Queen's representative was here and Sheila found the moment an emotional one. The older men took off their hats as the women stood up in their seats.

As she stood in silence, Sheila's thoughts slid back to the war, when, as a Wren, she'd driven a staff car up here for the long journeys by senior officers to the more out-of-the-way naval centres on the West Coast. Those days seemed a long while ago now, and Keith had been dead a long time. Why did she have to lose her heart to a man who was destined to be lost in a submarine on trials in the Clyde? The boat had been lying off Ailsa Craig, stuck in the mud, ever since.

A loudspeaker was crackling behind her, and then a sonorous voice announced the opening of the proceedings: 'My Lords, Lord Provost, Ladies and Gentlemen, pray silence for Sir Anthony Anstruthers, chairman of International Oil...' The hubbub was suddenly subdued. 'Sir Anthony Anstruthers.'

There must have been over 1,000 people there, she thought. The crowd rustled, the loudspeakers crackled, and then the self-confident and amusing words of International's chairman filled the arena. She could clearly see the VIPs assembled on the raised dais, which was flagged and gaily decorated with streamers. The women were huddled in fur coats, while most of the men seemed to be wearing car coats or anoraks. The trapeze line from which the champagne bottle was suspended hung in an arc from the top of the jacket to the stand on the dais. The English were certainly making a meal of this.

'It's a cold day, but it's fine…' So the self-assured man began. By all accounts, he was being a successful chairman, after his fire-eating predecessor, that man who had put up the backs of the oil sheiks and had been retired with an astronomical golden handshake. Anstruthers went on to recount the progress of the construction and the principal events in this two-year battle to catch next year's weather window.

He has conveniently omitted the callous strikes, Sheila thought — the mysterious murder of that welder; the poisoning of a simple society; the enmity in the village and the destruction of the countryside. What a hypocritical farce this ceremony was: typical English behaviour, this morning's ritual, with the hired band and the visitors from all over. At least they had listened to her, though. She had managed to bully the management into giving her 50 seats for the locals. West Coast had apparently been surprised at first but finally had succumbed to her blackmail: the Save Innochervie Organization might be mollified if invited to the launching.

Sheila glanced about her at the stands that were now filled. She saw Dougal moving down the aisle, coming to join her. She smiled, pleased to know she would have him by her side.

'How goes it, Sheila?' he asked, as he pushed into the next seat. 'All set?'

She grinned and nodded towards the dais. The VIPs were all there now. She recognized the tall figure of the chairman, and that mousy little woman with the unsuitable hat flopping over her eyes must be the secretary who was about to launch the monster… She had once stayed in the hotel.

'Just as well this is what the English think we Scots would like,' Dougal chuckled. 'I'm looking forward to the fun. Embarrassing if anything goes wrong.'

'Nothing will slip up,' Sheila said. 'They've rehearsed it often enough.'

'I knew they'd have the pipes,' Dougal said. 'Pity they couldn't have had the soldiers.'

'Cheaper this way, with McAllister's band. Hope they don't disgrace Scotland. Ridicule might teach these self-satisfied English a lesson. They would never take local advice…' She nudged the schoolmaster. Things were beginning to happen on the launching dais: the chairman was tapping the microphone and the speakers in the stand began to splutter.

'I now have pleasure,' Sir Anthony boomed, 'in asking Miss Charlton to name the Oil Platform for us… Miss Charlton…' Sir Anthony stepped back and bowed gallantly to the slim woman on his left. Miss Charlton was neatly dressed in a dark blue coat and dress. She stepped forward and lifted the champagne bottle, holding it horizontally to display its foil.

'I name this Oil Platform, *Sulisker One*…'

She's a self-assured lass, all right, Sheila muttered to herself. *I wouldn't have such a chip on my shoulder if I'd had her poise. Damn her eyes…* There was a suspicion of a smile at the corners of Sheila's mouth as she watched Miss Charlton release the bottle. The bottle struck the steelwork, bounced, and hung there, incredibly unbroken. There was a hush, then a ripple of laughter from the crowd.

'Bad luck for the platform,' someone said close to her. 'It'll never be any good now.' She felt angry at the small-mindedness of people. Funny, she thought, that she could react so, when she was dead against the project … but she hated superstition…

Sir Anthony was snatching at the spare bottle, which had been independently rigged for such an emergency. Sheila could hear him laughing over the loudspeaker, but now the hubbub of the crowd, the flutter of a press helicopter overhead and the whine of the cranes were drowning any further chat from Miss Charlton. She soldiered on, her lips moving inaudibly. The second bottle flew through the air. There was a dull 'plop', a showering of white foam, and a cheer from the crowd.

At first, Sheila could distinguish no movement on the slipway. Then, by closing one eye, she could discern the latticework beginning to shift across the background beyond. The platform was beginning to move down the ways, held in its red cradles. The huge cranes towered above on either side as they inched along, their tracks parallel with the ways. Then she heard the *thump! thump!* of the band as it struck up from somewhere to the right. Just the right moment to curb the crowd's impatience, for, at this rate of descent to the water, the launch would take some time. The tugs were there, waiting like sheepdogs, and tooting their hooters.

'McAllister's in his element today,' Dougal muttered. 'Hope they're all sober. He'll be making a bob or two.'

And then the band swung into the half-moon arena running down the side of the slipway — kilts swinging, pipes skirling, drums tapping, what more could the English want? A cynical smile was creasing Sheila. Half of them were out of step and she was reminded of the finale at the end of the circus.

Dougal was prodding the small of her back. This was her cue, the moment for which they had rehearsed for so long. The time had come for action. She took a deep breath, pushed past her neighbours, scurried down the aisle and ran out into the arena as the band moved past her, beating the retreat. The tempo changed suddenly as they moved into the 'slow march', three files of pipers parading with solemn dignity towards the far side of the arena.

Sheila heard the mixture of cheering and boos as she aligned herself in the wake of the marching column. She felt ridiculous, but then suddenly she was surrounded, not by policemen or the security guards, but by her 'ain folk!' Scores of them tumbled from the aisles, and rushed up behind her to give their support. She recognized the faces, some coming from as far away as Inverness and Caithness.

Her heart lifted: this was no jumbled mass of pathetic sheep following an unknown cause. These were decent citizens, whose only recourse to saving their way of life and their native land was to demonstrate publicly — the action went against the grain of these worthy people, but they were prepared to put up with the ridicule, if their protest could be heeded in high places.

'Good for you, Sheila.'

Dougal had moved in beside her, and was marching in step and swinging his arms with the best of them.

'Follow the band!' she shouted above the skirl of 'Scotland the Brave'.

'They'll be counter-marching.'

'What?'

'*Counter-marching.*'

At that moment, she saw the silver-knobbed cane of the drum-major wobbling high in the air at the head of the band. The kilted men in front of her suddenly began to slow, to stop as they flexed their knees for the 'mark time' of the turn. Then they were about-turning, marching back again, the pipes and drummers aware for the first time that they were being followed.

'Magnificent discipline.'

Sheila heard Dougal's remark to the soldiers now bearing down upon them. The first piper, eyes popping from his head, was too astonished to snatch his much-needed breath. He missed his cue and his pipes dispensed an agonized groan. The piper burst out laughing and dropped his bag. His surprised neighbour, following the cue, also lost his place and, before the band knew what was happening, the spirited 'Scotland the Brave' had degenerated into a mournful wailing of disappointed sheep bags. The resplendent drum-major, undaunted to the end, continued onwards, stave twirling manfully — but his band, a disorganized rabble, lay 20 yards behind.

Sheila could not speak. Above the noise, she hardly heard the yells, the laughter, the hilarious cries of 'Scotland for ever!' Donald Macgregor had seized his placard reading 'Save Innochervie', and was stubbornly trying to hold it aloft in the struggling mass of bandsmen, police and demonstrators. Dougal, tears streaming down his cheeks, was hugging her with joy. Then suddenly she heard screams behind her, from the spectators in the stands.

15

'Good day to ye, Mr Brodie.'

From his corner seat at the end of the second row in the VIPs' stand, Alan Brodie recognized the booming voice of Innochervie's Free Church Minister. This bigoted man was impossible to ignore if you lived in the village. Alan had met him at several meetings when International were still trying to keep the peace. The Reverend James Maclaren was now standing in the aisle and waiting for Alan to make room for him.

'Thank ye.'

The minister, clothed in his habitual black, squeezed his way into the seat next to Alan's. 'Not too late, I hope, Mr Brodie.'

Alan shook his head, in no mood to chat. The chairman of International was well into his speech. Anstruthers had always been a good speaker, but in spite of the loudspeakers it was difficult to catch his words. The press helicopter overhead, the whine of the winches and the trundling of the cranes along their tracks were drowning most of the ceremony. The racket was spoiling the efforts of the band which, in all conscience, lacked the dignity expected of it. When it first struck up, the incongruity of bespectacled middle-aged men in a variety of kilts had caused many a delighted Scottish chuckle. And when they had marched, if that was the word, into the arena, it had been problematical whether there were more men in step than out of it.

Alan's thoughts wandered as he watched the sun's first rays creeping across the greens and browns of the Saddle. The hills on the far side of the loch were stark this morning, so close he could almost touch them. There'd be rain before the day was out. But why wasn't Sheena here? For the third time, he searched the stands for the figure he knew so well. She should be down among the anti-brigade with her father. Donald Macgregor's sturdy frame stood head and shoulders above the spectators, opposite Miss Burns who seemed to be surrounded by the Save Innochervie brigade. Dougal Gordon, the schoolmaster, was in the kilt this morning, as were the majority of the locals.

An incredible woman, Miss Burns. She possessed a natural dignity and authority which impelled her raggle-taggle band of followers to heed her. Though she was heart and soul in the anti-movement, she was intelligent enough to know that the hotheads had to be curbed. In her green kilt she was a splendid sight down in the front row, with her rakish bonnet challenging this brash world she detested. Who would be their new leader, Alan wondered, now that Sim was dead?

Alan watched the high cirrus creeping across the clear, sharp blue sky. Now that Sheena had entered his life, he was more aware of the world about him. The colours were brighter, the blues bluer, the purple on the hills richer.

'There's a lot of our ain folk down there, Mr Brodie.'

Maclaren was pointing towards the front row of the spectators. A muscle was twitching in the minister's cheek and his fingers were restless where his hands gripped the rail in front of him.

'And what d'ye think of us, Mr Brodie?' the minister asked over his shoulder, as he watched the crowd below. 'D'ye blame us if we want to keep our independence?'

Alan felt irritated. Couldn't the man keep quiet? He was always trying to analyse the simplest of man's feelings — and Anstruthers was in full spate now, the loudspeakers crackling and battling against the whirring and grinding noise of the cranes. God, how he missed Sheena! They'd suffered their first disagreement yesterday, and she was not here this morning. He felt the pain of her absence, but the shock of Sim's tragedy had knocked her sideways. She had not kissed him last night — left him silently, pushing open the door of her parents' house. No word either this morning, but how could she get in touch with him when he had left the hotel at 6 o'clock? If only she had been here.

'Mr Brodie.' Someone was prodding him. 'Mr Brodie, what d'ye think of a people who won't give up their independence?'

'I name this Oil Platform *Sulisker One*.'

Miss Charlton's words sounded clear enough. Then, as the bottle bounced, unsmashed, against the head of the platform, there was a moment of silent disbelief from the crowd, before the reserve bottle of champagne was describing its arc through the air. Good old Sir Anthony — nothing went wrong when he was in charge. Who else would have thought of a fail-safe system? Alan pulled himself together. Maclaren was unlike his usual self today: introspection must be a strange exercise for him.

'We respect your views, Minister,' Alan said, 'though we may not agree with you. We've got a job to do.'

Maclaren grunted, and turned away from Alan as a burst of good-natured laughter preceded the clapping of the crowd. Then, at the right moment, the first faint skirl of the bagpipes rose, clear and distinct, above the hubbub. From the opposite side of the stand, hidden until now by the fascia boarding, appeared the leading files of the drum and pipe band. The crowd cheered, the cranes began to inch forward, and the slow journey to the water's edge began.

Who the hell was that? Sheila Burns? Sheila pushing past the spectators until she reached the aisle… Then, half-tripping down the gangway, she ran across the open space towards the rear of the band which had already crossed the halfway mark. A couple of bemused security men were closing in on her from the other side, but before they reached her Dougal Gordon, followed by dozens of men and women pouring from the stands, led this surge of humanity towards the courageous little figure at their head. Up went a banner, a white two-staved affair with a blue St Andrew's across it, heaving and tossing as it battled onwards. Donald Macgregor, his burly form unmistakable, was carrying the righthand stave, but the other seemed to be supported by someone of lesser calibre: 'SAVE INNOCHERVIE' in bold red letters flouted its message across the material.

Alan felt his hefty neighbour shoving his way past. The black-suited minister had at last made up his mind.

'I'll show ye, Mr Brodie.'

The Reverend James Maclaren bundled down the aisle and out into the melee in the arena. Alan watched the tormented man fighting his way towards the banner. He took hold of the other stave and held it high in his arms. Up came Macgregor's, and then the banner streamed high above their heads. A roar of delight swept through the stands.

Courageous fools. How could they arrest the world's hunger for energy, halt the surge of so-called progress? Pathetic idealists, tools of sinister interests, tragic in their faith that they could stop the ravaging of Innochervie. A handful of fanatics, hopeless in their cause.

The bandsmen were beginning to counter-march, their drum-major a colourful sight, as he flung up his stick on the turn: the tap-tap of the drum — and he was off again on his reciprocal course.

There was hilarious laughter from all sides as the leading ranks began to tangle with Sheila's demonstrators. An agonized wail arose from the deflating bagpipes; there were cheers and cynical encouragement from the crowd as the shambles developed; and then a roar from the delighted spectators as Macgregor and the Reverend Maclaren fought their way clear to the far side of the arena, their banners streaming beneath the giant steelwork of the creaking platform — and, suddenly, drowning all else, the irritating clatter of the helicopter, a big yellow brute, close above the tops of the cranes.

Alan stood on the edge of the boundary plank forming the edge of the outside aisle. The spectators in the stands had risen to their feet but, by craning his head, he could take in the whole scene.

The two security men were racing now, trying to head off the banner bearers, when overhead the roar of the yellow press helicopter drowned all else. Alan looked up and saw the cheeky bastard sidling in across the cranes, only feet clear of the fly jib. A blue police helicopter was there also, but too far out and too late, trying to fob off the impertinent intruder. What were they up to, those two? There'd be a collision, if they didn't watch out.

And what the hell was that, those sudden spurts of dust on the far side of the slipway? A flurry of black smoke, an orange flash, shooting suddenly upwards at the base of the crane — then the shock of the blast, slapping his eardrums. The crack of the explosion and the sudden jump of the crane at its base — the sequence of events would be etched into Alan's mind for the rest of his life. Then came two more blasts, in line with the first, on the far side of the platform.

The main beam of the huge Sky Mastodon crane jerked, and seemed to lift. The shock wave carried up the latticework of the crane, shaking the summit. Alan could see the astonished face of the operator, leaning from the window of his cab, as the whip carried the length of the fly jib. Then, agonizingly slowly, the length of the jib began to lean inwards as the structure was jolted from its tracks. A steely flash spurted from the base, where the drive motors were housed. Then the whole edifice began to fall sideways, all 400 feet of it.

It was the slow-motion effect of the disaster, like a sloweddown cine film, which mesmerized Alan where he stood immobile among the VIPs. For an instant, the spectators were silent, unbelieving, as the crane began to sag. Then, faster and faster, the jib began to droop, like a woodpecker's beak, as the crane upended.

The spectators in the stands tried to warn the oblivious multitude in the arena. Alan heard the yells and the screams around him, but it was useless: the Sky Mastodon was crashing across *Sulisker One*, which was still crawling down the ways.

The fly jib was folding like a stick of liquorice. The main beam came next, buckling at its centre, before disintegrating in a shower of sparks and dust across the cross-members of the platform. Then the base of the crane up-ended to crash, a crumpled mass, alongside the furthest node. Suddenly, the head of the fly jib was falling, a twisted mass of steel, towards the arena on the near side of the platform. The whole giant's package was collapsing on to those human ants scurrying, in sudden terror, from the annihilation hurtling upon them from above. He saw them check, then turn in retreat, like a breeze passing across a barley field. The crowd would be well clear but, to his horror, he saw with terrible clarity four left behind, separated from the others.

Two uniformed security men, one without his cap, were leading the race for safety. Looking upwards over their shoulders as they ran, their mouths open as they screamed their warnings, they were several yards ahead of the other two men. One was a burly, middle-aged man; the other, larger, dressed in black. On the ground, yards behind them now, lay the crumpled banner they had been carrying...

The first to reach safety was the sprinting Donald Macgregor, probably because of his fisherman's fitness. He was several yards clear when the cloud of dust sprang upwards to obliterate everything. One of the security men had stumbled, tripped and fallen. The other had vanished, as the Reverend James Maclaren, collapsing on his knees, was buried, crushed to oblivion by the steelwork of the fly jib.

Alan heard an explosion, a sudden hiss and a crash, probably an electrical fire. Then nothing but a holocaust, impossible for him to grasp.

16

It was the silence that was most unnerving — the terrible stillness as the horror was slowly absorbed by the crowd. Alan felt rooted to the stand. There was an eerie silence, except for the rhythmic banging of a steel girder that had torn free and was balanced across the edge of the platform. To reach that shambles, it would be quicker for him to nip round the other side of the slipway. The platform had halted, but was still yards from the water. He could cross the ways and double back to the arena.

Alan tried to thrust his way through the blocked gangway, but it was hopeless. He nipped under the handrail at the end of the stand and jumped the ten feet to the mud below. He slithered in the morass, then struck out towards the rear of the platform. He was shocked by the damage to the platform — even one of the nodes, those huge cylinders, seemed to be twisted. He crossed the tracks well above the crumpled wreck of the crane. He had begun running along the edge of the slipway when he came upon one of the jagged craters that had just been blown. He stopped for an instant, amazed by the regular spacing of the recent explosions. There they were, six of them, parallel, close to the slipway, and following the line of the underground power and telephone cables. He rushed onwards, aware also that the explosives must have been detonated close to, or inside, the six main flooding ducts to the ways. The tamping effect on the explosions must have been devastating. But how, for God's sake, had these explosives been detonated, let alone placed?

Then he was on the edge of the milling crowd. The first ambulances, sirens braying, lights blinking, were trying to reach the casualties. Police, mud-bespattered, white-faced, were taking charge and shepherding the crowd towards the buildings: it was a miracle that the arena wasn't a pool of blood and guts.

He'd phone MOD at once, if he could find a line — hopeless in Innochervie. He'd grab his car from the hotel and nip up to Begga Brig to the public box. He'd insist on speaking to Otway. With his authority, there might even be a chance of snatching the criminals before they ran to earth or escaped the country. He sprinted towards the main gate. The security man waved him through and slammed it shut after him.

'I'll see him at once. Send him up.'

Captain Charles Otway replaced the receiver. He had endured the longest Monday on duty in the whole of his 44 years. His phones had not stopped since Brodie's first summons late on Sunday night. He had not taken a day off for nine weeks. 17.25 already, Monday 1 November — six hours since Glasgow had reported the Innochervie catastrophe and nearly 18 since Brodie's call.

'Come in.'

He pulled himself to his feet to welcome the grey-faced man who had heeded the notice on the door: 'Knock and Enter'. Brodie looked years older since his last visit — he'd been a youth then in comparison. There was experience in the hard lines about his mouth and the open look about the blue eyes had vanished. The fellow was exhausted.

'Take a pew. The RAF were good to pick you up at Ullapool.'

Brodie nodded as he unbuttoned his coat. 'Seems days ago now, sir, since the disaster. I didn't even have a chance to find out the death toll. The longest part of the trip was getting into London from Northolt, but the most frustrating moment was trying to reach you. I had to use a public box at Begga Brig, but I couldn't find enough change. I was losing too much time, so I used 999. No trouble after that.'

'Police helpful?'

'Yes, but pushed. They have their hands full on the west coast.'

Otway reached to the bottom drawer of his desk. 'A tot before we get down to work? You could do with one.'

Brodie twitched a smile. 'Thanks.'

'Our security wasn't good enough, Brodie. There'll be a lot of questions asked. After all, you gave us enough warning.'

Two crescent lines compressed the corners of Brodie's mouth. He had every right to feel sore. 'First, the submarine collision, then the sabotage in *Explorer*. I reported as you'd asked, but I've heard nothing from MOD. Didn't you connect those incidents with the subversion at Innochervie?' There was bitterness in the question.

Otway stiffened in his chair. This man was not pulling his punches. The eyes that held his were angry.

'We've preferred to leave you alone, Brodie. I knew you'd contact me if you needed me. We decided to allow the enemy his head — to show his hand, make a mistake. We've had little to go on, because the unexplained incidents seemed to have no common denominator.' He leaned back in his chair, trying to ease the tension between them. 'But tell me your news first, Brodie. I'll give you my opinion tomorrow, after International's meeting.' Otway poured himself another whisky, pushed the bottle across the desk, and continued, 'Anstruthers has called an emergency conference of all his top people: the Minister of Energy will be there also. No one wants to see West Coast close down. Too much at stake. State investment's too high, let alone the unemployment that would follow. The DTI rang me: seems your chairman's got something up his sleeve.' Otway coolly appraised the man in front of him. He seemed more at ease now — the whisky was taking effect.

'My last few days have been fairly busy,' Brodie said. Then, for ten minutes, he let Otway have it. Otway jotted down the essentials on his memo pad — dates, times, places. Piece by piece the story fell into place — the loner, the driving force of the conservationists, Sim McIver, used by the Nationalists to enhance their political cause; the sudden influx of money; the influence of the anonymous, sinister men allocating their funds and ruthlessly disciplining those whose loyalty was in doubt. Sim, browbeaten and warned, terrorized into keeping his mouth shut. That afternoon, Saturday 30 October, when Sheena and he had spotted the strong-arm men leading Sim to the waiting van on the Hoyea causeway — and, most sinister of all, the threats to McIver about Sheena Macgregor's safety. Then, on Sunday evening, their discovery of Sim's body hanging from the rafters.

'I'm sure now it was suicide, sir.'

The captain lifted his eyebrows, pencil poised over the pad: 'After what I discovered from the police yesterday,' Otway said, 'I'm certain that McIver was scared out of his wits by those foreigners. I reckon that he had stumbled across their intention to destroy *Sulisker One*. If he squealed, they'd murder Sheena Macgregor. Sim told Sheena Macgregor, didn't he, that they had threatened her?'

Brodie nodded. 'We're going to get married.' The fellow was playing it cool.

Otway ignored the petulance. 'Why are you so certain McIver took his own life?'

'Reckon he suspected how the sabotage was to be carried out. It's a long story, but in the sheds at the back of his cottage there was a lot of unusual gear: five sets of GPO equipment and five hard hats were hanging on hooks there.'

Otway shook his head, bemused.

'I think those hats and gear were used by that telephone gang I saw on a Sunday morning months ago. And this morning I knew for certain: the six explosions ran along the line of the telephone cables. How they were triggered off, I don't know. All I'm certain of is that the explosives were laid by that spurious telephone gang. They must have used some sort of firing device. With today's technology, anyone could have blown the detonators by remote control.'

Otway was interested in Brodie's logic. He might as well be brought up to date. The captain spoke without emotion. 'The police roped off the area as soon as the spectators were clear of the yard. Their Energy Squad investigators were on the job by midafternoon, flown up from Glasgow — good going. So far, they're mystified how the detonators were fired, but they're certain that the charges were laid some time ago.' Otway peered wistfully through his window at the grey waters of the Thames swirling silently down past. 'We've absolutely no trace of the criminals — no abandoned car, no one held on suspicion. We have been looking for concealed high-frequency transmitters — easy to conceal in a suitcase or in the back of a car. We've drawn a complete blank, except that the detonators seem to have been wired to the telephone cables.'

'That should give a lead.'

'So far, a complete blank. Those Glasgow boys are good — but you've got to hand it to the opposition. They're a smart lot of bastards.'

'Sim McIver knew what was coming today,' Brodie said. 'I'm sure of it. He was torn between blowing the gaff and saving Sheena's life. He couldn't cope, poor sod — and he probably realized there could be a massacre if anything went wrong.' He stared at Otway. 'How many casualties?'

'Seven killed. Fifteen seriously injured.'

'God! So many?'

'The men killed, other than the crane drivers, were crushed by the fly jib. Two security men and the village minister.'

'The minister?'

'Yes. Maclaren was his name.'

Brodie gazed out of the window. Otway could feel the silence. When finally the younger man turned again, his face was taut. 'I saw it,' he said. 'He died on his knees.'

'What sort of man was he?'

'Bigoted and feared. He ran the Free Church at Innochervie; he was dead against the oil invasion.'

'Can't blame him,' Otway said. 'It must be pretty horrific to see a way of life callously threatened.'

'It will be interesting to see what effect his death will have on his people — it might even succeed in pulling the village together. Living, he couldn't do it: he was one of Innochervie's most divisive influences.'

'Brodie.' Otway leaned across his desk, clasped his hands and peered closely at the pale face opposite him. 'We've information that forces me to warn you that you're the next on the list as far as the opposition are concerned.' Brodie slowly turned towards him, but before he could answer Otway interrupted him. 'They'll get you unless you're cleverer than they are, Brodie — and more cautious.'

Brodie continued to stare out of the window. 'I'll take my chances, Captain. I'll stay with West Coast while the Sulisker project is on.'

'Whether International can continue after this disaster depends upon tomorrow's emergency conference at their head office in the Strand. Anstruthers has called a meeting for ten o'clock to take decisions on the future.'

'Will you be attending?'

Otway nodded. 'I'll be wearing the hat of DNI. I gather I'll be batting last, before Sir Anthony sums up. I'll be presenting the Navy's case, in face of the criticism chucked at us.'

'I'll be there, too,' Brodie said. 'I'm staying with my brother-in-law tonight.'

'See you at the conference, then. We can have a yarn after the meeting, when I know what's happening. Of one thing I'm sure, though — you had better take seriously the warning I've given you.'

Brodie raised his eyebrows — slightly contemptuous, but his superciliousness was understandable. The ease with which the enemy had won hands down, all along the line, must have disillusioned him.

I'll let him have it, Otway thought, *even if it hurts*. 'They'll get at you through your girl, Brodie,' he said, measuring his words. 'Just as they said they would when they warned McIver.'

Brodie jerked round and faced him. 'What makes you so positive, Captain?'

Otway fixed him with that steely appraisal that had broken better men than Brodie. 'The Glasgow police rang ten minutes before you arrived.'

'So?'

'McIver had left a letter addressed to you, cleverly concealed at the back of the drawer in the kitchen dresser. In it was a plea that you and Sheena left the district at once — for the girl's sake.'

'Why?'

'Because the foreigners had discovered that you and Sheena were close to each other — they already knew that Sheena had probably shared all that McIver had found out.'

'How much did he know?'

Otway was silent for a moment. Then he said, not raising his voice, 'McIver's letter was a last testament disclosing all he knew. The names of the enemy were obviously false, but there's plenty for us to go on. He reported on the workings of the organization, a branch of something called ACLA (UK).'

'But these people don't know *me*.' Brodie was more irritated than frightened.

'Why not? They have ways and means of discovering whatever they need to know. By the way, you found McIver's body hanging from the ceiling?'

'Yes.'

'Sure?'

'Of course.'

Otway rose from the desk and walked slowly to the window. The lights of the embankment were shining now. A barge with its navigation lights glowing brightly in the darkness slid silently downriver. 'The police found the corpse cut down from the rafters and laid across the table. The pockets of the shirt and trousers were turned inside out and the croft had been ransacked.'

Otway walked slowly to the door and ushered out his silent visitor. 'If you change your mind, Brodie, let me know. See you in the morning. Good night.'

17

'Filthy night, sir.'

Alan Brodie smiled grimly and nodded his thanks to the security guard holding the door open for him. He paused on the top step outside the portal of the northern entrance to MOD and buttoned up the collar of his raincoat. The massive sculptures on either side of the steps, each man straining to ride his leaping dolphin, glistened in the rain. The traffic slushed down Whitehall, and the pavements splashed from overflowing gutters. He screwed up his courage and stepped out into the night.

Margaret was his only sister, married to an accountant. Alan would be glad to spend the night in their flat off Great Portland Street. He turned towards Northumberland Avenue for the Underground entrance on the embankment. It was depressingly dim and wet here, the first sleet slatting against the beacon lights skirting the Thames. A north-easter was driving in his face, more soul-destroying than anything in Scotland. Hunger and coldness were beginning to have their effect, he knew. Big Ben had struck eight: over nine hours since the nightmare.

He resented DNI's impersonal attitude to the appalling incidents happening on the west coast. Apart from Otway's personal warning, what the hell had they achieved? They'd been seen off all down the line. So futile had their efforts been that perhaps Otway *was* telling the truth and they were indeed giving the enemy his head. He would have to think hard about police protection, but he'd accept it only for Sheena's safety. She'd never leave Innochervie, he felt sure, but supposing the police insisted? He ought to be up there to look after her. Those ruthless bastards could strike at any moment, for so secret were the counter-measures that not even the local constabulary had been put in the picture. MI5 was handling the whole affair.

'*Standard* — read all abaht it...'

The evening paper would give him something to think about. The banner headlines were glaring at him: DISASTER AT SCOTTISH RIG LAUNCH — SABOTAGE SUSPECTED.

As he fumbled for change in the pockets of his sodden raincoat, he could not help noticing the pathetic dregs of humanity crouching by the Underground exhausts. Gripping their bottles and their plastic bags, the meths drinkers were rolling themselves up for the night in their newspapers, trying to catch the buckshee warmth. As Alan stepped out into the lighting of the entrance of the Underground, he was aware of three shadows flitting from the darkness beneath the bridge. So there were other fools out on this filthy night...? He would be thankful to reach Margaret's place. Thank heavens he didn't have to change.

'Great Portland Street.'

His change rattled down the dispenser. It was quicker to buy a ticket than going through the performance of collecting coins for the automatic machines. The pale-faced clerk pushed the ticket through the plate-glass aperture.

Alan moved on, an automaton on the assembly line — but, tonight, no doubt due to the weather, the station was deserted. He stepped onto the escalator and began his descent. A warm draught flushed upwards along the empty escalator. He took off his raincoat and watched the advertisements drifting past — West End shows; seedy films; firm-busted models in acrobatic bras; bathing beauties adroitly embellished by passing graffiti artists… He stepped off at the bottom, but for a moment was unsure of his route. As he turned to read the directions, from the corner of his eye he noticed that he was no longer alone. Three men were descending the trundling staircase. They were in a hurry, by the way they were nipping down those steps.

Alan walked on, through the opening to his right. As he reached the platform, he felt the pressure wave and then the train rattled into the platform. Good — he had expected the usual wait. The doors slid open and, thankfully, he slumped into the first seat of the empty, leading carriage.

He was extracting his evening paper when several figures flashed past the windows, to scramble through the other door at the rear. He heard a rapid conversation in some foreign language and he glanced round to see what the commotion was about. Bloody foreigners — even if they'd taken over London, couldn't they be less ostentatious about it? Three men were seated at the rear. One, the largest, was on a seat facing forwards; the other two sat alongside each other, facing the tunnel wall side. They avoided Alan's glance, and began chattering amongst themselves: Middle-Eastern gentlemen, by the looks of them…

Alan checked his route from the Underground plan above his head: Temple, Blackfriars, Tower Hill, Aldgate, Liverpool Street — and straight through to Great Portland Street. The doors hissed and opened; hissed again and slammed shut without Alan noticing the passing of his journey. The evening paper was certainly revelling in Innochervie's tragedy.

Blackfriars now … and an old woman, tired-faced, and loaded with plastic bags, entered the carriage. Poor old soul, a-late-night cleaner probably, on her way home. London Transport was not making much of a profit tonight. The largest of the other three passengers moved up to a seat behind the leading door. He sat on the same side and Alan, without turning deliberately round, could not see him.

The advertisements flashed past and the train rumbled into the darkness again. In the mirror effect of the window opposite him, Alan could study from behind his paper the man behind him. The man was paunchy, blue-jowled and with a fashionable Mexican moustache. Alan was not too adept at identifying Middle-Eastern nationalities but, at a guess, this customer was probably Syrian. His hands were stuffed into the pockets of his brown overcoat. At that moment, he turned and caught Alan's eye. Their glance held for a fraction of a second. In that instant, Alan knew that the man was summing him up and trying to identify him. There was a glint of satisfaction in those black eyes and a twist of a grin. Alan put down his paper and stared ahead, as the train pulled into Cannon Street.

The old woman shuffled out on to the deserted platform. The doors closed and, as the train clattered into the tunnel, Alan heard the footsteps of the other two foreigners padding up behind him. What were this lot up to? He was alone with these characters. They had waited for the train to enter the tunnel and now they were surrounding him.

Alan glanced at the alarm cord. If he pulled it, what could he say? There was no law against sitting where one chose. And yet, at this moment, he sensed that his life was hanging in the balance. These bastards were out to get him, though they had spoken not a word... They were waiting their chance, only seconds were needed to slip a knife blade between his shoulders. He jumped to his feet and spun round to face them, just as the train bucketed into Monument, the station for Bank — and there, thank God, were standing half a dozen businessmen, jovial and late home after a working dinner. Alan turned swiftly as the doors opened, but the big man was barring his way.

The man gasped as Brodie's elbow jabbed his solar plexus. The businessmen entered and, in the confusion, Alan pushed his way on to the platform. His counter-attack had surprised his shadowers and the doors slammed shut again. He stood and watched the red lights of the rear coach disappearing into the tunnel. Thank God for that. He'd continue in the next train — it was too wet for a bus and he'd never find a free cab; he had slipped those bastards and he was safe now...

There were several passengers in the next train but they were all in the first carriage, a smoker. Alan was thankful to be on his way again, but to collect himself he was glad to be in the second coach, this empty non-smoker... Tower Hill next.

Then, as the train drew up, three figures slid slowly by the window. Alan jumped up, but the men were walking slowly through the doors.

He had no doubts now. But as his hand shot upwards for the emergency cord, a wizened old man entered by the rear door. Alan was safe until the next station. The men hustled their way past him and sat down on the far seat. The smallest of the three, a sly bastard, if ever there was one, wore a perpetual smile. There was a bulge beneath the armpits of the other two, but the third character seemed too incongruous for a professional killer. Dressed in the cavalry twill of an army officer, he would have passed as a poor man's version of the King of Jordan. But even he was big — a formidable customer... They were watching him, but they were not grinning now. Alan would get out at Aldgate and scoot like hell for the exit...

Brodie faced them, his back to the doors. They held his stare, then, as the train slowed, they rose to their feet. Alan glanced at the little man dozing at the far end of the carriage — no help there. He felt the doors sliding open behind him. He stepped backwards, out on to the platform, not taking his eyes from his pursuers. He turned quickly to his right and began running...

Suddenly he knew his error — the exit was at the opposite end of the platform. He slithered to a stop and noted the interested stare of the driver. Nothing for it but to double back and charge his way through... The train drew out, its lights disappearing into the tunnel. Alan swung round to face his killers.

The three men had spread out across the deserted platform. On the kerb side, the big man, the leader. Against the wall, the 'King of Jordan'. And between them the little runt, licking his lips and crouching to spring, steel glinting in his hand...

No use shouting... As Alan charged towards them he knew, suddenly, that they would kill him as he tangled with them. He panicked for an instant, stopped, then inched backwards from them, until he felt the wall of the tunnel at his back.

Less than five yards now and they were advancing remorselessly towards him. He realized he had one chance only, and he took it. He yelled, thrust up his hand and gazed past them, towards the far end of the platform. They stopped in their tracks, hesitated, and glanced behind them... In that second, Alan rolled swiftly over the white lip of the platform. He felt the gravel beneath his feet, and saw the gleaming steel of the conductor rail. He crouched low and scrambled towards the mouth of the tunnel. He was blinded by the darkness, but somewhere, far away, a red pinpoint of light pierced the blackness. He tripped and felt the chippings cutting the palm of his hand — there was a crack, and the whistle of a bullet whanging over his head. He struggled to his feet and scrambled into the darkness of the tunnel.

The panic that had threatened to engulf him was now replaced by a deliberate effort to calm himself as he groped his way along that terrifying black hole. *It's me against three strangers to this city; three men who don't know London, let alone understand the Underground system. The odds are on your side, Brodie, so pull yourself together ... but there is one disadvantage: they have guns.* The concave concrete burnt his fingers as he felt his way along the tunnel and into the inky blackness. At the back of his mind was the fear of falling again, with that conductor rail somewhere, less than a yard away, waiting to incinerate him with hundreds of thousands of volts... He struggled onwards, the shouts of his pursuers louder now...

Another flash behind him, lighting up the tunnel. The crack of pistols and the bullets singing overhead. They'd be bloody lucky to hit him under these conditions and he ducked instinctively, crouching as he stumbled onwards. He was gasping now, his heart hammering as he panted for air. If he could reach that red signal light before they caught up with him, close enough to kill, he still had a chance ... and then he saw the twin lights coming towards him from round a curve, a shower of blue sparks spurting from the conductor shoe of the approaching train. He slithered to a halt as he felt the pump of air against his ears. He flattened himself against the tunnel wall, gasping for breath. By the glow from the approaching carriages, the conductor rail gleamed at his feet, less than a yard away. There would be little to spare between him and the coaches — but at least his pursuers were suffering the same terrors. And they could not shoot while taking care of their skins. He shut his eyes and held his breath, waiting for extinction...

The racket of the train suddenly diminished. Alan jerked round to watch the centipede string of lights sliding off to the right. They were suddenly extinguished, cut off by the tunnel wall. There must be a junction there — to Aldgate East. He heard the foreign voices shouting behind him. He turned and ran onwards towards that red pinpoint of light. The next train would come through, direct: when the signal turned to green, the next train from Monument would run him down from behind. There was a staccato double crack, the flicker of pistol flashes and then the whine of a bullet ricocheting along the roof of the tunnel. *God, I'll never make it*, he thought, and he dashed into the darkness, hugging the wall as he stumbled onwards.

The driver of train number 671, Frank Trewby, had been working on this line for over 15 months. For five days of the week, year in, year out, on the afternoon shift, he had been transporting London's commuters. He yawned as he pondered that they no more relished their rush-hour battle than he did carrying them through these dark tunnels. He was surprised at the lack of passengers this evening, but then the tourist season was finished. As he shoved over his dead man's handle, his thoughts went back to his last holiday he'd spent in Paris, in the days before inflation had spiralled so viciously. In Paris he remembered that the Métro was better lit than London Transport's system. The French drivers could see ahead and could take emergency action more quickly. Driving through the darkness, Trewby felt almost expendable, the control of the train elsewhere, in the tentacles of the computerized signal system... So here it came, for the fifth time round, crappy old Liverpool Street. Smilin' Joe, the inspector, was often here for a quick puff, but today he was absent. Frank Trewby missed the cheerful face. They always passed the time of day and Joe usually had a story or a joke to share.

The signal flicked to green again. On again, into the tunnel for Aldgate ... then back again once more for the return to Hammersmith and he'd be on his way home. The train plunged into the darkness. Another couple of minutes and he'd have to slow down for the red signal protecting Aldgate East junction. He shuffled, and settled more comfortably into the corner — he was getting stiffer in his left thigh: old age was creeping on. There was the signal. As he watched, it changed to green... He opened up to full speed.

What the hell was that, up ahead, streaking across the light at the entrance to the junction? There was someone on the line, running straight towards him... He released the handle. He slammed the brakes to emergency...

Alan Brodie had only one thought in his mind. That signal must be protecting the Aldgate East junction from the west-east train. He'd noted the Underground plan in the non-smoker. He'd *have* to reach that before the next Aldgate train or he'd end up as strawberry jam...

He didn't give a damn for the bullets singing past him now. He'd be bloody unlucky to be hit by one of them because the marksmen must be firing blind. Shots echoed down the tunnel and more bullets whistled overhead. He half turned to catch the sound of his pursuers. The clattering and the shouting seemed nearer now — 30 to 40 yards, at a guess. He forced himself onwards, his lungs gasping for air... He'd never reach that beckoning fight, never make it at this rate — why the hell hadn't he bothered to keep himself fit up at Innochervie?

Terror was beginning to grip him — an animal panic suddenly swamping him. He was sobbing for breath and now he was stumbling dangerously as he fought his way forwards — and then he felt the sudden pulse of air as the pressure wave hit him — and men's voices, shouting somewhere ahead. The red signal, so near now, flicked to green — and the whole scene became suddenly unreal, a ghastly, tortuous nightmare.

They were gaining fast on him now, those assassins — he heard them swearing and the big man, probably, was yelling at them, goading them on… A rattle of shots whined about him. He saw suddenly the lights of a train approaching from ahead … less than 40 yards away, swinging round the curve.

Alan flung himself forwards, oblivious to the conductor rail, towards the widening of the tunnel where the lines gleamed — there it was, the junction, right on top of him… He staggered towards the sheen of the rails in the Y-junction. Train no. 671 was bearing down upon him, its rattling carriages a rising crescendo… If it bore off to Aldgate East, he'd be safe.

Train 671 clattered across the points, lunged towards him. He hurled himself to the right, into the safety of the junction where it started to widen. He collapsed against the end coping of the wall as the train swung by, the lights through the windows of the empty carriages flickering against the tunnel wall. As the rear coach rattled past, he heard a screeching of brakes behind him, the bucketing of carriages as they concertinaed. There was a tortured cry and screams of terror. An electric-blue flash flickered through the tunnel — then, quite suddenly, an eerie silence that was broken only by the throbbing compressors of the train.

Alan picked himself up and staggered towards the dim halfmoon of light ahead — there it was, the entrance to Liverpool Street. Along the edge of the platform, faces were peering ridiculously into the tunnel towards him. He heard the shouts and, seconds later, he'd reached the beginning of the platform. There were lights here and, on the line, a train purring, waiting for the 'reds' to change. Then, along the whitened edge of the platform, people were running, their hands outstretched towards him... Everything was hazy, gyrating crazily, and he could not breathe...

'Steady, mate — steady... Give us your hand...'

A uniformed figure had jumped off the platform and was edging cautiously towards him...

18

Captain Otway had not been looking forward to making his contribution at International's Emergency Conference. If its Chairman, Sir Anthony Anstruthers, had not expressly requested the attendance of a naval representative, Otway would have been much happier catching up on his paperwork at MOD.

The meeting had proceeded remarkably smoothly, for Anstruthers was a master at handling people. He had opened the meeting and summarized the extent of the disaster at Innochervie. *Sulisker One* was so badly damaged that, even if it was repaired, it would miss next year's operating weather window and probably the year after's, as well. International could not afford this scale of income loss on capital. Seven killed; and West Coast reeling, punch-drunk and incapable of ideas for the future. Sir Anthony had catalogued the list of disasters but, before he sat down, he had intimated that there was a shaft of hope. As the minister had emphasized when he'd thumped on the table, the object of the exercise was to save International and the Sulisker project. There were too many jobs at stake; too much capital, both public and private, invested in *Sulisker One* for the project to be abandoned now, without exploring every possibility for saving the development of the oilfield they had discovered at such cost and effort.

The heads of the various sections and departments had all said their piece and the lamentable story had fitted like a jigsaw. At the moment when *Sulisker One* was being successfully completed to catch next year's operating window, catastrophe had come. To repair the platform, even if the steel could be obtained on time (an impossibility with delivery dates of over 18 months), clearing away the mess would take months. But at the end of it all, men's jobs and lives were the price.

The Minister of Energy, too evasive for Otway's taste, had brought them up to date with the sovereignty problems that were proving impossible to resolve internationally.

The discovery of oil around the coasts presented problems both in international and national politics. The Department of Energy was busy trying to have its cake and eat it, thought Otway. And in domestic politics, governmental help was utterly inadequate for local authorities trying to cope with the oil boom.

As usual, the problem was one of money. The taxpayer could not be fleeced for ever. The banks were not prepared to lend now, because of political and economic uncertainties. Even conservation was expensive: however much the locals wanted to preserve their coastline (longer than the whole of the French seaboard) the problem was one of cash, as much as sentiment — but there was much to be learned from the Norwegians, who had learned the hard way in the Stavanger area. How to mollify Scottish resentment was a difficult problem, too. Local housing profiteers forced up the rents, while foreigners from all over the world lorded it in the streets, in the bars, hotels and dance-halls — and up went the prices, sky-high.

Anstruthers was winding up now, his shrewd eyes slowly absorbing the team gathered around him.

'I've asked a representative of the Directorate of Naval Intelligence to put us in the picture, gentlemen, regarding security in the future. After yesterday's catastrophe, I think we should know where we stand regarding the safety of our platforms. When Captain Otway has finished, I'd like to have a further word with you all, because I need your support over a difficult decision.' The chairman sat down.

Otway rose to his feet. As the clock at the back of the conference room chimed 12, the door in the far corner opened and a figure he recognized slipped quietly into one of the rear seats. Brodie caught his eye, and held up a bandaged hand. Otway smiled briefly. What trouble had Brodie landed in now?

'Gentlemen, I'm not here to make excuses,' Otway began. 'I'm here to give you the facts.'

He felt immediately that he had a grip on this sane, common-sense audience — but there was heavy weather ahead. The Royal Navy was being blamed for the inadequate protection.

He let them have it, good and strong. To maintain one ship on patrol, two others were needed in reserve — one refitting, the other giving leave. The areas to be patrolled were vast: our Home Fleet, based on Scapa Flow during the war, could not adequately cover the inhospitable wastes of the North Sea up to the edge of the Arctic Circle. How could today's Navy cope, with the funds made available to it by a British public which had been lulled by its politicians and effete intellectuals into a false sense of security?

Britain had its responsibilities to Europe now, as well as its own defence, NATO claimed its resources, so the whole strike force was committed to the deterrent. What was left of the surface forces was fully stretched countering Russian probes around the coasts, or in showing the flag in sensitive areas overseas. To be brutal, the Navy was incapable of protecting Britain's mercantile fleet against determined attack, though the oilfields were provided with deep cover by the Royal Marine Commando, able to react at instant readiness. If there was any cover left, the ships were better deployed in surveillance of the North Sea, rather than patrolling the north-western and Irish coasts. Even with the RAF and its Nimrods, the Navy was forced to admit that the demands made upon it were beyond its resources.

'If the country won't give us the ships or a Fleet Air Arm, gentlemen, the Royal Navy cannot possibly give the protection you ask for. What we can do is to make it unpleasant for anyone who attacks a rig. A policy of reprisal if you like, like the stalemate of terror provided by our Polaris fleet.'

'Bit late, if you happen to be a rig,' someone was muttering from the middle rows.

In the silence that followed, Otway sensed that the speaker was voicing the opinion of his audience.

'Give us the ships and you know that the Navy will be there,' he finished. As he sat down, he knew, at least, that he had told the truth. The silence in the room underlined the doubts in so many minds. Anstruthers rose again to his feet and from the chairman's table he nodded his thanks to the naval representative.

'And now, gentlemen, you've heard how we stand on the brink of total disaster. A cross-member of *Sulisker One* has been badly damaged and a node destroyed by the crane. The time it would take to repair the platform would cost us more than the price of the structure. By the time the steelwork has been x-rayed, we will have lost over a year — think of the loss of income and the interest charges on the capital cost, and you will realize that the costs of delay now would be more than if West Coast gave us the platform. Before we do part, I am about to ask you for a quick decision on what I consider could be the saving of the situation.' He drank from the glass in front of him, his eyes sweeping round his audience. He inclined his head and smiled briefly at someone in the back of the hall.

Otway noted Brodie's acknowledgement and then the chairman began his summing up.

'Thirteen days before the disaster, I was approached confidentially by our French friends with whom we are associated in Union Compagnies Ciments. They were just completing their concrete platform, *Liberté*, when their customers, a Norwegian-Danish consortium, decided to pull out — further appraisal had proved disappointing and, what with the uncertainty over government taxation, the consortium could see no profit in the enterprise. UCC wanted to know if we would be interested in *Liberté* for future development of our Sulisker Field. With our *Sulisker One* steel platform almost ready, I declined with thanks.'

Anstruthers was peering over his bifocals at his silent audience. He leaned across the table: 'At midnight last night, I telephoned the chairman of UCC and asked whether *Liberté* was still available...' He paused to lean back, the better to watch the reaction to his announcement. 'Their concrete platform is immediately available at its yard at Largs. It is a complete package, ready in all respects. Our senior geologist tells me that the sea bed, in his tentative opinion, is suitable to take the weight of *Liberté*. Leaving out the obvious details, gentlemen, my question to you is this: do we, or do we not — subject to all technical specifications and details being satisfactory — buy this concrete platform? The cost is within our means, our secretary tells me, providing the banks agree. We could catch next year's operating window, if we act now. We can work out the details as we proceed with the formalities with UCC.'

A voice was raised from someone in the middle of the room, but Otway could not identify the speaker. 'Is it your intention to fit her out at West Coast, sir, on site at Innochervie, with our own prefabricated modules?'

'Yes, but we must tow her up as soon as possible: it's getting late now. We won't need many alterations. She's right for the job.'

'Bit dicey, isn't it, to shift her now, with the winter gales coming on?' the speaker insisted.

Otway sensed the irritation in the chairman's voice. 'I'm asking only for a decision of principle, subject to all the problems being resolved. Do we, or don't we, buy *Liberté*?' He sat down abruptly and announced, 'I suggest you form discussion groups. In 40 minutes I shall seek your decision. Over to you, gentlemen.'

As the meeting broke up into its separate groups, Alan Brodie watched a sole figure separate itself from the front row. As Captain Otway passed the chairman's table, Anstruthers took his elbow and led him to one side. The two men stood apart, Anstruthers talking, Otway listening. They both turned towards Alan. Otway nodded briefly and then Anstruthers turned away to talk with his directors. Otway picked his way through the throng and, nearing the door, beckoned Brodie to follow.

Otway was seated in a leather-backed settee at the far end of the corridor outside the conference room.

'What the devil has happened to you, Brodie?'

'You were right, sir, but they tried too damned promptly for my liking.' He gave a brief report on the events last night. 'If they can react so quickly and are so well-informed on.my movements, what about my girlfriend's safety?'

'Sheena Macgregor? You have every reason to be worried, but you refused to listen.' Otway's eyes narrowed. 'Have you got involved with the police?'

'They drove me to outpatients at St Mary's, then took me to my sister's. They waited until this morning for my statement. I tried to cover up as best I could, but I gave them your name and telephone number when they asked me why I was in the tunnel. The Circle line was still blocked this morning, while they shovelled up the remains of my hatchet men.' He stared down the corridor, the sound of those screams still echoing in his mind.

'I'm giving the orders now.' Brodie was snapped back to the present by the impatience in Otway's voice. 'And if you don't accept them, I'll take steps to see that you're put away by the police until this lot blows over.'

Alan felt the tension mounting. This dreadful mess in which he found himself was none of his doing. 'Who's behind all this?' he demanded. 'And how the hell are they so well informed?' He continued before Otway could reply. 'Who put the wind up McIver and threatened Sheena Macgregor?' His voice rose in anger: 'And while I'm speaking my mind, sir, what have your Energy Squad been up to while Rome burns?' He held Otway's gaze.

'Okay, Brodie,' Otway said. 'For both our sakes and many others, I'm taking you fully into my confidence — and if you leak a word of it, I'll pull you in under the Official Secrets Act.' He crossed his legs and turned to the settee, his eyes fixed on the ancient print of that majestic ship, *Queen Mary*, hanging on the opposite wall. 'Why do the Russians spy on our rigs and patrol trawlers? Why do they use expensive nuclear submarines to do so? One reason is that the more data they can bank in their computers, the more selective their targets when they decide to strike. Their information on the Sulisker project must be furthering someone's interest, whether it's their own or one of their pawns. They are adept, as you know, at using others —

155

we don't know the answers yet, but things are beginning to gel.'

'Meaning?'

'The reports from our agents in Europe are beginning to add up. Those two ships in Gdynia, which your unfortunate namesake discovered, have sailed. They've been traced, flying the Panamanian flag, to Beirut.' He was speaking quietly now: 'We've a particularly reliable woman, an Armenian married to a VIP in the Egyptian FO, who has a hunch that these ships may soon be putting to sea, probably for the western Mediterranean. They appear to be ultra-modern container vessels, but no one can board them because security measures are so tight. The Israelis mounted a cut-out raid, but even *they* failed to board. Their men were mown down on the quay. We reckon they are warships and we're giving top priority to this report. With the cash resources at the disposal of these Middle-East gentlemen, there's no knowing these days what activity to expect next. These hijacking horrors prove that human life means less than nothing, even for their own people. One thing we do know — the man running one of the outfits is a character we've met before. He has organized the worst of the international crimes ... a king-sized bastard if ever there was one. We've been trying to get him ourselves for a long time now — goes by the name of Faqus — "L" to his friends.'

'Who's he working for, sir?'

'His boss heads up the executive committee of some sort of Middle-Eastern consortium, we reckon.'

'What's their objective?'

Otway shook his head. 'Our Armenian lady hasn't been wrong yet. She reckons a massive operation is being mounted with a dual objective: to force the world to solve the Palestinian problem and to embarrass the West's energy crisis.'

'But why all this rough stuff up at remote Innochervie, sir?'

'Just a sideshow, to slow up our oil production. Every little helps.'

Alan was silent. There seemed to be no end to this horrifying business. 'The companies have always been worried about an attack on our rigs in the North Sea,' Alan said. 'Reckon they've every reason to be, but such an incident would be an act of war.'

'Would it,' Otway asked, 'if the attack was dressed up as some fanatical Arab coup?'

Otway was right. The West had never retaliated yet against the senseless carnage by hijackers. Half a dozen RN Offshore Patrol Ships, with 3-inch guns to cover the North Sea — what could the patrols do?

'Why d'you think McIver hung himself, Brodie?' Otway asked suddenly. 'Merely because he was an alcoholic depressive?'

What was Otway driving at?

'He was being terrorized beyond his powers of resistance. He knew that they'd have a go on launching day. They would fix up Sheena Macgregor if he went to the police.' Alan's words were controlled, but he felt the hate mounting against this vicious gang. 'The enemy has won all down the line, Captain…'

'Maybe. But time is *not* on their side now. They're nervous, or they would not have returned to Hoyea so promptly. You have got to leave Innochervie, even if West Coast continues … and your girl too.'

'And if *Liberté* is taken on?'

'All the more reason for leaving. We want you alive. You're useful to us.'

Alan was silent. His world had been centred around that little port.

'Sir Anthony spoke to me just now,' Otway said.

'About me?'

'If *Liberté* is acquired, he wants you to join it to carry on your work there. It has got to be finished off, and even in Innochervie you'd be safe. The concrete platform is like a fortress.'

Alan was thoughtful. 'And my girlfriend?'

Otway smiled, the first sign of warmth for some time. 'I've asked Sir Anthony to make an exception in your case. She'll be taken on as an assistant secretary. There are three women there already. She can live on the platform with the others.'

The door was opening at the end of the passage. The secretary was beckoning them. 'They're taking their places, Captain Otway. Thought you'd like to know the decision.'

19

ACLA's Force Commander dismissed his driver inside the entrance to Quay 17. 'Wait for me by the main gate,' he ordered. 'I shall be about eight hours.'

Kommandant Faqus watched the white Mercedes receding down the cobbled road. He turned and strode briskly towards the new quay that had been recently completed to take the three new ships, the pride of the Attack Commando of the Liberation Army. Emerging from the screen of the vast new warehouses, he reached the security barrier to Quay 17. He submitted to the routine check of his pass by the German guards. He nodded perfunctorily, as he acknowledged their smart salute of recognition, then walked on to the end of the new basin. He felt satisfied now that his security arrangements were at last being strictly carried out.

08.50 precisely, 15 November. He paused in the freshness of this pleasant Alexandrian morning to size up the three ships lining the western side of this magnificent basin. His tight mouth relaxed with approval. There they were, at last, all three concentrated and ready for his inspection after the final, frustrating delay of fitting the new FSD complex in *King Feisal* and *Eastern Star*. These weapons, high velocity mortars, had finally been proved — trials of the solid projectiles had been 100 per cent successful against concrete targets set up on the beach west of Fuka.

The grey sides of the ships gleamed in their fresh paint, the buff upperworks being smart, as well as functional. At night, the silhouettes of this strike force must be as unobtrusive as possible. *Third World*, the HQ support vessel, was nearest him, leviathan in contrast to her consorts. The Russians in Odessa had made as good a job of her, as the Gdynia yards, of *Feisal* and *Eastern Star*. He'd inspected her last week and was well satisfied. Her ultra-modern satellite communication systems and support logistics could not be bettered. As with the other two, her Russian engine room crews could steam in the deep oceans for months on end, thanks to their nuclear propulsion units. The ships' maximum cruising speed of 28.5 knots made his command a formidable strike force.

Faqus strode briskly past the slab side of *Third World*. He was determined to be at *Star*'s gangway promptly at nine. He was amused to see a seaman at *Third World*'s stern signalling to *Eastern Star* that he was approaching. He'd arranged to meet the three COs in the captain's cabin of *King Feisal* at noon, so he'd inspect *Eastern Star* first. He did not drink, so could dispense with that ritual. He was determined to keep up with today's timetable: lunch on board *Eastern Star* at 13.00, then the staff meeting at 14.00 in *Third World* to finalize the training programme. He would insist on finishing at 17.50, because — a rare event in his hectic life — he had an appointment this evening for which he would not be late at any cost.

Kommandant Faqus glanced at the clock on the after bulkhead in the captain's state-room of *Third World*. 17.20. He was beginning to feel fidgety after his strenuous day, but, as he listened to the clipped English of Klaus Dietrich, ACLA's chief of staff, he felt satisfied that the training programme would remain on schedule. Next spring, just four months away now, in mid-March to be precise, his force had to be operational. The boss had said so. Faqus had only one fear — and that was crossing the path of the chairman of HQ's Action Committee. The boss brooked no inefficiency, and his ruthless single-mindedness and fanaticism made him the most formidable character 'L' had ever known.

Eastern Star (105,000 tons) and *King Feisal* (80,000) were magnificent ships, each the complement of the other in this powerful strike force. With their large slow-turning propellers, they could knock up 36 knots, thanks to their nuclear power and fine lines. Both were nominally modern container ships, their squat, ugly funnels and bridges sited forward, within 300 feet of their sweeping bows. *King Feisal* was a replica of her larger sister.

To all appearances, abaft the funnel, the upper deck was packed to the gunwales with containers, reaching as far aft as the twin cranes on either quarter. All the containers were protected from the weather by heavy, netted tarpaulins. The outboard observer would never realize that the upper deck loading was a hollow rectangle, the sides being formed by the outboard containers. The hollow interior was concealed by the same overhead protective covering as used on the outboard containers.

At the touch of a button in the ship's machinery control room abaft the bridge, the inboard overhead covering unrolled into athwartship recesses, fore and aft. The operation took just eight minutes. On further command, actuated by hydraulic rams, two-thirds of the for'd containers could slide along rails, with the aid of ball bearings, into the hollow at the after end of the upper deck. When this was complete (18.5 minutes), two-thirds of the upper deck — the centre section — had been transformed into a flat, upper deck surface. The after half of this deck area contained the flush-decked lift surface for the 12 VTOs, stowed in their hangar two decks below. These Russian single-seater supersonic fighters, copies of the plane the British had pioneered, could be raised from below and be in the air within four minutes. If ranged on deck, standing by for a strike, the squadron could be airborne in 43 seconds. The pilots were all Russians, Germans and Americans out of work in their own country and disillusioned by their way of life.

'The choppers will be uncrated tomorrow, Kommandant,' Dietrich was saying. 'Stress trials in both ships have been satisfactory, but there is considerable down-draught in *King Feisal*, caused by the projection of the crane jibs, we believe.'

Faqus nodded. The helicopter pads, on a built-up deck at the stern, formed a roof above the container assembly. The choppers, four in each ship, were housed inside dummy containers, the floors forming the lifts. The cargo in the containers seemed harmless enough. They provided storage for bulk provisions to feed the ships' companies and embarked commandos. *Eastern Star*'s complement was 300 sailors and 1200 troops; *King Feisal*'s, 250 men and a commando force of 900.

The assault landing craft and the high-speed attack craft were housed in the boat hangars, above the sloping ramps leading out through the square transom. In heavy weather, the emergency stern doors could be lowered, when steaming down following seas.

'Ammunitioning?' Dietrich asked, raising his eyebrows in question at Faqus. 'End of month?'

The Force Commander nodded. The Russians had kept their delivery date. The missiles, small arms and spares were waiting in a guarded store at the end of Quay 17. So far, the Israelis had not sniffed the scent...

The magazines, below the waterline, were armoured and provided with flooding arrangements. The ammunition was as near as possible to the weapons it served. The 90 mm stuff was in concealed mushroom units on the fo'c'sle heads, the stalks of the mountings extending vertically at battle stations. The bridge decks bristled with 20 mm. And amidships, in hidden sponsons along the inboard side of the permanent containers, the multi-barrelled mortars were ranged in their two batteries — the COIs (crude oil ignition) and the FSDs (fixed structure demolition) side by side. Well aft, and below the hangar deck, were the kerosene tanks for the VTOs and choppers.

'Embarkation of troops next Thursday, sir?'

Faqus found Dietrich's constant questioning irritating. He was paid to plan the details, so why did he need continued reassurance?

'Yes, and we'll sail for our first training cruise as soon as Captain Olsen and Captain Trenik are satisfied.' Faqus wanted to shake down the troops in the comparative calm of the Mediterranean, before seasoning them to the Atlantic. This was the reason he had asked for top priority in the building of the off-shore terminus at Burat-el-Sun, east of Tripoli. *Feisal* and *Star* could lie-to inconspicuously there and the capital city provided the pleasures that these mercenaries needed. 'The sooner we get to sea,' Faqus told his assembled staff, 'the better it will be for morale. They've been long enough in camp.'

Even Cairo palled after weeks in the desert sun. The 2,000 men of all nationalities, highly paid mercenaries, were now toughened up and disciplined under their German NCOs. The Arab-Israeli wars had provided ideal battle training and the troops were all set for action.

Faqus glanced at the clock. He rose from his seat and picked up his cloth sun hat. He'd deliberately arrived in civilian clothes, but his unconventional rig did not diminish the respect accorded to him by his officers as they rose to their feet.

'See you in two days' time,' he said as he left the state-room. 'I'll give you further schedules for your training programme. Thanks — I'll find my own way ashore.'

Joseph was waiting for him in the Merc. A merciless and reliable killer, he had been with Faqus for over four years now. 'Shepheard's Hotel,' he said. 'Step on it.'

'L' felt elated, now that the planning was nearing fruition. He was on target and the Boss could have no reason to complain. He lolled into the comfort of the back seat, as the car surged through the main gate.

In December and early January, when the Western World thought of little else but Christmas, he'd take his force into the Atlantic. Gibraltar and Tangier were security risks, so he'd pass his ships through independently. Their movements would become routine — and, soon, unremarkable. With *Third World* waiting for them 300 miles out, the force could exercise there for days without interference. He'd be ready by the spring, no doubt about it now. There was only one problem — the time required for his force to become operationally efficient. The longer the process, the greater the chance of ACLA's intentions being discovered by the enemy. He had been disturbed by the boss's latest intelligence report. A leak of information had possibly occurred after the successful operation in that north-western Scottish port — an impossible name for 'L' to pronounce.

The execution squad had been ordered to eliminate the high-risk individuals, but its first attempt in London had failed — this was disturbing, because British counter-espionage must soon sniff something. There were two persons involved, apparently, a young petroleum scientist and his girlfriend. The squad would not be so clumsy on its second attempt, the affair now being priority one. But he, Faqus, had informed only Petrov, his second-in-command in *King Feisal*, of this incident.

'Take the night off, Joseph,' he said. 'Shan't need you tomorrow. Pick me up here.' He always kept his private life to himself.

The car door opened and the commissionaire smiled obsequiously. Now that the Canal was open again, the traditional courtesies of the past were returning swiftly to this superb hotel. He tipped the man and was thankful to reach the air-conditioned entrance hall. Pandering to normality, he wandered slowly through the reception rooms and bars, as if searching for a friend. He strolled back to the hall-porter's desk and ordered a taxi. 'Entrance to Khartoum Avenue,' he ordered. 'It can drop me there.'

Shushanik herself opened the ornate glass door to him. She smiled and beckoned him inside, his training forcing him to absorb swiftly all the details — the same revolving fans, the cane furniture, the glass-topped tables and the ferns — and somewhere, invisible, the tinkling of an indoor fountain. He heard her throwing the bolt across the door as she silently closed it behind him. He turned and faced her, the only woman he'd truly loved in his whole life.

'Ahmid is in the Lebanon,' she said. 'He's away for ten days, so I've given the servants a week's holiday. Allah's on our side for once, my dear.' She gave that delicious throaty laugh of hers.

He went up to her and took her hands. 'You haven't changed, Shushanik. It's been a long time.' The memories of that camp in the German forest swept through his mind — that, and the other meetings they'd shared over the years. She was, he supposed, his one weakness, the one chink in his steel-plated armour. The other females had been necessities, nothing else.

'It's pointless asking you to have an aperitif.' She smiled as she took his hand. Together they slowly mounted the wide staircase to the bedroom overlooking the gardens. They stood by the window, looking out at the coolness of the waving palms.

'I'm here for a while yet,' he said as he slipped his hand to her shoulders. 'We could see much of each other.'

The whisper of her silk gown slipping to the carpet was the only sound. She led him gently to the bed. 'We'll talk later,' she said. He shook himself from his tropical suit and gazed down upon her. She was as exquisite as always.

20

'*Merde*! So it takes a Frenchman to understand English weather.' Raoul Ghio, Controller of *Liberté*, was perusing the weather report handed to him by the radio office. 'Take a look at this, Alan.'

Brodie and Sheena Macgregor were leaning against the rail outside the navigational control room of *Liberté*. Sliding slowly past South Harris, at a snail's pace of three knots, this huge concrete oil platform was already past the halfway mark of the 337-mile tow from Largs to Innochervie. Four hundred yards ahead churned the wakes of four ocean-going tugs, with *Dalrymple Navigator*, Iain Macgregor's new supply boat in the centre as command ship. Leading the way, like a proud mother hen, the old wooden offshore boat *Seamew* navigated on her transponders along the line she had surveyed last month.

Alan glanced at the tall Frenchman, whose round face, with the vivacious, dark eyes of the Niçois, exuded friendly amusement. Six feet three, with a massive chest, he had worked for seven years with Cousteau in the Mediterranean. Ghio had chosen *Seamew* to carry out the emergency survey because the wooden boat was ideal for his requirements. A man of many talents, he had enjoyed rigging up the three responders in the fish-hold and establishing communications with the beacons he had hurriedly set up along the promontories ashore. For his soundings he had used the new system which gave an oval shadow, instead of the usual 'along the line' method. His depth-finding was therefore much more practical for a wide structure such as *Liberté*. Underway, she drew 20 fathoms, so a clear depth of 22 had been surveyed. *Liberté* was now 78 hours, 255 miles out from Largs.

Raoul was holding out Port Patrick's last weather forecast, transmitted at 08.33 today, 11 January: 'Gale warning, imminent', it read.

'Bit of a let-down,' Alan said, 'when we're served by the most sophisticated weather forecasting in the world. Glasgow promised us fine weather from last night onwards.'

A melon slice of a smile creased Raoul's face, but he resisted any 'told you so' comment. The Frenchman had taken a long time to give way to the company's pressure to tow the platform north at this time of the year. Only when he knew they could navigate inside the shelter of the Minches did he falter in his opposition — and then only if five days of settled weather could be forecast. He had insisted that a record be kept of his objections, and of his agreement which he had given only because of the urgency of the operation. If *Liberté* could not be towed north now, to complete the module modifications at West Coast, she would miss this year's operational window.

Alan grinned. 'You'll not allow us to forget this. I owe you that beer.'

Raoul grimaced, before deliberately spitting to leeward. 'Keep your English draught beer — I'll stick to my Pernod.' He turned to concentrate upon the chatter between the tugs which was coming over on the RT: '...five degrees to port.'

Brodie recognized the sing-song of Donald Macgregor as he took *Seamew*, under the pilot's supervision, along the surveyed track, the responders accurately transmitting the course through the track recorder and the auto-pilot which had been recently installed. Alan stood alongside to watch the dawn stealing across the hills of South Harris.

'It's difficult to believe, isn't it?' Sheena said softly, staring at the beauty. 'Hard to realize that we're together again, away from the terror and suspense.'

From this control platform, over 350 feet above the sea, the tugs looked like toy boats as they laboured to maintain the speed of advance. Alan still could not absorb the gigantic proportions of this pre-stressed concrete monster which, from seabed to summit, towered to 750 feet, the derrick top rearing 90 feet above him from where he stood.

Sailing day, last Tuesday, 8 January, seemed far in the past now, and the period after he had returned to Scotland from London felt eternities ago. MOD had refused permission for him to fetch his gear from the Errabeg. Otway had even sent the police to bring Sheena down to Largs to join Alan in *Liberté*. She had settled quickly, helping out with the paperwork, and Raoul had been swift to acknowledge her efficiency. She shared a cabin with the other two secretaries on the command deck, and Alan doubled up with the radio officer.

'Seems a long time since October,' she was murmuring. Her eyes were mischievous, reading his thoughts. 'Remember the little seal?'

He smiled, content that soon this phase of the Sulisker project would be completed. He'd find another appointment and then they could build a home together. The clearing-up operation had begun immediately the decision to buy *Liberté* was taken on 2 November. *Seamew*, old though she was, was the only suitable boat available, so had been chartered the next week. Fitted out in three days by Raoul and his cronies, on 7 December she began her survey of the track from Ailsa Craig, past the Mull of Oa and Skerryvore, and through the Minches to Innochervie. At sea for Christmas, Donald Macgregor had reached Innoch Head on the last day of the year.

'I feel great, Sheena, now that your Innochervie is trying to live peaceably again.'

He gazed up at the wads of oily clouds gathering from the southwest. They were high up, their edges hard as they swept in against the low cumulonimbus drifting towards them from Cape Wrath. The eastern sky this morning had been slashed with purple.

'Even Mum is patching it up with Dad,' Sheena said. 'He said that it took the death of the minister to force the village to work together again.'

Alan watched the white horses breaking far below, where the gulls wheeled and squabbled for the gash. The events of Innochervie had been paradoxical. The villagers had huddled together behind the cemetery wall on that depressingly wet day, when they laid the remains of the Reverend James Maclaren to rest. In death he had achieved what he had been unable to do in his life. With McIver dead also, the antis could no longer fight the monster. Sheila Burns kept the flag flying, but there was no heart now in resistance. Dougal Gordon, the liberal schoolmaster, had proposed a truce with the pros, and in a spirit of compromise the management of West Coast engaged all the labour they could from the crofters and storm-bound fishermen to clear up the mess after the catastrophe.

When the village heard that *Liberté* was northward-bound to bring work and life again to the little port, the community began to pull together and to work with a will. But, Alan wondered, how long could it last? Feelings ran deeply and it needed only another incident to re-kindle the strife. Innochervie, under Dougal's quiet leadership, knew that, to protect its future, *Liberté* simply had to be fitted out in time to catch this summer's weather window.

Management had wisely decided to alter as little as possible, the main modifications being to the derrick and to the accommodation. There had been no need to construct expensive modules which would have to be towed out in barges to the exposed waters of Sulisker, there to be hoisted on board for welding into place. *Liberté* was 99 per cent complete in itself.

By the end of March, all the pipelines would be completed. *Explorer* was now on stream and only the line to *Sula*, the exposed weather storage buoy off Stornoway, was not finished. The barge was working flat out, all £5,000,000-worth of it, to finish the lay on time. By April oil would be flowing, though *Explorer* was a risk that authority was now ignoring. By the end of May, *Liberté* must be ready for her tow to Sulisker where she would be settled on site. The divers were already working on the site survey and it seemed there would be no difficulty. The bottom was as good as the geologists wanted. Trials next, and, by the end of July, *Liberté* should be on stream.

It was already ten o'clock. Alan walked round to the leeward side of the control platform. The wind had backed rapidly and was north-easterly. The cold was eating through their sweaters and it looked as if rain was on its way. The breeze was whistling through the concrete structure and the tugs were working hard to keep their tow moving.

The French were certainly way ahead with their know-how of pre-stressed concrete. *Liberté* was a miracle of engineering — her gigantic size and her underwater weight of 400,000 tons meant that she would be able to withstand hurricane-force winds. Her 16 180-feet cylinders forming the base would act as oil storage tanks once they had been flooded for settling at a depth of 360 feet on the seabed. Four concrete pillars, nearly 600 feet high, reared upwards from the base to support the production and drilling decks. Drilling could be carried out through three of these columns, but the fourth would house the machinery and pumping gear. International had paid £35,000,000 for this most modern of platforms, but the bankers had insisted on strict controls now that money was so tight.

It was incredible, Alan mused, that over a third of *world* costs were spent on North Sea exploitation. Emulating Shell and Exxon, International would be linking its future fields to a central pumping system at the Butt of Lewis, then across to Eddrachillis Bay, where it would join the main line for the Sutherland storage depots and a refinery yet to be built on the west coast. The feeder line to the *Sula* exposed weather storage buoy would run out from the Eye peninsula. No wonder these costs were astronomical, but the Western World was hungry for energy. In America every man, woman and child spent an annual £2.10 towards research and control of ecological problems in the air, the sea and on land.

'Bye.'

Sheena's hand pressed lightly on Alan's shoulder. She was off to her work in the admin office, two decks below. He watched her going down the ladders, as much at home here already as she had been in *Wanklyn*. Alan decided to take a few turns round the catwalk before settling down to his own paperwork.

The wind was freshening, but remained north-easterly, as it added its braking power to the spring ebb now running against them. He watched the flights of seabirds flapping their way stolidly towards the cliff of South Harris. He heard *Dalrymple Navigator*'s hooter as she altered to the course of her consorts. Her towing span slid across the protective steel arc spanning her open stern. Toots of acknowledgement floated upwards from the other tugs and then, slowly, the wakes described a gentle curve to the new alteration of course to the eastward. From his side of the platform, the northern tip of Skye was blue against the haze now shutting down to the eastward. He could not see the mainland now, but the mountains behind Gairloch were disappearing in the lowering clouds. He felt the chill in his bones. He was cold to the marrow, but now there was a heaviness in the air and a clamminess he had not noticed before. He shivered and entered the warmth of the navigational control room where Raoul and the Clyde pilot were crouching over the charts.

'Alan.'

Alan had liked the look of the Trinity House pilot, Captain Buchanan, from the first moment he had taken charge after the monster had been manoeuvred into the Clyde. A short man, with laughter lines at the corners of his eyes, he had a fund of ludicrous yarns in his repertoire. Nothing was sacred to him. His comments on life in general were a stream of profanities, but those on the unreliability of the weather were even more obscene. There was only one worse calamity — the incompetence of some foreign shipmasters.

'Mornin', Mr Brodie. The weather in your neck of the woods is certainly not living up to its reputation.'

Alan smiled. Ross and Cromarty were God's own country for him — and its weather was part of its life. 'What's the barometer doing?' he asked.

'Falling slowly.' The mocking banter in Raoul's voice was absent. 'We've a difficult decision to make, Alan.'

'We're only making two knots,' Captain Buchanan said. 'If the wind freshens much more, we'll be lucky to maintain that speed and still stay on the line.' He took off his cap and scratched his balding head. 'I'd like to be past East Bank and through the Sgeir Graidach narrows by dark.'

Raoul's finger traced the track running across the Admiralty chart. 'We've an alteration abeam the bell buoy of Sgeir Inoe. Only a mile on 124° before we alter round again to 081°. Then we're relatively safe for our final run north to Stornoway and across North Minch to Loch Innoch. We can always anchor once we're through the narrows and are safely past Sgeir Graidach.'

Alan noted the rock-bound passages, barely a mile and a half wide, which gave *Liberté* the depth she needed. If they passed through before dark they would sight Sgeir Inoe rock, but it would take another hour to clear East Bank and the beacon guarding Sgeir Graidach and Eugenie rock.

'Okay, Pilot,' Raoul said. 'We'll make the passage of the narrows in daylight: I don't want to be caught just here, if we're in for a real *tempête*.'

The French word seemed more sinister than its British equivalent. Alan would leave them to make their own decision. Thank God, he had no part in it, but he could understand their anxiety — to be caught out here, between the entrance to East Loch Tarbert and that menacing coast of Skye, was a seafarer's nightmare. He'd bash his in-tray and return after lunch to see what lay ahead.

Before taking the lift back to the navigating platform, Alan took a stroll outside along the recreation deck. It was raining and he was surprised how little headway *Liberté* had made. He could still hear the weird siren of Eilean Glas lighthouse, 141 feet high on Scalpay islet, only three miles away. *Liberté* had gained little in these two hours — the bell buoy of Sgeir Inoe was spasmodically tolling its mournful dirge. He'd nip up top to see what was going on.

Sgeir Graidach rock seemed close, right ahead, its pinnacle less than a mile and a half distant. He'd be able to judge things better up on the navigation deck. He'd take the leeward stairway to be protected from the sheets of rain slatting in now from the southwest.

He sheltered for a moment in the lee of the navigation room. Inside, Raoul and the pilot were huddled in the far corner, working out the alternatives. It was almost 14.30 now, and down below the tugs were well off course as they struggled to hold *Liberté* into the wind. Their wakes frothed and the tows splashed across the wave-tops where the wires sprung taut with the strain. The seas were curling white, midget waves from up here, but it must be blowing because, even in the lee of North Harris and Lewis, up here it was certainly force six, gusting seven. To the westward, the hills and the mountains were black against the lowering sky. Already the sun was well down, sinking fast on another day. It would be dark early tonight, well before official twilight at 16.53. Alan pushed open the door and stood in silence, listening to the orders being passed on the RT to the tugs.

'I've told *Seamew* to keep dead on the line,' Iain Macgregor was reporting, 'but if the wind continues to freshen, I doubt if we can hold you — *over.*'

'*Dalrymple Navigator*, this is Pilot *Liberté*. I read you, Iain, loud and clear. It's important here, to keep her on track. What are the chances of turning her, and making up under the lee of Harris? We could anchor at the mouth of East Loch Tarbert — *over.*'

'Couldn't hold you, Pilot. I'm towing 40° off track now. Once she gathers leeway, there'll be no holding her. You'd be on Graidach before you knew it.'

Another voice cut in brusquely: 'Pilot, *Liberté*... This is Pilot *Seamew*...' There was anxiety in the Glaswegian voice. 'I'm turning to 081°. I'm dead on track now, but at this low speed I'm having to stop and start continually. It's impossible not to make leeway now; I'll hoist a cone when I'm off track.'

'Okay, Dick. Message received and understood. I'll have a word with the Controller, then come back to you. Iain, could you lay out anchors for us in this, do you think?'

There was a long silence, the loudspeaker crackling above the frames of the windows in front of them. The tugs were bucketing in the seas, as they took the waves on their port bows. The tows streamed, wet with flying spume.

'Not much time before dark, Pilot,' the Scottish voice was saying. 'But we'll have a go. Reckon it's our best chance. Can you pass us a line? *Over.*'

'Won't reach you up wind, Iain, not even with our line-throwers.'

'Pilot *Liberté*, this is Pilot *Seamew*. I can take your lines to the tugs for you. You'll have to look slippy.'

'Thanks, Dick. We'll drop our emergency anchor underfoot,' Buchanan said. 'Might hold her temporarily until you can take the weight. Don't want to ballast down unless we have to. We've got shale, shingle and the odd rock showing on our chart. We'll damage the skirt if we touch. Stand by, *Seamew*, while I have a word with the Controller ... *out.*'

Raoul Ghio was standing at Buchanan's elbow. He nodded to Alan to join in the discussion.

'You're the seaman, Captain Buchanan,' Ghio said. 'I'm an amateur sailor, but I can recognize an emergency when I see it.' He nodded to the eastward where the wind, having backed rapidly, was now south-westerly and driving the seas on to Graidach and the islet of Eilean Trodday. The lighthouse reared 160 feet above the sea and soon it would be winking its groups of two flashes, white, red, green every ten seconds. There were too many visible rocks less than a mile and a half off; and if *Liberté* fell away from her charted track, she'd be aground in minutes, the 30-fathom line being less than eight cables to the southward. '*Merde!*' the Controller swore softly. 'This is precisely the situation I tried to avoid.' Raoul beat the table with his fist. 'So you wish to anchor, Captain Buchanan?'

'Yes, Controller. The gale has caught us four hours earlier than expected — it's backed too fast. You have two choices, sir: to ballast down or anchor. See for yourself...' He nodded again to leeward.

'Anchor, then.' Ghio was not pleased. He bent his broad bulk over the ship's intercom: 'Tell the mate to stand by the emergency anchor and to take *Seamew*'s lines.' The working deck loudspeaker buzzed. 'Mate here, skip. What's up?'

Ghio was in action now and Alan could understand why he'd been chosen by Cousteau. The pilot was interrupting: 'Right, sir, let go the emergency anchor.'

There was a long delay and then a faint rumbling as the cable rattled out, clear of the concrete base. Ghio picked up the machinery room phone.

'Chief? We may need to ballast down. Stand by the valves but do nothing until ordered. Okay?'

Alan could hear the croaking Scottish voice crackling from the earpiece. Impatiently, Raoul hung up. 'We've only flooded once and that was on trials, Pilot.'

Alan watched the little *Seamew* manoeuvring upwind, close under the working deck. As she stemmed the seas, a line snaked through the air to be snatched successfully first time on to the platform. Out went the manilla and then the boat eased forwards towards the furthest of the four tugs, the bight of the manilla splashing in the seas as it was paid out from *Liberté*. To Alan it all seemed desperately slow, but in reality the operation was well handled — and all the while Buchanan was craning over the pelorus, his eyes straining along his anchor bearings.

'The emergency anchor is not holding.' He spoke in a matter-of-fact way, as if expecting the inevitable. 'Veer as much as you can, sir.'

Seamew was surging back towards them now, her first line passed. She turned broadside, in a wide arc, to take out the next line. As she swooped into the foaming seas, Alan saw the first of the huge anchors splashing into the waves, as the tug hauled the 6.5-inch wire towards her counter.

'Let go, when you're able.' Buchanan was talking to the tug. 'As soon as you've enough wire.'

'Okay, Mr Buchanan — we'll not waste time.'

'We're dragging fast.'

Buchanan's tanned face looked up from the bearing ring. 'If the first anchor checks her, we've a chance — but stand by to ballast down as fast as you can.'

Alan watched the flashing light of the bell buoy: it was almost sunset and the night was shutting in already. *Seamew* was off with the second messenger before the first anchor was let go. Buchanan crouched low, swiftly taking his bearings.

The tension on the navigational bridge was now tangible. Two men, one keeping the log, the other operating the sounding machine, worked silently in the corner. The radio officer stood motionless, waiting for orders. In the centre was Ghio, huge, restless, furious at the slowness of the operation … and then *Seamew* was back again, ably handled, making no mistakes even in these mounting seas.

'That's slowed her up,' Buchanan said.

Outside, through the leeward windows, Alan could see *Liberté*'s crew huddled in the lee, watching the tugs as they struggled to save this giant from driving ashore. Buchanan, relief on his face, said, 'We're barely moving sir. The second sheet anchor should hold her.'

It was now past sunset and the light was failing rapidly. The flashes from Eilean Glas light flailed across the windows. It was past twilight before the third tug had let go the last anchor. The platform trembled, as, on the working deck, they hove in to take the weight.

'She's holding, sir.' The pilot looked up, a crooked smile on his face. 'We've stopped dragging.' He snatched another set of bearings for his final fix. 'I'll stay up here for a bit, if you don't mind. But we ought to be prepared to ballast down, in case anything goes wrong.' And Alan saw the pilot's glance to leeward.

It was dark, but through the windows Alan could see the columns of white spray leaping against Graidach and Eugenie rock — and, to the southward, the seas were battering the stranded hulk of a wreck which had been driven ashore on the rocks of Fladda-chùain.

'It'll be a long night, Alan.' Ghio stretched himself, then moved to the stairway. 'I'll have my supper early and have a yarn with the mate. We haven't seen the worst of it yet, so we'd better get some sleep.'

Alan nodded, then pushed open the leeward door to snatch a breather before going below. The wind hit him as he peered round the corner, a gust that almost bowled him over. In the darkness he could see the navigation lights of the tugs, white, green and red, bucketing in the seas below. These maids of all work were keeping up to windward, for there was little sea-room for them now. Alan wondered how long they could remain here, fully exposed, before they would have to seek shelter up to windward. This was no place to be caught out — but if they were forced to leave, *Liberté* would be very much on her own.

21

Before turning in, Alan saw Sheena to her cabin. The wind strength was increasing hourly, and now the cables and anchor wires were snatching in the short seas building up across the Little Minch. At each snatch, the cement structure quivered through its length. Sheena was obviously troubled by the ferocity of this gale, but he had reassured her about *Liberté's* strength. Pre-stressed cement was ideal material for a structure that relied on its immense weight to anchor itself to the seabed. He took comfort in the information he had acquired of *Liberté's* strength — the older the concrete, the harder it became, and it lasted virtually for ever. Lloyds had given it its certificate of fitness — a comfort tonight, when the fundamentals of an untried design were being put to a practical test.

Immense research had been carried out for *Liberté*. An accurate picture of the weather pattern of the Sulisker bank had been the first essential, to calculate accurately the gigantic forces exerted by hurricane-plus winds; the techniques of building pre-stressed concrete were studied; so were the nature and mechanics of the seabed, so that it could support the enormous weight of some 400,000 tons ballasted, when spread over a small area.

Alan slept fitfully. Then, in his restlessness, he gradually became aware that something was wrong. The pounding of the storm continued unabated, and the platform was trembling rhythmically from the shocks of the seas breaking upon it — but why this list?

'Sparks?' He called across to the radio officer's berth, but there was no reply. Alan snipped on the light, but the cabin was empty. He scrambled from his bunk and was slipping into his clothes and thick Norwegian sweater when the klaxons sounded. What the hell was up now?

He grabbed his engineer's torch and lifejacket, then slipped into the corridor. The alarm was still sounding imperiously, summoning all hands to their emergency stations. He raced down the passage and up the ladder to the deck above, to find Sheena. He was rapping on her door when she came quickly out in anorak and trousers, her lifejacket clutched in her hand. He took her by the arm and hustled her towards the lift where a queue of men waited, struggling into their orange lifejackets.

'Come on,' he said. 'It'll be quicker up the stairways.' He barged against the exit door on the leeward side. They clattered up the stairway, careful on the slippery steel. As they reached the nav. deck, the fury of the gale tore Alan from the rail to which he was clinging. He pulled Sheena into the shelter by the door. He could see their orange lifeboat, but only a couple of men had so far arrived at their station.

This gale was a savage thing: the wind was shrieking through the derrick above them, flailing the exposed gear on the working platform. It was blowing so hard that even up here the spume was flying, wet and cold, against their faces.

'*Inside!*' His cry to Sheena was carried away on the wind. He grabbed her, flung open the door and shoved her into the relative calm of the nav. room. Buchanan was standing by the windward windows, binoculars to his eyes as he peered to leeward where Eilean Glas was blinking intermittently. He wedged himself against the corner to counteract the list which seemed to be growing more acute now.

'That you, Alan?' Buchanan asked.

'Yes — anything I can do?' Even in here, they had to shout above the clamour of the wind.

'Nip down to the control room and tell the Controller that there's a tug coming out — bloody fool, what's she think she can do in this?'

'Where are the others?'

'They ran for shelter three hours ago — under the lee of Loch Grosebay.'

'Why the list?'

'When we began ballasting down, the computer went on the blink, just as the bypass valve in the flooding box jammed. The chief's trying to fix it now, but he'll have to get a move on.'

'Dragging?'

'Fast,' Buchanan said. 'It's a race against time.'

Alan's silence prompted the pilot to continue: 'We've 40 foot of water under us in this patch, so we can safely ballast down another 20 feet. The extra draught and less windage should give the anchors a chance. But the chief's got to get a hustle on.'

'And if we drag into that shallower water?' Alan nodded to leeward, where Sgeir Graidach and Eugenie rocks were waiting.

'We'll touch on East Bank first — only six cables under our lee.'

There was no need to add the details. If *Liberté* touched, the skirt would be damaged — and the resulting delays would mean the schedule would be lost — the chief *must* conquer the fault or the platform could even be totally wrecked.

For the first time that night, Alan felt the kick of fear, as *Liberté* shuddered from the onslaught of the raging seas. 'Stay here,' he yelled into Sheena's ear. 'I'll be back.'

Below in the control room, Raoul Ghio stood aloof, away from the cluster of men at the panels. Sparks, a grey-faced man in his late twenties, leaned against the doorway of the radio room. Stranraer radio was on the air, the taciturn Hebridean operator clearly audible, even in this weather.

'PAN — PAN — PAN,' he was announcing to the listening world as he alerted the emergency services. 'Oil platform in difficulties.' Laconically, *Liberté*'s position was being broadcast to the helpless lifeboats and helicopters. Nothing could operate in the fury of this dark night.

A sudden, violent tremor vibrated throughout the platform. Alan staggered across the floor, while Ghio braced himself against the shock. Buchanan was speaking on the intercom: 'The westward cable's parted,' he reported, tense now. 'The others will go if we can't reduce the windage. Suggest it's time for our *Mayday*, sir.'

Alan felt the increasing list as *Liberté* lurched further from the wind. Then the second cable parted, and even above the raging of the storm, they heard the crack of the parting wires.

Ghio nodded at his radio officer. Seconds later, the *Mayday* signal was being passed.

'Pointless taking to the boats, sir,' the mate yelled into Ghio's ear — and he nodded towards the black line of rocks to leeward. 'Better to stick it out here... Everything depends on how fast we can ballast down.'

'We've still got one anchor,' Buchanan called from above. 'If only we can lay it up to windward, that might check the drift... I'm coming down.'

Seconds later Buchanan staggered into the control room, his face grim as he faced the Controller. 'If we could weigh our kedge that's underfoot, and take it up to windward, we might stand a chance, sir. It'll be impossible to gain distance, but at least we might stop falling off to leeward.'

Ghio glanced at his mate. '*Dalrymple?*'

'Iain Macgregor's about the only man who could do it, sir. And he's out there now.' They peered through the spinning clear glass screen, searching for the lights of the supply boat. There they were, white and green pinpoints of light smearing across the window.

Ghio picked up the mic. '*Dalrymple Navigator*, *Dalrymple Navigator*, *Dalrymple*... This is *Liberté*. D'you read me? *Over*.'

Macgregor's voice broke through: 'Loud and clear — *over*.'

'Can you get a line over to us, and take our kedge up to windward — as far as you can? We'll let you know before we reach the bare-end ... *over*.'

'Roger. I'll close you up wind and pass a line. Report when you're ready — *out*.'

Events moved rapidly — as the mate scrambled below, taking the bo'sun and several hands with him, the chief broke in on the intercom: 'Chief here, sir. I've sorted out the problem — I'm continuing to ballast down.'

'Thanks, Chief,' Ghio replied. 'Fast as you can. We're running out of depth.'

'Understood, sir.'

The platform was quivering now, but the list had not increased.

'Ready on the working deck,' the mate was reporting.

'Okay, Mr Mate,' Ghio answered on the intercom. 'Stand by *Dalrymple*'s line.' He picked up the RT mic.

'Ready when you are, *Dalrymple*.'

'Stand by.' Macgregor was in command now. They watched through the window as the little ship dipped and disappeared in the seas that raged nearly 400 feet below the control room. She had just disappeared beneath the crane extension when the flash of a Coston gun lit up the tug's flying bridge — a cotton line was at that instant flying downwind, into the latticework of

Liberté's working platform. On this thread depended their lives and the future of International… They waited in silence for the mate's report. The tug disappeared, lost beneath the overhang.

'For Christ's sake, Smith,' the mate's voice yelled, his intercom evidently switched on. 'Grab the fucking thing!' Then silence again…

'We've missed it,' the mate shouted angrily.

'Tell 'em to try again.'

Ghio glanced to leeward, through the misting windows. 'Got another line, *Dalrymple*?'

'Only one more, *Liberté*. Stand by.'

A flash in the darkness, the silence, the waiting … and then a shout as the mate cut in: 'We've got it. *Heave in.*'

The men in the control room were crowding at the windows. Then slowly, barely moving, the tug appeared again, the floodlighting on her working deck a shimmering pool as the sheets of water broke over her. Yard by yard, she fought her way out into the bedlam of the gale, away from the platform — and astern of her, the manilla streamed, a glistening scythe of spray.

'One hundred fathoms out,' the mate called out. 'Standing by with the wire.'

Raoul Ghio repeated the information, but Macgregor cut in, the first sign of stress discernible in his voice. 'Manilla's safe inboard,' he reported. 'Can I haul in yet?'

'Haul away.'

Alan slipped below. They'd be needing help now, down on the working deck. He gasped as he battled out into the wind and found the stairways. The air was full of flying spume. He reached the deck and lay back on the 4.5-inch wire now being backed up on the revolving drums of the windlass.

'Watch what you're doing,' the mate yelled to his gang. His hands spiralled above the silhouette of his head as the wire veered, fathom after fathom, over the lip of the working deck and into the blackness below. It was difficult keeping a foothold on this slippery deck.

'Avast veering.'

The windlass clanked to a stop.

'Back up and heave in on the anchor wire.'

The mate's cry was carried away in the wind. The windlass eased. 'Heave in on the wire.'

The kedge went over, hauled in by the supply boat, veered from *Liberté*'s end.

'Twenty fathoms to go.'

The mate was barking into the intercom. 'Tell *Dalrymple* we're reaching the bare-end. She can let go when she likes.'

Seconds later, the wire went slack. *Dalrymple Navigator* had let go. There was no more that anyone could do. Silently the weary gang climbed back up the ladders, into the shelter of the bridge. For Alan, this was the longest night of his life. He longed for the dawn.

Alan never knew how long he had dozed, with Sheena's head against his shoulder, in the corner of the nav. room. He had dropped into unconsciousness when the dragging stopped. But now he was awake, aware of the light stealing across the sky through the east-facing windows. Small black clouds were streaming by, but the hammering of the wind seemed less.

'The guts have gone out of it,' a voice said near him. 'The wind's veering.' Buchanan's wan smile emphasized the exhaustion on his face. Alan gently woke the girl beside him.

'Let's go outside,' he said. 'The gale's blown itself out.'

They stood by the rail, but the wind was still gusting hard. Down below, a supply boat was plunging into the seas, while close to her starboard bow an orange anchor buoy dipped in the troughs. On the bridge of *Dalrymple Navigator*, a man stood in his oilskins. Alan raised his arm in salute. Macgregor saw him and waved in return.

From the north-westward five little ships were approaching downwind, wallowing as they nearly broached. An ancient, wooden drifter was in the lead, racing to join the supply boat from which she had been separated during the night.

22

Heidi Stettler watched the cold sunlight stealing across the mirror of her dressing-table. At about coffee time, the winter sunshine would disappear behind the shoulder of Ben More and would not reappear until two in the afternoon. This cottage of hers, tucked away up a sandy lane which wound up the glen from Garra Brig, was her solace and her consolation. Today, more poignantly than for a long time, she needed the serenity that Curlew Cottage gave her.

She checked the page in her red-backed pocket diary: 18 January, '10.30, Kevin Strong, 22, lonely, sensitive, from Shoreditch.' She glanced at last Friday's newspaper lying on the bedside table. That small paragraph emphasized the impersonal callousness of an oilman's life.

'Oilman killed,' she read aloud. 'Kevin Strong, 22, of Shoreditch, London, a welder on International's *Explorer* rig, suffered a fatal accident yesterday. His clothing was caught in machinery which severed his right arm. He was brought ashore by emergency helicopter to Ullapool hospital, where he died from his injuries.' She allowed the tears to stream down her face, thankful that she would be free this afternoon.

Half-past ten had come and gone. She must pull herself together. This was not the first time one of her 'friends' had been killed on the rigs. Welders, drillers, derrick-men, they all ran risks — but the divers in particular gambled their health for the fortunes they won from the black gold beneath the ocean bed.

Kevin had been such a decent boy. The fact that he had come from Shoreditch brought back Heidi's own memories, not always happy, of the time when she first came to England — way back now, 20 years ago. She'd never known her father — he'd disappeared one night, arrested and carried off to the camps, never to be heard of again.

She stood before the mirror, dabbed at her eyes and tossed up her hair above her head. Were those grey streaks showing again at the base of her twisted blonde hair? She could hold her ageing in check at the moment, but what in ten years' time? She'd have to think hard on that, or perhaps one day marry. She never starved, was never lonely, for the men she served came from all over the world — and there were some real men amongst her clientele, good men who would cherish her. Then she heard the scrabble of tyres on the gravel outside. She zipped up her robe, shook her hair into place and edged to the window. A red Ford had drawn up at the door. A man was stooping across the seat and reaching for his travelling grip. She would recognize those broad shoulders from the other side of the world.

He lay on his side, then propped himself up on one elbow to look down at her. She could certainly satisfy a man, and he wondered idly what life would be like if he were married to her — or would that spoil everything?

Heidi and he had known each other for 12 years now, since they first met in London when he had been diving for the PLA. Now, after his spells on the rig, it was seldom that he did not visit her during his seven days' freedom. With the money he was earning, he could afford to keep some of it for his own pleasure — though Doreen's alimony was taking a big enough proportion. He savagely jabbed away the memory of her, intent on not wasting a minute of his precious time with this big-hearted, sensual woman.

'Let's talk,' he said. 'Haven't seen you all these weeks.'

'October,' she murmured. 'During that lovely weather — before Kevin was killed.'

He sensed the wistfulness in her voice. But, though pangs of jealousy struck him at times, he did not resent the other men she took to bed with her. What right did he have, anyway?

'You're not listening, Jake.'

'Thinking about you.'

'Nice things?'

'Depends — nice for me.'

'How?'

'The other blokes. The way you live ought to bother me.'

Her arms tightened about him. 'They're good to me when you're not around — most of them.'

'It's the ones you're *not* so sure about that worry me. D'you often choose wrong 'uns?'

'Difficult sometimes. Once they've arrived, it's hard to get rid of them.'

'You ought to vet them first in Ullapool — a sort of grading system.' He realized, too late, that the bitter laugh which escaped him had wounded her.

'I know, Jake, but I can't join the lot in Ullapool. They take their money and accept the risks. Me, I'm selective. What's up with you anyway?'

He was anxious, worried for her safety. 'What sort of bloke last bothered you? How long ago?'

'Usually the foreigners,' she said, 'not often the Scots. The man who scared me most was a southern Irishman who arrived with his sidekick — both divers.'

His arms tightened around her. 'Go on,' he said.

'I told the Syrian to wait in the car. He was okay — and they shared the afternoon. The Middle-Eastern gentleman paid well.'

She was teasing him — he knew her so well now.

'Go on.'

'Nothing, really. The Irishman was low class, and I'm sure he was IRA. Reckoned he was a Romeo, but his talk was better than his performance... He asked about *Explorer*, come to think of it.'

'*My* rig?'

'Asked a lot of questions. How many men? Was there work there? What did they pay?'

'Anything else?'

'No,' she said, and he sensed her impatience. 'Oh, yes — he asked the names of the bosses. Wasn't interested in the roustabouts, drillers or floormen — just the tool pusher and the office men, the drilling superintendent and the engineers. But I wasn't interested. Bored with him and his antics. Wanted to go to sleep. Wasn't like you, Jake!'

'What about his sidekick in the car?'

Her eyes were shining with excitement as she continued to mock him. 'Much better, he was. Wasn't sleepy with him — never knew what would happen next, because he'd interrupt with his questions too, just as he was becoming interesting — big and strong, he was — my God, he was tough.'

'Same questions from him?'

'Yes, but I could remember only you and Joe Wadham — *Explorer*'s tool pusher, isn't he?'

'Yeah — good bloke. D'you give our names?' He was alert now, anxiety clouding his contentment.

'Only yours and Joe's.' She paused. 'They both asked if I knew a man called Brawdy — didn't register with me.'

'Brawdy?'

'Said they wanted to meet him if they could — drilling engineer, apparently. Owed him money, they said.'

Jake shook his head. He didn't care for foreigners, especially inquisitive ones — and, least of all, those who treated Heidi as an information centre.

'I'd get you out of this, if I could,' he said. 'I'll live with you one day, even marry if you like.' What the hell was he saying?

'I'm hungry.' She sliced some venison and they washed it down with Guinness.

'See you,' he said, and kissed her.

'Tomorrow, Jake?'

'If I can make it. See you.'

He levered himself into the rented car and drove off down the lane. She was still waving from the doorway as he lost her in the rear mirror.

It was usually the same with divers. They always lived dangerously and drove too fast. This first run ashore, with nearly 1200 quid, plus £250 a week living expenses in his pocket, was more than most men could resist. Jake had knocked back three doubles with Dave, the manager of Offshore Diving Ltd, who had given him some good news. They'd raised Jake's pay by 20 per cent, because the oil moguls could not find enough experienced underwater men.

He leaned against the grubby bar of this Ullapool pub, a dump of a place freshened up hurriedly a year ago when the boom was certain. This was a drinking saloon, where beer was chased with spirits. Once a man became involved in a pool, a round could cost 30 quid — but at 25p a nip, hell, what did it matter? The kids were grown up, leading their own lives —

and Doreen? God, Doreen. He knocked back the malt whisky to the dregs … ach! That was better! He reached for his chaser.

'You deal, Jake.'

His turn again — the faster the better at this American pool, but the stakes were too high. He was bored with this lot. He'd dip out after this deal.

In the end, they refused to leave him. Pete Mackay threw an arm about his shoulder and swayed with him to the bar, the other five at his heels. Divers were great guys, close as a nun's —

'Jake, you old bastard, where've yer been all me loife?'

He looked up and there was Romeo O'Toole, the best diver on the east coast and the highest paid this side of the Atlantic. He had given up contract work and was diving for himself now — and Jake wondered whether he could risk the same step yet. O'Toole was one of his oldest mates, but his pace had been too hot during their shared runs ashore.

Romeo lived up to his name. A woman was clutching his arm as she rhythmically pawed his chest, her hand inside the opened shirt. She gazed up at him, her eyes brittle as her false eyelashes fluttered absurdly. His fame always spread quickly through Ullapool when he was ashore. He always took a room in each of the port's four hotels. With Scotland's ridiculous licensing laws, he could booze through his 24 hours and enjoy his oats at the same time. At the Stage Coach, Ullapool's most modern atrocity, rearing high in its cellular splendour, he had once booked the honeymoon suite. He had smuggled his girls in for the night and they'd certainly had a ball. He had tried the same tactics on the next night, but the manager had flung the girls out when the occupants in the next room complained. And now that the prostitutes were moving into Ullapool, the Rent-a-Girl agency was raking in the lolly.

'What'll ye take, me boy?' O'Toole flung up his arms suddenly, contemptuously ridding himself of his female encumbrance. 'A coupla chasers 'fore we get down to the hard stuff?' He slammed the palms of his hands on to the bar top and glasses rang the length of the saloon. 'Drinks on t' house,' O'Toole waved. 'It's time this fuckin' morgue was shook up.' His bellow drowned the laughter. 'Who's drinking with O'Toole tonight?'

Jake watched as they gathered round the expansive Irishman. Here he was, burning up the £160 a week he was earning now. How long could he last, at this rate of drinking? A bottle of whisky a day was the norm for him when he was going at it hard. His weather-beaten face was now unhealthily blotchy, there was a puffiness beneath the eyes and the suspicion of a double chin that had not been there before. Jake tossed back the Scotch, and followed it up with the sweet stout. One more and he'd be on form, up with the others.

This was the only way to live, he supposed, if you gambled your health and your life for hard cash. Bloody stupid, though, like the Australian, Barry Fields, who blew his £150-200 every time he came ashore. Barry had never failed to spend his last night ashore, cooling off in the overcrowded cells of Ullapool's inadequate police station. The booze did the damage — the chicks were part of the fun, picked up, used, discarded — that was the way the girls liked it, and the fellows too.

The rounds were circulating fast. There must be nearly 15 in the party, since the last lot had attached themselves — recent acquaintances of Romeo's, and as sexually potent, he'd boasted, with his roar of self-esteem: 'Jake, me old timer, meet me buddies. O'Toole's no racist — we're all comrades together, ain't we boys?' He waved his arms towards the four men — not a Brit amongst them. 'This is Bruno from Holland,

and Helmut from East Germany, Fawzi from Libya, and you, you fat bastard, where'd yer father come from, if yer ever 'ad one?' His bawdy laughter erupted once more.

The large man nodded and grinned. 'Sean Thomas,' he shouted, 'from Dublin.'

Jake sank his drink and moved over to him. The Irishman had the build of a useful diver.

'Where you been operating, Sean?'

'Across at Nigg — the Cromarty one. Wanted the channel surveyed for the latest platform. Bloody awful place, Nigg.'

'I've heard so. Worse than this?'

The Irishman laughed, a grating, unpleasant sound. 'Arsehole of the empire, mate. Dregs of humanity there, hellish dump. You can live in the old Greek accommodation ship, or on the van site — take yer pick. The chicks are the scum of Scotland, and two out of three of the operatives end up eating and sleeping in a glass. Fuckin' 'orrible.' He knocked back another stout to deaden the pain.

'What are you doing here?'

'Looking for work. They tell me there's plenty at West Coast.'

'Yeah, now that the concrete job's moved up there. They're pushed to catch the window.'

His three companions were edging closer.

'Do they pay well?' the Syrian asked, his yellow teeth bared in a grin that showed flashy gold fillings.

'If you're a worker,' Jake said. He knew he'd made a mistake, by the instant reduction of noise.

The boozy Dutchman lunged towards him and clapped a heavy hand on Jake's shoulder. 'I've worked on the McAllister barges, Mister,' he shouted aggressively. 'We laid more pipe in one day than any other company could in a week.'

'Say that again, Bruno,' a squat Italian hissed, breaking into the gathering circle. 'Nobody works more than us. We knock pants from under you fuckin' Hollanders.'

Jake felt the sudden tension and saw the flash of a knife. He wanted no part in a punch-up. 'Okay boys, cool it,' he shouted. 'Don't wreck the joint.' The four foreigners were edging closer to each other for mutual protection. The Irishman, Thomas, had slipped his hand inside his shirt. Jake could see the bulge where they packed their shoulder holsters. He was getting out of this.

'Romeo,' he yelled across the crowd, as they formed opposing camps. 'Let's clear out of this dump.'

He wagged his head, and collected up his chicks. 'Where'll we go, Jake? D'yer know a daicent 'otel what'll welcome Romeo?'

'There's a good place at Innochervie,' Thomas yelled. 'I was there once. Food's good, Tartan beer, and whisky galore.'

'Too bloody far, Sean,' Romeo shouted as his glazed eyes focused slowly on the clock. 'Quarter past seven already. Wanna eat.'

'Ullapool gets on my tits,' Thomas persisted. 'Besides, what's West Coast like? There's work there, Jake says.'

'Only 55 miles by the motorway,' O'Toole hollered. 'Three-quarters of an hour, if we take our own cars.'

'You can sleep there too, Romeo,' Jake shouted, grinning. 'The Errabeg hotel is okay.' For himself, when the night was well on, he'd slip out and drive back to Garra Brig.

'What we waitin' for, then?' O'Toole brushed through the crowd of drunks spoiling for their punch-up.

Outside the air was soft and cool. Jake shook the muzziness from his head, and tried to focus on the stars sparkling in the clear, cold night sky. He heard doors clunking as the owners identified their five cars in Ullapool's parking reservation.

'Get in,' he muttered to the four men standing by his red Ford. 'Three smallest in the back.'

'Belt up.'

He let in the clutch and was off, engine racing, towards the road leading to the new Ullapool-Innochervie motorway. He'd have to watch his driving, but once they were out of the town it was unlikely he'd be breathalysed on the motorway. His passengers were silent as the car swung along the pale ribbon of concrete towards the hills.

'Makes a difference, this road.' Thomas wanted to talk. The stale stench of booze wafted across from the passenger seat.

'Not bad, three-quarters of an hour to Innochervie. They did well to take the motorway round the back of Ben More, to the eastward and into Glen Cassley.'

'First time for me. Don't know this part — but I s'pose they've wrecked the beauty.'

Jake was surprised at the music in the sing-song of the Irishman's last word. So he was human, after all.

'Inevitable, if you slice a road of this width through the Highlands. Reckon they've tried their best, but it's massacred the head of Loch Shin and along Reay Forest.'

He heard them snoring in the back seat, but Thomas was too damn talkative. Jake was thinking of Heidi, whose lane he'd be passing soon. This bloke was irritating with his perpetual questioning. Jake found himself talking about his work, his months on *Explorer*. Then the man was at it again, demanding, pumping. Suddenly Jake was alert — wasn't this the experience that Heidi had shared? Names of individuals in International: who was this guy, anyway? And what was his business, if he was the same fellow who'd pestered Heidi? First time in these parts, Thomas had said.

He swung the Ford into the long sweep towards the head of Loch Shin, where the river joined the little loch. Four miles further on, halfway to Loch Merland, was the turning to Curlew Cottage.

'Garra Brig' — the blue sign bore down upon them and Jake swung off to the left. He found the lane, and minutes later pulled up outside the cottage.

'Shan't keep you long, mate,' Jake said. 'Popping in here for a moment to see a friend.'

He'd stopped the car close to the little gate, and left the engine running. Heidi was standing in the porch, hand on the light switch.

He got out quickly and passed through the light of the headlamps. Her eyes questioned him. 'What's going on?' she asked quietly.

He closed the door behind him.

'Why've you brought him here?' she demanded. Her eyes were blazing.

'That's all I want to know.' He kissed her. 'Don't wait up. I'll be back.'

'Jake.'

But he pressed her down to the settee and left, slamming the door behind him. As he climbed back into the car, the porch light went out.

'We'll soon catch up with the others,' Jake said.

He slipped into first. The passengers were awake now and he tried to keep the conversation going, but it was not until they bordered Loch Stack that Thomas spoke again. His tone was matter-of-fact now that he had sobered up.

'I've had an introduction to a bloke at West Coast,' he said. 'Might help me with a job.'

'Oh, aye?'

'If you know him, Jake, could you point him out?'

'Sure, but I only know the rig men — not the office boys.'

'He gets out to *Explorer*. Link man between International and West Coast,' the Irishman said.

'Name?'

'Brawdy. Alan Brawdy.'

Jake's mind was clear now, as keen as ever it was at 300 feet. 'Don't know the guy.' He revved the engine, changing down for the bend. 'There are the others. Told you we'd catch 'em.'

He kept the conversation going for the whole journey to Innochervie, as he held the Ford close behind the red beacons of Romeo's Merc.

'That's the place,' he said, relieved to see the hotel on the shoulder of the hill. 'The Errabeg.'

The other four cars had parked at the back, because the front drive was packed. Romeo was trying to quieten the girls, while the party, 15 strong, swayed towards the front entrance. Jake felt himself now, and he paused to watch the bay where the sea moved restlessly into Loch Madach. The setting moon was casting a sliver of gold across the pewter surface where the waves were breaking lazily upon the causeway to Hoyea.

'C'mon, Jake,' someone was shouting. 'We'll find a bird for you, mate.' The thumping of a group escaped through the curtained windows of the largest room.

The girl on Romeo's right arm began howling, 'Scotland for ever.'

'Shut up, you noisy bitch.' Romeo flipped his forearm as if shaking off a wasp. 'If we want to sleep here tonight, we gotta be posh.'

'No sleep for us, Romeo,' the blonde on his other arm giggled.

'We'll be needing rooms — and if they can't put us all up, we'll have to share. Our money's as good as theirs.'

They barged through the double doors. Jake stayed until last, uncomfortable, sensing trouble. This lot were three-quarters cut and could shift with the wind — and as swiftly. He followed them into the entrance hall where a formidable middle-aged woman was rising to her feet behind her desk. Her pursed lips emphasized her disdain.

'I'd like to speak to the manager, ma'am.' Romeo's hands hung like hams by his side. He was focusing hard, doing his best.

'I'm Miss Burns, the manageress,' the woman said. 'Sorry, but this is a private dance. There are no more tables.' Her eyes swept over them. She disliked what she saw.

'You got me wrong, ma'am.' Romeo slapped his hands on the registration book. 'We want rooms for the night. How many've ye got?'

The hall was silent except for the rhythm of the group throbbing through the glass doors of the dining-room.

The woman was no fool, thought Jake, as he watched her perusing the register. Miss Burns was facing a delicate situation and she knew it. Romeo was towering over her, watching her finger tracing across the pencilled names. Even from where he stood, Jake could see that not all the rooms were taken.

Her face jerked upwards as she faced the giant above her. 'We're fully booked,' she said. 'No rooms. I'm sorry, sir.' She flipped the booking forms to one side, behind the typewriter. 'You can have a drink at the bar.'

The tension was broken by murmuring from the rear of the party. 'Aw, 'ell, Romeo,' an American drawled. 'Tell the dame we've got the bucks.' He added, 'Ain't our dough good enough for her, heh?'

Romeo had steadied sufficiently not to stumble over his words. 'You're not full up, ma'am. You've got the rooms, ain't ye?'

'Sorry — no rooms vacant.' She was sizing up the girls again. 'Goodnight, sir.'

Jake tried to stop them, but the booze had taken hold as the infuriated swarm headed towards the music. Romeo swept the girls along, booming at the unfortunate manageress as he rolled past. 'We've come a long way, miss, and we're gonna have a ball.'

Jake hesitated, worried by this ugly turn: he was known here because of his *Explorer* association. Thomas, the Irishman, was bawling at them, egging them on, but Jake followed them as they pushed open the doors. Fawzi, the short Libyan, stayed close by the door. The noise of the group hit them, and then the laughing of the crowd. The music wheezed to a stop. The dancers halted where they stood. Jake would never forget the surprised faces, frozen like statues — some in amusement, some in disgust.

Sheena Macgregor felt ridiculously happy as she felt the pressure of Alan's knee beneath the white tablecloth of the VIPs' table. The group wasn't bad, the food was good, and the managing director of West Coast had made his farewell speech. *Liberté* had arrived in Innochervie only two days late. Divers had been flown out by chopper from Ullapool and, on the afternoon of 12 January, they reported that there was no visible underwater damage even to the leeward sections. The tow had begun again on the morning of the thirteenth, in spite of a force five blowing from the west. The tugs had brought her across North Minch and safely in through Innoch Narrows on the afternoon of the sixteenth, two days ago. And to celebrate the triumph for them all, the local community, West Coast, Cul Mor Services, and even International had forked out to pay for tonight's fun and games.

She had never felt so happy, now that Alan's and her worries were over. They'd be able to look for somewhere to live, after all. Raoul was on her left, with Buchanan's attractive daughter eagerly chatting him up. Opposite was Black, *Liberté*'s mate, and next to him Toby Sheridan, the Lieutenant from Innochervie's most recent acquisition, the Offshore Patrol Ship, HMS *Kittiwake*. Toby and Alan had made friends in the RNR, but Sheridan had made the Service his career.

'D'you think, Mr Ghio, that those smaller crude oil boxes would have stood up to your gale?' West Coast's managing director was leaning across the table, as they discussed the new concrete developments.

Raoul was not to be drawn. 'Difficult to say, but she wouldn't have grounded so early. Her 300-foot tower might have collapsed if she had grounded. It would depend whether the compartments were empty or not, because when they're full the platform weighs 10,000 tons.'

'She only draws 30 feet and that's the main advantage,' Alan was saying. 'It doesn't need a deep water construction site, but when it's offshore it stores over a million barrels — not a bad idea.'

The conversation was boring Sheena now. Would they ever stop talking shop? She wanted to dance again. Sheena placed her hand on Alan's sleeve.

'There'll be over a 100 platforms by 1985, they say,' Raoul added as the group's leader twanged his electric guitar.

'Everyone on the floor, ladies and gentlemen.'

She pulled Alan up and smiled at Sheridan's wife, who was being lifted to her feet by the mate. Alan had accepted West Coast's invitation for tonight and brought Sheena here without seeking security clearance. She knew that this deliberate flouting of Otway's orders was niggling at the back of his mind, but neither of them could face the next three or four months in *Liberté*, virtually imprisoned, until the rig was safely settled. Alan was fed up with having a detective on his back all the time. Otway had promised them a routine break every ten days, but only a chopper lift-out was allowed and then only to service accommodation at Dingwall. Roll on July — they'd had enough of this job. All she wanted now was to live with him, and settle as far away from Wester Ross as possible.

The group had done its best to play an old time medley. They paused, and struck a chord. Sheena saw Toby leave the managing director's wife at their table and steer towards them. It was great to have him here now. His presence up here and that of Jill, his wife, during the dreary weeks ahead would make all the difference.

Alan had locked his hands about her, as Toby struggled through the press. And then the band was off again, to the waltz of 'Tulips from Amsterdam'. Toby was grinning at them but she could not catch his words above the din. The crowd swept them on again and Sheridan turned back to look for Jill.

'I'm sorry I dance so badly,' Alan said.

A hubbub broke out by the doors and the rhythm of the band suddenly went to pieces. She tried to see across the floor to where a crowd was gathering. The men had been drinking and a big Irishman was calling the odds.

'Look, there's Jake O'Keefe.' Alan was smiling, amused at the interruption.

Sheena stood on her toes. 'Who's he, darling?'

'Diver friend from *Explorer* — good bloke. Must be up from Ullapool for a run ashore.' O'Keefe caught his eye and Alan waved to him.

They were shouting now, and Sheila Burns was signalling from the doors to the group's leader. The music started again, and the couples on the floor slowly began to circulate. Alan propelled her forwards and steered her safely around an enormous woman and her diminutive partner. Alan and she had almost made the circuit when she saw Jake again. He was standing on the perimeter and obviously waiting to talk. But she let Alan merge back into the meld. There'd be plenty of time for chat. Now O'Keefe was threading his way across the floor towards them.

'Don't look behind,' Alan was murmuring into her ear. 'Jake's after us.'

'Just when we're enjoying ourselves.'

He steered her away from one of the drunks barging in upon them with the bird he'd brought with him. If she'd been one of the village girls, Sheena would have recognized her, but with the arrival of some flashy professionals from London it was impossible to know them all. Cul Mor Terrace was virtually Brothel Row now — and there was nothing the village could do about it.

'You clumsy bastard.'

'Alan … shh!'

He was angry, more on account of the man's bad manners than his clumsiness. Then they were hemmed in by several couples, their breaths stale with drink. Sheena was being jostled and she began to feel angry.

'Hey, watch it,' she cried. 'You've torn my skirt.'

She felt the material rip as the man's heel caught the hem. Alan had tripped too, and she tried to hang on to him as he overbalanced against a lumbering drunk.

'Watch it, you clumsy sod,' an Irish voice shouted, and then Alan was separated from her. She saw him struggling with two men — one the Irishman, the other a foreigner. They were punching him hard, jabbing him viciously in the stomach, and he was doubling up with pain. She screamed and saw O'Keefe and Toby Sheridan fighting their way towards Alan. She was being separated from the struggling men when someone grabbed her wrists from behind. A hand was clapped hard across her mouth and suddenly the lights went out. She fought for breath, suffocating from the sweaty stench of the hand smothering her face. She felt herself fainting, and tried to scream as the room spiralled about her...

23

'You'd better go below, Number One,' said the captain of Offshore Patrol Ship 14, HMS *Kittiwake*. 'I'll finish your middle.'

Lieutenant Toby Sheridan watched his First Lieutenant disappearing down the ladder. The flu was hitting them all, one by one, but last night's pier-head jump made no allowances for sickness. In the present crisis he wondered what good *Kittiwake* could do up here, when all the action was in the North Sea.

Sulisker Bank was a godforsaken patrol area — weather foul, utterly desolate. He had the echo on his radar now. *Liberté*, which had settled without incident on site at the beginning of June, was already on stream and pumping oil through its pipeline to Lewis. Not bad going, after the frenzy at West Coast during the spring to have her ready for the tow northwards by May. And now, almost dawn twilight on 20 July, it was Jill's birthday — as usual, he was at sea, but she, too, had probably heard the midnight news.

'Bring her round to three-five-o,' he ordered down the voicepipe.

He watched her jackstaff cutting across the horizon as the little ship began to swing. It was unusually dark tonight, with no moon, but this was midsummer and the nights were short. *Kittiwake*, named after a World War II sloop, was the third vessel to be converted for this purpose — she was an ex-deep sea side-trawler with superb sea-keeping qualities. With a 3-inch gun mounted on her fo'c'sle head, she was more of a communications centre and morale booster for the rigs than anything else. She was too slow to be of any use on the east coast, but her white ensign lent authority to the proceedings should there be any disputes out here.

The BBC late news had been sober diet for the ship's company. The international situation had been as grim only during the Cuba emergency, when he was a boy. In some ways today's crisis was worse, because Russia had now caught up with the West, all along the line. She had stockpiled wheat last year, buying wherever she could — and why had she been so unusually co-operative at the disarmament conferences? Now, with the Arab Oil Consortium and the Palestine Liberation effort beating the drum, the Russian Black Sea fleet was being truculent the length and breadth of the Med.

It was heartening to know that, even under this neo-communist British government operating beneath a socialist banner, the people could still be irritated by threats. Parliament, with only the usual fellow-travellers dissenting, had declared a state of emergency and ordered the first step towards general mobilization — but, wondered Sheridan, as the first silver streak began to steal across the eastern sky, could the reserve fleet be manned in time? The Home Fleet was already on war station 'somewhere in the North Sea'. The Russian Baltic squadrons were rounding the North Cape and concentrating somewhere west of Altenfiord. The RAF were shadowing and had them taped, but at any moment there could be a catastrophic encounter with the Russian fighter escorts. Protection was beyond the Royal Marine commandos now. Every major unit of the Royal Navy was out there, disposed to prevent somehow the destruction of our vulnerable platforms — an impossible task, but at least the squadrons could concentrate in the most valuable fields: Forties and the cluster of fields around Brent. The situation would be explosive, if the two fleets met. The big gamble was whether the British Polaris would retaliate. The Fleet was ready, but the ball was in the politicians' court now.

The WT office was calling on the inter-phone: 'Main transmitter warmed up and operational, sir.'

'Very good.'

The captain (OPS) had given him only one order: 'Your job is to report the enemy,' he'd said. '"Alert West" is your enemy report. Press the radio tit first. Fire your cannon afterwards. That's all you have to do.' He'd smiled apologetically as Sheridan had left his office. 'You're on your own out there at Sulisker. Someone's got to be there, but I'm sorry you'll miss the fun.'

Toby Sheridan felt bitter about his billet. The whole of NATO was concentrating in the Channel approaches and the North Sea, but here he was, with his one piddling Bofors and two 20-mm — forgotten, buggered and bewildered, on his own to defend this deserted Sulisker complex.

The last three months had been hectic. West Coast had finished *Liberté* in time and she'd settled smack on *Explorer*'s site, in the most perfect weather, on 6 June, an auspicious day. The concrete platform was now pumping out half a million barrels a day through the pipelines to Lewis and the EWSB terminal. But all those hectic weeks had been overshadowed by the tragedy of Sheena Macgregor's disappearance.

It was almost six months now since the appalling fracas at the Errabeg. He and that diver friend of Alan's (O'Keefe, wasn't he?), had managed to hold off the unidentified attackers. Alan had been kicked in the balls and had passed out, but after the confusion had died down and the light fuses had been replaced, there had been no trace of the girl. She'd vanished and her kidnappers had never been found. Airports and docks had been covered throughout the islands, but only last week Alan had told him that the police had called off the search. Sheena was now officially listed as a 'missing person'.

Alan had been detailed to check on the first readings at *Sula* and had asked whether he could bum a lift in *Kittiwake* on her passage to Sulisker. Though the course for the terminal buoy was to the westward, Toby had guiltily agreed. So, when halfway across to *Sula*, *Kittiwake* ran across *Seamew*, on course for *Sula*, Toby had been relieved to transfer his passenger.

Toby had felt an intruder as he had watched the two men greeting each other, apparently unemotionally, on the wooden drifter's bridge. Prospective son-in-law and stunned father, both were desolated by the loss of Sheena. Jill had wept — unusual for her — when finally the police had given up. Though Toby and she had done all they could to comfort Alan, only through immersing himself in work had he managed to survive the tragedy. He had felt responsible because he had broken security. He had marooned himself in *Liberté*, devoting himself to ensuring that the platform made the operating window, almost as if Sheena's reappearance depended upon the project's success. Yesterday, silent and morose, Alan had seemed ten years older. His face was gaunt and grey, and a restless fire burned in his eyes.

Brodie had never talked much of his work. He had always been something of a mystery, but Toby had never forgotten the night that Alan had seen him off from *Liberté*, before the Errabeg incident. He had drunk too much whisky, and, for a moment, as they'd stood together by the lift, he'd suddenly turned towards Toby. He was obviously bottling something up inside himself and his grey face had been haggard with strain. 'If anything happens to me, Toby, get Sheena out of here — fast.' He had spoken quietly but urgently, and gripped Toby by his elbow. 'And ring this number — Captain Otway, MOD.

Understand? Give me your word?' But it was Sheena who was missing now.

On the passage yesterday with Alan, they had discussed the motive behind the Errabeg kidnapping. This was only the second time that Alan had hinted of the silent war being waged underground. Toby had sensed that Brodie was leaking the barest minimum in case of further accidents.

It was obvious that an execution squad had tried to eliminate Alan and Sheena. The couple were a source of potential danger because of their association with that poor fellow McIver whom Alan had found hanging. The attempt to kill Alan had failed, but what were they doing with Sheena — if she had not been murdered? Alan remained convinced she was still alive, and Toby remembered those tortured eyes yesterday, staring towards the horizon. Alan reckoned that the Errabeg attack had a second motive — to stir up again the hatred between the conservationists and the oil lobby. The village had barely settled down to bury their differences when those drunks and their tarts had savaged the Errabeg, the institution of which the village was quietly proud.

The enemy had almost succeeded, so incensed had Sheila Burns been at seeing the values to which she clung suddenly violated in public, and under her own roof; but she had heeded the warnings of the others not to play into the opposition's hands. Instead, the village had condemned the incident and, more intensely than before, had buckled-to in their joint desire to ensure that *Liberté* caught the window.

Donald Macgregor had played a large part in uniting the community again, Toby Sheridan realized as he moved across again to the radar screen. The luminous circle glowed in the darkness, the strobe sweeping across the face of the PPI. He was in short-range, now that the rig was closing fast. There was *Liberté*'s blip, edging down the bearing of his course-line.

The Macgregor father was a fine man, one of the rocks upon which the village depended now that the community had lost its minister. Iain, his son, was probably the most respected of Cul Mor's skippers, after the part he'd played off East Bank — a remarkable feat, that. The old man had said nothing, but he was obviously proud of his son's seamanship. Iain had sailed in *Dalrymple Navigator*, two days earlier, with a couple of geologists and a diving team under O'Keefe's charge.

Dalrymple's Loran and Decca fixing was vital for the accuracy needed in exploring this Sulisker Field. Now that *Liberté* was on stream so successfully, the quicker the rest of the field could be exploited — just as Shell and Esso had done at Brent and Cormorant — the better. Sulisker would be a mass of rigs soon, with all its pipelines leading to one focal point and pumping station.

'279° — bridge.'

'Bridge?' The voice belonged to their new RP2, just joined from Portsmouth.

'Echo bearing 279°, 13.5 miles.'

Sheridan switched to long-range — sure enough, a good contact. No land on that bearing.

'Track and report. It's *Dalrymple Navigator*.'

She was just where she should be. Nothing bloody well happening up here. He might as well fix himself a cup of cocoa while he made up the 02.00 log. Where would the watchkeeper keep the kettle? Log reading first, and then he'd concentrate on the cocoa. He glanced at the log and the barometer, checked the ship's head and completed the columns — 02.00, weather fine, vis. three miles — another hour and they'd see for miles.

He found the stuff for his cocoa at the after end of the bridge, in Bunt's locker. The kettle smelled foul and the cups were dirty.

'Bosun's mate,' he rapped down the wheelhouse voicepipe. 'On the bridge.'

'Aye, aye, sir.'

He handed the cups and kettle to the ordinary seaman. At that moment, the VHF crackled from the screen loudspeaker. He glanced at the clock: 02.21 — early yet for *Liberté* to be so awake.

'Ops 14, Ops 14… This is *Dalrymple Navigator*.'

'Loud and clear. Good morning, Iain.'

Macgregor sounded in a hurry. 'Ops 14. A container ship has passed me to the southward, steering about 110°. She's steaming every bit of 25 knots.'

Inward from Canada perhaps, and bound for the Baltic. More and more traffic was passing north-about, now that the Straits of Dover were so crowded.

'Thanks, Iain. Get her name?'

'No. Just thought you'd like to know.'

Macgregor sounded apologetic, as if he'd disturbed the peace of the night for nothing. All the Macgregors were on first-name terms now with *Kittiwake*, since Sheena's disappearance.

'Thanks, *Dalrymple*. No problem.'

'There's one thing bothering me.' The RT was silent for an instant.

'Carry on, Iain. Hear you loud and clear.'

The RT went mushy again, with too much background interference. Macgregor had reduced to low power, by the sound of him. He was speaking softly and was difficult to hear.

'She's going like hell,' he reported. 'She's darkened overall and she's carrying no lights.'

24

The Force Commander sat upright in his chair inside the control room on the upper bridge of *Eastern Star*. Faqus was watching his second-in-command, Kurt Haagen, checking his side arms and the Verey pistol strapped to his hip. Kurt could not be bettered. If things went wrong it would not be Haagen's fault, of that Faqus was certain.

'One minute to go, sir.'

'Very good.'

Faqus momentarily caught his second-in-command's eye. They'd trained long enough for this moment, D-day, 02.19, 20 July. The strike force was committed and the computerized plans were being followed to the second. *King Feisal* had passed her signal to report that she was safely past Eilean Trodday and was altering course for Rubh' Ré, on her final run-in up North Minch. The operation was proceeding without a hitch, the only incident being the irritating encounter a few minutes ago with that supply boat to the northward of Sulisker Bank. He had been right to leave the vessel alone. It was too early yet to disclose his hand.

'Ten seconds to go, sir.' Haagen was staring at the big second hand of the clock on the bulkhead. 'Zero.'

'Action stations,' Faqus ordered calmly. 'Range all aircraft. Man the assault craft.'

Haagen pressed the red knob and the alarm klaxons brayed throughout the ship. 'L' glanced at his wristwatch. The southern wing of VTOs should be on their way south in less than 90 seconds to concentrate with *Feisal*.

'Good fortune, Kurt.' Haagen saluted, his face set. He turned on the soft soles of his commando boots and moved swiftly below.

'Course 123°.'

The quartermaster's acknowledgement to the Action Officer of the Watch was as calm as if the ship was on routine training. '*Liberté* bearing 104°, range five miles.' The action plot was reporting every half minute now.

'Stop both engines.' The order was precise to the second, and the ship began immediately to lose way from her 32 knots, to give the handlers all the help they needed. Unlike a carrier, a VTO was embarrassed by wind along the deck.

'Echo bearing 132°, range three and a half miles, small ship, sir.'

'Investigate and hold.' The routine checks carried on, Captain Olsen as unflappable as ever.

Faqus cursed beneath his breath. These small craft could wreck the operation and shatter the deception plans. *Eastern Star* had officially been routed from Montreal and the St Lawrence, bound for Stockholm with general cargo, a passage which could explain a course north-of-west. So far, no one had asked questions, which was just as well with massive Russian forces deploying at this moment in the North Sea. He glanced again at the 01.00 intelligence report while he slipped the ear-protectors across his head. The roar of VTOs taking off for Target South drowned everything. The reflections from their blue and orange exhausts flickered weirdly across the deckhead of the control room.

The Russian deception plan was working better than anyone had hoped. The troop movements along the length of the Iron Curtain had certainly produced the expected American reaction. NATO ground troops were moving forwards to their battle areas. In the North Sea, the Soviet Arctic Fleet was at this minute surrounding the main concentration of oilfields. Faqus's Action Information Office had reported up-to-the-minute details of the Royal Navy's Home Fleet deploying to their war stations, from Harwich to the Faroes. The Russians were moving southwards and were west of Stavanger now, conveniently shadowed by three squadrons of Britain's latest missile destroyers and the strike squadrons of the RAF.

Even up to the last moment before sailing, Faqus had been the only man in the strike force to know with certainty the identification of the targets which they were to attack. The Arab nations enjoyed a long memory. They had never forgotten Isaac Kort, the previous chairman of International Oil, who had so publicly ridiculed the Sheiks' oil policy. Not only had Kort stood up to the threats, but he had openly declared, throughout the political halls of power, his support for Israel. Kort had been an unabashed leader around whom the enemies of the Arab alliance had swiftly rallied. So Faqus had not been surprised when the boss had pinpointed the objective for Operation Castor's attack. International's existence depended on its Sulisker gamble — and the Russians were solidly providing moral and physical support. One more heave and the economy of the Western World would collapse.

'Permission to deploy southern wing, sir?'

'Deploy.'

He watched the southern wing circling the ship, before it disappeared into the darkness of the southern horizon. Perfect — they'd rendezvous to the second with *Feisal*, who was at this moment reporting herself dead-on for track and distance.

'Echo bearing 132, range three miles, identified as small trawler, sir, type unknown.'

Another one? Annoying — could be an embarrassment. He glanced to the south-eastward and stiffened in his chair. A light was blinking on the horizon.

'What's he making, Yeoman?' While Faqus waited, his mind was working, weighing up the imponderables.

'Stand by Evocets,' he ordered. 'Captain, stand by to destroy the radar target, bearing 132°, range three miles.'

Faqus watched as the surface-to-surface batteries swung silently in their mountings, the missiles elevating until they locked on.

'Missiles on target, sir.'

'Challenge being repeated,' the Yeoman reported. '"What ship and where bound?", sir.'

Through his binoculars, Faqus could see the small ship now, a black smudge on the horizon. 'He can have the Evocets as his answer,' he said. 'Open fire, Captain.'

He heard the slight hiss, felt the barely perceptible shiver as the 12 missiles were launched, while *Eastern Star* lost way.

'Away assault boats and the helicopters, Captain. Fly off the northern wing. Stand by to attack.'

His binoculars held the darkened smudge. As he focused his right eyepiece on to the red and green side lights of the unfortunate vessel, the international broadcast loudspeaker was spluttering behind him.

'*Alert west... Alert west... Alert...*' an English voice was reporting in plain language. There was a flickering of fire along the length of the black outline. A blue-white flash of light soared momentarily across the south-eastern horizon. A sheet of flame leapt upwards, and the silhouette disappeared. He turned and moved out of the wings of the bridge There was a hang-up with No 1 LCI. One of the falls had jammed — yes, goddammit, it had to be Kurt's boat. He was having trouble with the girl, who was struggling to remain in the ship. He cursed softly. He'd been against Haagen's scheme from the start, but Kurt was an obstinate man and, after all, it was he who was leading the assault.

'Get a move on,' Faqus yelled from the wings. 'Shoot her if she won't go.'

Kurt was drawing his pistol when the falls suddenly freed — the Macgregor woman was bundled across the gunwales and into the LCI which was already disappearing from sight.

'All boats away.'

He absorbed the report floating downwind from the boat deck. It was as well *Liberté* was less than four miles off now, for a long trip in the LCIs always produced sea-sickness amongst the commandos … and the wind must be almost force six and increasing. He watched the arrowhead formations surging away from the ship, their bow-waves froths of white in the greying seas.

Up in the van were Haagen and his female guide. Faqus smiled to himself — the Macgregor girl had soon been tamed. When the squad had captured her, the boss was all for liquidation. But when Intelligence, successful as always, had persuaded her to talk, it was realized that her knowledge of the geography of *Liberté* would be invaluable. A model of the concrete platform had been fashioned so that every nook and cranny was now familiar to the demolition party. Sheena Macgregor was in the leading LCI now, and, until those few moments ago she had seemed, under those drugs, to be cooperative. Pity there wasn't more time — he'd have tried some persuasion of a different kind himself.

He picked up the Ops mike. 'All boats stay clear of the platform and lie off,' he ordered. 'Attack only when ordered.'

He laid down the RT. He'd sit back and watch the VTOs go in. There they were, just visible, concentrating at 900 feet. Hutch, the Yank, was a first-rate squadron commander. He suddenly put down his nose and began to dive. The other seven, following in staggered formation, streaked after him. Faqus could see the violet fire from their exhausts as they tore past. Hutch was pulling out at 300 feet, levelling off now: at less than 600 feet his cannons began to judder. Faqus could see the shells shattering as they hit their targets in the accommodation units — crimson spots of fire in the twilight.

'Stand by the FSD,' he ordered. 'Target, the concrete towers.'

He watched the broad barrels of the mortar batteries elevating beneath the starboard gunwales.

'On target.' The barrels were quivering in their mountings, counteracting the ship's motion.

'All aircraft clear of target area, sir,' the captain reported up to him.

'Engage with FSD.'

He heard the boom of the charges, and the noise of the projectiles whistling through the air. He watched the burning superstructure of the platform, flames licking along the paintwork of the derrick tower. Men were running for the lifeboats, like bewildered ants whose nest had been disturbed.

Raoul Ghio had not slept well. The weather was too muggy up here for him — give him the dry heat of the Mediterranean, any day. He turned on his side again to ease the sciatica in his right leg. He could hear the morning shift on the working deck — on stream now and producing more than expected. The clock by his bunk glowed two o'clock. Another few hours only. Sleep was elusive tonight.

He jerked to wakefulness again, roused by the strange electric blue light lingering across the deckhead of his cabin. He heard a distant succession of thuds — certainly not thunder or lightning, and he reluctantly sat up, trying to summon enough energy to pull on some warm clothing and see what was happening outside. He must have dozed off again, for he was woken by the loudspeaker above his head.

'*Liberté*, this is *Dalrymple Navigator*.' Iain Macgregor sounded worried — unusual for him. 'D'you hear me? I can't raise *Kittiwake* ... over.'

What the hell was he worrying about? The naval ship wasn't due until sunrise.

'*Liberté*, please raise *Kittiwake* for me ... over.'

Raoul spoke irritably into the mic. 'Okay, Iain — I'll call her. What's the trouble?'

'I can't understand...'

The sentence was never finished. As Raoul tried to catch the Scot's message, a deafening roar of aircraft began to drown all else — and from the westward, of all quarters. He threw down the mike, tore on his clothes and rushed on deck. A vessel lay stopped not far off, an ugly black container ship. She was darkened and showed no lights. *Merde! What the...?*

He hurled himself back into the control room next to his cabin. As the first cannon shell struck, he lunged at the emergency alarm push. He could hear the bells ringing down below, wrenching the lads from their quarters. His whole world was collapsing about him, as slivers of shattering glass spattered about the room. He felt the smack of exploding incendiaries, the punch of shells pumping into the framework of the exposed control room.

He hurled himself towards the companionway as the roof caved in above him, a blazing wreck of dripping polystyrene and twisted aluminium. What the hell was going on? Who was attacking *Liberté*? As he passed the open door of the burning radio room, he glimpsed Sparks calmly standing by the emergency transmitter, his clothes smouldering from the heat as he pumped out his Mayday.

'Get the hell out of it,' Raoul screamed at him. 'Abandon platform.'

He forced himself downwards, fighting against the growing heat. There was only one thought in his mind now — had the drilling string been severed? Had the automatic shutdown of the BOP been successful? Had the chokes closed in the bottom of the well? If there was a blow-out now, the sea would catch fire — and the wind was increasing from the north-westward. Someone stumbled against him, a man who had once had a face. His voice was familiar, that of the Danish chef, but he was unrecognizable as he tried to cover the remains of his battered head with fingers that ran with blood. Ghio tried to support him down the stairway, but a merciful bullet put an end to his agony. His knees crumpled and Raoul left the body there, at the foot of the ladder. He reached the head of the working deck as the last of the planes swung off into the darkness of the southern horizon. For a moment, the subsequent silence seemed as unreal as this shocking holocaust.

The bosun was getting No. 2 boat away while Harry, the tool pusher, was roaring at the gang on No. 1 boat. 'Get yourselves away, Dave, up to windward,' and, as he let go the brake, the automatic falls took charge and the boat slipped quietly from sight, down the vertical guides, on its descent to the seas surging 200 feet below.

'How many left?' Raoul shouted.

'Dunno — reckon about 20, sir.' Harry was slithering across the working deck to reach his boss. The wind was fanning the burning paintwork, but already the heat was decreasing.

'We've still got the inflatable, Harry.'

'Only one — the others are ripped to pieces.'

The one essential question remained now in their minds, as they supported each other across the hot plates and staggered along the derrick floor.

'You take the blow-out preventer, Harry,' Raoul gasped.

Ghio saw Harry beginning to wrestle with the valves as the first mortar salvos splayed upon the towers and the base of the derrick. Raoul felt the main structure juddering from the hail of solid shell striking the concrete towers far below. As Raoul threw himself flat, instinctively shielding himself behind the massive bulk of the draw-works engines, an explosion obliterated the derrick floor from his sight. He never knew how long the inferno lasted. He realized only that the barrage had finally ceased. Numbed by the suddenness of the attack, he dragged himself upright, his limbs trembling.

He glanced across at the shambles of what had once been the derrick tower. The latticework had folded, twisted beyond recognition, while the fire still raged furiously through the contorted steelwork. Its roar was now the only sound above the wind, as Raoul slowly picked his way towards the control panel for the blow-out preventer.

The derrick floor was a charnel house, the plates slippery with oil and blood. Of Harry there was no trace, save the flaps of glass fibre from his hard hat. The stench of burning human flesh was unbearable and Raoul staggered to the edge of the floor, hauled himself up to what was left of the handrails. He retched uncontrollably as he stared uncomprehendingly down to the working deck far below.

The towers were a mangled mass of pocked craters, the ferro sticking through like bones from a fish's carcass. On No. 3 tower, the whole width had severed about 80 feet below where he stood. How long could this gargantuan structure stand these abnormal stresses now? And as he slowly began to absorb the reality of the catastrophe, he saw three formations of small craft clustering like water beetles around the landing sponsons at the base of the towers.

Dark figures were swarming across the landing jetties and disappearing into the entry ports of Nos. 2 and 3 towers. Then, sometime later, he heard shouting behind him.

About 15 men in dark green uniforms were advancing towards him, automatic weapons in their hands. Their faces were blackened and they moved silently.

'We've been looking for you, Captain Ghio,' the leader said. He waved the barrel of his automatic at Raoul's chest. 'Get going.' He was roughly manhandled down the remains of the external ladder to the recreation deck below. About a dozen of *Liberté*'s men were drawn up in a line against the mess-room bulkhead. They were in a desperate state, some of them bleeding profusely, the shock of their ordeal showing in their listless eyes. He was shoved from behind and staggered against Ralph, the electronics engineer, who tried to prevent them both from falling. Raoul turned to face their executioners.

A squad of commando-type soldiers were mustered there, drawn up in a hollow square. Their commander was checking a diagram which an aide was holding before him.

'Girl, where is the main pumping room?'

The officer nodded and the pathetic figure of Sheena Macgregor was dragged forwards. She was white with exhaustion, bedraggled, listless and barely able to stand. Raoul would not have recognized her, even if she had not been dressed as the others. It was only her Scottish accent and the black hair escaping beneath that ridiculous baseball cap which identified her. She showed no sign of recognition as he called to her, frantically, '*Sheena!*'

A savage blow across his face from a pistol barrel sent him reeling backwards. He felt the blood in his mouth, and spat out broken teeth.

'Come here, Ghio.'

The English seemed strange from these foreigners, but he kept silent as they dragged him towards the officer.

'Take the others up to the top deck.'

As the prisoners were marched away, the leader approached Raoul and shoved his face close.

'You've got half an hour before the demolition charges blow. Where are the keys to the pump room and the flooding box? This bitch says she can't remember.' He swung the butt of his automatic across Sheena's chest. She cried out in pain.

'*Where are the keys?*'

Raoul bit his lips as the gun smashed against his cheek. He was condemned anyhow, so what did it matter what they did to him? Even if they tried to topple *Liberté*, the platform would run wild at any moment — with luck it would take these *salauds* with it.

'Okay, Ghio. You've asked for it. Take him and the girl down to the machinery space.'

As they were dragged out into the night, the cold wind whipped against his bleeding face, numbing the pain. Someone forced Sheena's wrist against his own. They were strapped together and then shoved down the crazy, toppling staircases. As they reached B deck, a signalman with a portable RT stepped forward and handed the transceiver to his officer. Raoul watched as the cruel mouth set. 'Understood, *Star*,' the leader snapped. 'Returning to base immediately.' He threw the instrument at the operator and turned to his squad. 'Bind the prisoners to the rail,' he ordered. 'Man the boats.' He waited for the last man to finish pinioning Raoul and Sheena to the steelwork of the sagging safety rails.

'Enjoy your last few minutes,' he said. 'If your RAF doesn't finish you off, the demolition charges certainly will. I'll tell your people that you're still alive and well here.'

Raoul heard him clattering down the stairway. He was laughing as he hustled below to the descent cages.

25

Skipper Iain Macgregor shouted across from the bearing repeater in the starboard wing of his bridge: 'One-three-eight — steer one-four-o, George.'

He hurried back into the wheelhouse, shouting over his shoulder, 'Sparks, get through on 2182. PAN-PAN-PAN, explosion one-three-two from my position.' He dipped his head into the radar's visor. 'Range 11 miles. Investigating.'

The throb of *Dalrymple*'s diesels working up to full power set up a vibration throughout her hull, but on her new course she was settling down nicely with the wind abeam.

'Call the lads.'

By the time both watches were on deck, morning twilight was well forward, and the eastern horizon was pale with the new dawn. To the south, the darkness was intensified by the cloud sweeping up from the south-west. He heard the sound of aircraft somewhere ahead and then, to his amazement, pinpoints of fire speckling the horizon on *Liberté*'s bearing. As he watched, a crimson glow billowed upwards, then spread outwards, orange and red along the horizon line.

'*Mayday — Mayday — Mayday — Platform Liberté, Platform Liberté...*' The voice trailed off, as a strange stuttering sound interrupted the background roar. What the hell was going on this morning? *Kittiwake* was not answering — and now something terrible was happening.

Stornoway came in: '*Liberté, Liberté, Liberté*, This is Stornoway Radio. What is the nature of your emergency?'

Iain listened for *Liberté*'s reply, but there was nothing, no answering call. He felt the back of his neck bristling as the cause of the disaster became only too clear.

'Give me 2182, Sparks. Stornoway Radio, this is *Dalrymple Navigator*, *Liberté* has been attacked and is burning.'

'*Dalrymple*, This is Stornoway Radio. Message received. Continue reporting. All services being alerted.' The operator hesitated, then came in again.

'The Navy's coming through direct, *Dalrymple*, Assistance is on the way. You may expect Nimrod aircraft.' The operator sounded flustered, the background clatter of a busy station being clearly audible.

'Roger. Anything else, Stornoway?'

'We've got an emergency here on our doorstep. Keep off the air. *Out*.'

Iain was surprised at the unusual tone of Stornoway's operators this morning. Normally they were an unemotional bunch.

'*Dalrymple*, out.'

Iain could see the top of the platform now, his eyes mesmerized by the dancing lights of the fires. It must be an inferno on board that structure — the poor sods.

'Stand by the inflatables.'

There was no need to check his position, now that *Liberté* was illuminating the horizon. As he moved out to the after verandah, he heard the roar of low-flying aircraft passing overhead, invisible, flying westwards.

He picked up his binoculars. He caught his breath as he sighted the huge platform — must be four miles off.

'Seen that ship, skip, broad on the starboard bow?'

He turned quickly, and noted the rows of lights along her decks — a big container ship, steaming fast, with starboard light showing brightly, about three miles off, well clear.

'Thanks, George.' He turned back towards *Liberté*. As he watched, he saw three red flares lobbing in a parabola, before floating gently downwards.

'Parachute flares.'

He nipped to the radar and picked up the two small echoes … ten degrees to the northward of *Liberté*'s bearing.

'Bring her round to port, to 096°, George. Someone's in trouble over there.'

Alan Brodie thought that his world was disintegrating, as he was thrown from the bunk in the visitor's cabin always available in *Sula*. His first reaction, as he grabbed the lifejacket hanging in the cupboard, was that the terminal buoy was exploding. He did not bother to get dressed but tore down the corridor, which collapsed about him as he aimed for the emergency escape door. He felt a blast of heat and fell flat, tripped over by a man lying across the plates. He regained his feet and stood for an interminable moment to find his bearings, to think. As he stood there he heard the rustling and licking of flames. Then, all about him and very close, the shriek of jet aircraft swooping across the crane's jib-head. At that instant, the tanker which had been fuelling since 23.00 caught fire as the floating pipelines burned. In seconds, she was a volcano of flame. Great gobs of orange, purple and crimson flared upwards in the black smoke billowing in the night which was now as bright as day. And as he watched, the fo'c'sle head of the second tanker, going astern as she turned, swung away to starboard. Only minutes before she had slipped her head-ropes, her loading completed.

'Abandon *Sula* — take to the boats.'

From somewhere he heard John Tregonnel's voice. After leaving *Explorer* Tregonnel had become the boss of what, seconds ago, had been his proud terminal buoy. Alan rushed down the outside stairway to catch the lifeboats already sliding from sight. He hesitated, and turned back to the other side… Far below he could see the orange shapes of two inflatables, one capsized, with men in the water struggling to right it; the other, milling around in circles, was picking up those who could hold on to its rope hand-holds…

'For Christ's sake, jump.'

Tregonnel was standing on the outboard side of the safety handrail. In one hand he held his lifejacket. With the other, he held on to the top rail. Strips of glutinous molten polystyrene dripped from the melting roof above them.

'*Jump, Alan!*'

He watched Tregonnel thrust with his legs against the rail. The man plummeted down, tumbling head first before hitting the water 80 feet below. Alan hesitated, looking for some other way of escape; he dashed round to the other side, against the spin of the buoy, into the wind.

A darkened vessel was standing off, less than two miles distant. A V-shaped flotilla of small black boats could just be seen receding into the darkness towards the waiting ship … and, as he watched, a succession of flashes flickered horizontally from somewhere amidships.

The roar of the flames was drowning all else. The paintwork of the melting steelwork had caught fire and the heat and smoke were billowing upwards in suffocating clouds. The boats to leeward were being overtaken by the blazing oil which was creeping upwind. At any second this monstrous oil drum on which he stood, waiting to be fried alive, would explode like a pressure kettle as the heat from the steel plates descended towards the level of the crude. He forced himself over the windward side of the circumference and watched the black surface spinning slowly beneath him. He loosened the upper toggles of his lifejacket — he could break his neck otherwise. He shut his eyes and jumped.

The Force Commander stood in the starboard wing of *Eastern Star*, the extension of the RT mike trailing on the deck behind him. He was watching the last of Kurt's flotilla hooking on to the automatic falls — too slow — he wanted to be off now, for the success of the attack had been beyond belief. He glanced across at the fire flickering at the base of the wrecked concrete platform, one tower of which was completely fractured. The whole outfit would erupt in eight minutes — if it wasn't wrecked by a blow-out before then. Even so, there'd be pollution from the exploration wells, if the divers had succeeded in blowing the pipelines.

'Command — Akbar. Command — Akbar.'

'Come in, Akbar.' Faqus had been waiting with growing anxiety for *Feisal*'s action report. Her captain had never been a loquacious type.

'Mission successfully completed. It was unnecessary to bombard and all boats have been recovered. Southern installation destroyed and one tanker sinking. Sea on fire. Am retiring in execution of previous orders.'

'Interrogative pipelines?' Faqus rapped.

'All divers recovered. Pipelines severed and oil escaping under full pressure.'

'Roger. Your ETA for rendezvous?'

'As planned. *Out.*'

Good. *Feisal* would be under way now. She was right to quit, her objective successfully achieved. Operation Castor would be 100 per cent wrapped up, as soon as *Star* and *Feisal* had joined.

Third World was waiting south of Iceland — *Star* should be off now, fully illuminated, once she'd rounded the Butt and was out of sight of land.

'Boats clear of the water, sir. All choppers recovered.'

'Proceed to rendezvous, Captain,' he called over his shoulder.

'Full speed.'

He heard the ting-ting of the order instrument. He felt suddenly exhausted as the tension eased. He watched the inferno blazing across the surface of the sea as the wind fanned around the remains of the concrete structure. He felt supremely confident now — both the VTO wings had homed successfully on *Third World* and the northern wing would be landing shortly on her spacious flight deck. Once she had recovered both VTO squadrons she would steam at full speed towards *Star* and *Feisal*. Within five hours the final transfer of landing craft and the bulk of the commando would be completed. *Star* and *Feisal* would then deviate, sailing independently on their legitimate seafaring business — *Feisal* was bound for Havana, *Star* for Montevideo. He'd fly back by civil airline as an ordinary passenger to Rome and from there to HQ for his report to the boss... He felt the wind increasing across the lip of the bridge as *Star* worked up to full power.

He glanced back at his handiwork for the last time. The charge would be activating in minutes. He saw a couple of red flares off to the northward and the lights of a small ship, dim in the twilight. He did not even bother to raise his binoculars — *Star* was on her way now, racing for safety before the enemy had time to retaliate. The damage that Isaac Kort had wreaked upon the Arab world had now certainly been avenged.

'Illuminate the ship,' he barked from where he stood. 'Switch on navigation lights.'

'Chopper Rescue — this is Stornoway Lifeguard.'

'Pass your message — *over*.'

'There's nothing you can do for *Sula*. Proceed to *Liberté* — *over*.'

'Roger, *out*.'

Pilot Officer James Kent had already sighted the orange glow on the northern horizon. The Butt was well astern now, while below him the white horses broke lazily in the half-light of approaching dawn. The wind had backed to the north-west and it was blowing hard.

'Stand by for a descent to the platform,' he yelled across to his sergeant. 'There's a man and a woman on one of the decks.'

Eight minutes later, the Sea King B for Bravo was hovering over the smouldering *Liberté*, close upwind of the trail of smoke and flames licking to leeward in the three-quarter gale blowing. He edged nearer, taking the chopper down as far as he dared. He nodded as Sergeant Ross suddenly pointed through the opened door.

'Down you go.'

He watched his instruments, lined up on the silhouette of a twisted crane-jib. Ross was spiralling now, but then he reached the deck. The wire suddenly slackened. This was a damn sight easier than cliff rescue — not so much down-draught.

Ross was taking his time, struggling on the rail with something. The wire tautened as a limp body slumped on the hook. The sergeant was signalling and then the winch motor whined as the ACI hove in. Seconds later, Ross was scrambling through the door, unhooking and hauling a semi-conscious girl across the lip.

'The platform is going up any minute,' Ross yelled. 'The guy down there says he can hook on by himself.'

Pilot Officer Kent snatched more height, the better to judge the descent of the recovery wire. The big man was gazing up at them, hands outstretched for the hook, almost in supplication. He was reeling on his feet and trying to follow the swinging wire. Suddenly there was a gush of violet and purple flame, a blinding flash, and the whole platform disappeared in a holocaust of fire and smoke.

Pilot Officer Kent wrestled with B for Bravo, which was bucking from the blast. He pulled her clear, upwind, away from the horror. No man could survive that inferno.

'Stornoway Lifeguard. Chopper Bravo.'

As he waited for the shore station, he glanced once more over his shoulder to the silver-streaked ocean now greying with twilight. Behind him the sea was ablaze, the flames flickering like fireflies as the oil spread to the south-eastward in an ever-widening stream.

26

One of the Nimrods sighted the raft first. Listening on 2182, Donald Macgregor had picked up the position towards which he was now steaming at full speed — dead-ahead and in transit with that fiery torch less than two miles off. He could hear the RAF personnel reporting to Stornoway, as they made their reconnaissance.

'Angus, be ready for anything,' the middle-aged skipper told his brother-in-law. 'Reckon we can help.'

He had never, in all his years at sea, been through such a night — and from what he'd heard on VHF, neither had his son Iain, who was trying to cope at Sulisker.

'There they are, skip.'

Angus was leaning through the other window of the pillar-box wheelhouse and pointing across the drifter's starboard bow. 'A couple of points to port, Donald.' The older man pulled his cloth cap firmly down on his forehead. It was cold and the old girl was rolling her guts out in this beam sea. He called down the midship hatch to the other two. It wouldn't be long before *Seamew* would be on the edge of that blazing oil. The sea was afire across the north-eastern horizon and, in the centre of the flames, a tanker was burning. Angus knew that he could not prevent Donald from trying to help — but in this wooden drifter, what could they do? Thank God his brother-in-law was a capable seaman and a sensible man.

The chill of the flying spray brought Brodie back to consciousness — aided by the cold and the bumping of the inflatable, as Tregonnel opened up the throttle of the outboard. There were five others in the rubber lifeboat. They were all silent as they made up to windward, trying to escape the sea of fire spreading across the oily waters and creeping up to windward, even against the tidal stream. John Tregonnel sighted the drifter first and it was his mini-flare that brought the old boat round, rolling in the seas, to pluck them from the water.

'Ye'll soon be warmed up, Alan.'

Brodie was too shocked even to smile, as friendly hands guided him down to the warmth of the saloon. They stripped the frozen survivors and wrapped them in thick woollen blankets. Alan felt his strength returning as the hot tea coursed down his gullet. His legs stopped trembling and his mind began to work once more.

'All of ye that can, give us a hand on deck.'

The sodden clothes around the coal-burning stove were at least warm, as the survivors flung them on again before scrambling up top — the wetness was rapidly forgotten as the drifter yawed down-sea towards the fiery lake. Donald was taking *Seamew* up to windward of the blazing hulk of what had been one of International's 70,000-tonners. Of the *Sula* terminal there was no sign.

Donald Macgregor saw them first, the cluster of men huddled by the after rail on the tanker's poop deck. They seemed safe for the moment, but the fire had spread almost the length of the ship — the tanker had swung away to leeward and her stern was slowly creeping up to windward. She was now surrounded by a sea of fire, the southern edge of which was less than two cables from her square transom rearing 80 feet above the blazing sea.

They dared not jump, Donald realized instinctively. This was the classic horror of the wartime tanker crews. The swimming survivors would dive below the surface of the water, but, forced to come up for air, would be suffocated by the lack of oxygen, which was being consumed by the fire.

The men were frenziedly signalling towards a couple of glass fibre craft, the lifeboats from the other tanker who was now lying prudently clear, several miles to the northward. The ugly orange boats dared not edge closer. The heat was almost intolerable even for *Seamew*, who was a strongly-built wooden hull, well insulated, her crew high above the surface — but even now the paint along her gunwales was beginning to blister. Donald could smell the varnish from the scorched sides of his wheelhouse.

Only 300 yards — less than two cables, to pass under that transom. The poor buggers were hopping from one foot to the other as the plates became red-hot beneath their feet. A few more minutes and they'd be roasted alive.

'Angus, get the hose going — play it on our wheelhouse.'

He spun the wheel in his hands and sheered *Seamew* towards the two orange lifeboats. From the corner of his eyes he saw his own survivors sheltering behind the wheelhouse from the heat. He heard the splashing water beat upon the windows.

'Ditch the diesel drums.' No need for the reserve fuel now — safer overboard.

He wrenched open the leeward door of his wheelhouse and shouted to the hands: 'We're on fire, port side. Jump as I pass close to those lifeboats.'

The stupefaction on their disbelieving faces made him angry. He spun over the wheel and swung *Seamew*'s starboard quarter within yards of the first lifeboat.

'Jump, ye silly buggers — jump.'

He glimpsed the figures leaping from *Seamew*'s gunwales — all gone, thank God — now he had no responsibilities other than himself and his *Seamew*. He pulled her round, steadied on the tanker's stern, and wound up the revs to full. The old girl was rocking beneath him as her massive Gardner trundled up to full power. He shipped the strop over the midship spoke for a second, nipped outside and adjusted the pulsing hose to smother the deckhead of his wheelhouse. He jumped inside again. The leeward door was opening and Alan Brodie was pushing through it.

'Get a line ready,' Donald shouted angrily, as Alan began wrapping sodden blankets about them both. 'Forget the bloody heat.'

The boat was juddering, pitching into the swell that lunged beneath the tanker's stern — the oil was calming the surface, so at least no waves were breaking. He could hear nothing but the crackling of the flames licking along the drifter's timbers as she forced her way onwards. Half a cable now — no second chance if he bungled this. Too fast and he'd overshoot. Too slow and *Seamew* would burn up before she reached safety.

He peered upwards through the window, which he'd slammed shut. The survivors in the tanker were dangling bights of ropes from the rail — already the first men were slithering downwards. He slammed the throttle to stop, paused, and pushed the lever to astern. *Seamew* shuddered and lost way as he manoeuvred her plunging stern beneath that huge, cut-away transom.

'*Jump, for Christ's sake!*'

He heard Alan shouting where he huddled in the shelter of *Seamew*'s high bulwarks, those sturdy planks he'd fitted so long ago. Men tumbled from above, collapsing where they fell on to the planks of *Seamew*'s fo'c'sle.

'*Jump!*'

A man was looking down at them, paralysed with fear. Donald heard the crackling of the flames as *Seamew*'s port side suddenly erupted into flames. He staggered from the blast of heat and felt the searing pain of his scorched face. *Full ahead —* that poor sod could only blame himself — mustn't lose the ship and the others for the sake of one man.

He felt sick as his head began to swim. He shook it, trying to clear his mind. Slowly he turned the wheel away, away from this inferno. And where were the others, those who'd jumped?

He tried to sight those lifeboats as he swung *Seamew* away to starboard ... blind, useless in this scalding, choking smoke. He could not breathe, his lungs scorched by the blistering heat. A mist swam before his eyes, fiery and whirling crimson — a terrible pain stabbed his chest. He cried out and Alan, one hand on the wheel, caught him as he fell.

27

Captain Otway glanced across the expanse of the operations room deep below ground at the Combined Services' Headquarters. He had been summoned out here by his director, and they were sitting side by side at the back of the tiers of seats among the rest of the staff who had been working in watches since this emergency had started.

Since the balloon went up the previous week, when the first signs of the Russian movements into the North Sea were confirmed, the senior staff had been brought to stand-by notice. Otway had been sleeping in the Old Admiralty Building and this morning he had not been surprised at being shaken at 02.25. He had been driven out in a staff car to find that the Director of Naval Intelligence was already waiting for him. 'Chief of Staff wants us here,' DNI had said. 'The First Sea Lord may want briefing on the Sulisker background.'

Otway was always overawed by the silent efficiency of Britain's Defence HQ, the nation's nerve centre which controlled defence and retaliatory capability. Events moved with such rapidity these days, that Britain's ability to defend ourselves and to hit back had to be centralized in as few hands as possible.

Today, the complete Defence Council was present, the Secretary of State for Defence, the Right Honourable Ronald Pugh, MP, heading the team. He sat in the centre of the amphitheatre facing the vast map on the illuminated wall of this underground hall.

This year it was the turn of the Army to provide the Chief of the Defence Staff. Field Marshall Sir Philip Lumby, GCB,

DSO, filled this exacting appointment. A large, thoughtful man, he was sitting on the right of the Minister for Defence. On either side of these key figures were disposed the political heads of the three services, the Secretaries of State, each with his own service chief alongside him. Admiral Sir William Bowes, GCB, DSC, Chief of the Naval Staff and First Sea Lord; General Sir Ranelagh Crabbe, GCB, DSO, Chief of the General Staff; and Air Chief Marshal Sir Peter Beresford, GCB, DFC, Chief of the Air Staff.

On either side of this semi-circular hall were grouped the staffs of each service. All the desks in the hall faced the massive illuminated map which extended the length of the wall facing them. The whole of the northern hemisphere, with Britain in the centre, was presented in clear geographical projection.

As Otway glanced across at these men, he recognized once again that the respective services had not produced their chiefs by accident. They were men of exceptional calibre and depth, and, in particular, 'Bill' Bowes. Fortunately for Britain at this moment, he was respected and liked by his two opposite numbers in the Army and Royal Air Force. Too often in peacetime, inter-service jealousies for the available cash clouded judgement and performance. Bowes was a slightly built man, almost inconspicuous in a crowd, but he was blessed with an acute intelligence, well able to cope with the Treasury and the party politicians, thank God...

'Nimrod Charlie's report coming in, sir.'

General Crabbe, Chief of the General Staff, leaned towards his chief, the Field Marshal, as the teletape message began streaming across the display unit on the left hand wall of the room. At the same instant, a green light began blinking on the wall map in a position to the north-west of the Butt of Lewis.

Nimrod Charlie, position 355 Butt of Lewis 15.4 miles, SITREP follows: ONE. Platform Liberté *badly damaged and ablaze. No sign of life. Wind north-west, force seven, sea on fire. Supply boat* Dalrymple Navigator *has picked up survivors. TWO. Have investigated SULA buoy area: terminal buoy destroyed, sea on fire, one tanker, laden, burning out, another escaping in ballast, to the northward and safe. THREE. Drifter* Seamew *has taken off several survivors from burning tanker believed to be International's* Pamir Barque. *FOUR. SULA is priority one disaster area because spill is drifting to leeward towards Sutherland and Wester Ross...*

Otway surreptitiously glanced round at his brother officers. There was no sound in the spacious hall save the Duty Wren Officer working busily about the plot, as she supervised the movements and the positions of the ships and aircraft when they were automatically altered by the computer. Everyone, from the Chief of the Defence Staff downwards, felt sickened by the results of this attack upon the defenceless ships and structures so far distant in those wild waters. The services, for all their modern technology, had been powerless to prevent this slaughter — men on the ground, boats in the water, planes in the sky were what counted in the final analysis...

The Nimrod's report was still flickering across the screen:

FIVE. Am carrying out square-search to north-westward and westward of present position. Dalrymple Navigator *reported darkened ship in vicinity of* Liberté *platform, but only ship in sight is fully illuminated and steaming opposite course 290 to westwards. Two other vessels on radar, 224, 23 miles, 258, 37 miles from my position. Will investigate and report. Stranraer reports one container ship northward bound from North Minch, but intend to ignore her while carrying out search to westward. SIX. Long distance radar indicates one other ship to north-west, 320 miles, steering 120 from south-east Iceland. SEVEN. No trace of Offshore Patrol Ship* Kittiwake. Dalrymple Navigator *reports she witnessed Ops sinking by missile fire from unknown source. EIGHT. On completion of search, will remain in area until further instructions are received. TOO 0301. Message ends.*

'How long since *Kittiwake*'s "Alert West"?' the First Sea Lord asked. The question was matter-of-fact, but there was steel behind the calm exterior. Bowes could be an acid little man when he needed to be ... then woe betide anyone who crossed him. His Staffie, a burly Rear-Admiral, was glancing at the log of events arrayed on a panel to their right: '48 minutes, sir. It will soon be twilight up there.'

'When will that oil reach the coastline?' asked Field Marshal Sir Philip Lumby, the Defence Chief. 'Ranelagh will let you have some of his reserves to clear up the filth, Bill, if you need help.'

'Thank you, sir. I wish I had enough ships to contain the spills. What's the pollution situation?' The First Sea Lord turned again towards his naval staff.

A young commander stood up. 'First reports indicate, sir, that the wells were successfully storm-choked 9,000 feet down by *Liberté*'s operators, before the platform was partially destroyed.'

'Needed guts to stay behind and close down the wells,' murmured the General.

'And being shot at while the whole outfit blazed around them,' the keen-faced Air Marshal added. 'Ghio and his men were a gallant lot... Sorry, Bill: didn't mean to interrupt.' The Air Chief glanced apologetically at the commander for him to continue.

'Oil from the *Liberté* platform seems to be escaping from its damaged storage legs and from the pipeline, which somehow has been fractured. The one helicopter which managed to lift off the only survivor, a woman, reported that there were several seepage points along the pipeline to Lewis.'

'Any chance of containing this spillage?' the Defence Chief asked briskly. Sir Philip was in a hurry.

'Certainly, sir, if we could get enough ships and tugs out there in time. We could burn up the oil before it reaches the coastline. The remedy is the same for the *Sula* EWSB, sir, where things are much worse. If that lot gets ashore, it'll be a disaster for the Summer Isles area. Detergents will harm the marine and wild life more than the oil pollution.'

Otway closed his eyes for a moment, trying to recall his memories of that beautiful stretch of country. He had flown up there following the Sulisker disaster, as he had wanted to see for himself, after listening to Brodie's impassioned pleas. The petroleum engineer had been right. This final onslaught bore the stamp of a well-planned military operation.

In DNI's opinion, there was little doubt now who were the perpetrators of this appalling affair: that ACLA organization had openly boasted that one day it would avenge the harm done to the Palestinian cause by the one-time chairman of International Oil. ACLA had certainly kept its word. In addition to vengeance, it had dealt a blow for the cause of Arabian oil at the same time … and how the Russians must be laughing! The West's energy drive would be slowed up for years by this interference with the Sulisker field — but the commander had not yet finished.

'In the *Sula* area, sir, we reckon over 50,000 tons of oil has escaped. Our fire-fighting tugs are concentrated on the east coast where the bulk supplies of detergents are stocked.'

The commander was pointing out the threatened areas along the coastline: his illuminated trace was slowly picking out the fishing villages and the sea lochs which were in imminent danger: Summer Isles, Enard, Eddrachillis — and the 'V' trace was now opposite Loch Innoch, the entrance to Innochervie itself. 'If the wind continues from this quarter, sir, it seems impossible for these areas to escape.'

'Thank you, Commander,' Admiral Bowes said quietly. In the ensuing silence, Otway realized that every bay, inlet and rock pool, every loch on the west coast, was almost certain to be smothered by the slimy, black oil creeping towards them. If the fleet had not been concentrated in the North Sea to deal with the Russian confrontation, things would have been different. The oil could have been contained at sea: surrounded, burned up and dispersed before the incomparable coastline of Wester Ross and Sutherland were fouled.

Oilmen said that detergents did more damage to marine life than if the oil were to disperse naturally. In time, they stated, the thick globules of bituminous material would break down and disappear through natural causes. But every family knew the frustration and the misery caused by the black filth on the rocks and on the sands — let alone the destruction of the flora that graced the lovely coast. And what of the bird life and the fish?

Otway realized cynically that there were more important priorities in life — and two of them were the defence of the United Kingdom and the halting of the forces of evil trying to destroy the nation. Though Sulisker and *Liberté* were just outside the 12-mile territorial limit, *Sula* was unquestionably within our sovereignty. Otway looked up as a grey-faced Wren officer, worn out by exhaustion, approached with a telephone extension.

'Call for you, Captain Otway,' she murmured. 'From Innochervie. A Lieutenant Brodie, he said he was. Insists upon talking to you only, sir,' she added apologetically.

'Thanks. Put him through.' Otway could hardly recognize the weary voice as Brodie's.

'What is it, Brodie? I'm pushed at the moment.'

'Thought a direct report might help, sir. I was on board *Sula* when we were destroyed.'

'Did you see who attacked you? Air or surface?'

'We sighted a darkened ship. She was lying off and looked like a modern container ship.'

'Size?'

'Large — about 80,000, I'd say. She was showing no lights, but I thought I saw assault craft in the water. Can't be sure, because we were being gunned the whole time by low-flying aircraft and from the ship herself. Bloody awful, sir. We hadn't a chance.'

'What about the tanker, Brodie? Think carefully. Was she fired on or did she explode from the effects of the burning terminal buoy and the blazing oil?'

'Not certain — but I think the planes shot her up. All her crew would have been fried alive if it had not been for *Seamew*, the oldest supply boat up here.'

'Haven't much time, Brodie. Get on with it.'

'Skipper Macgregor took his wooden drifter under the blazing tanker's stern, sir. He picked off her survivors, but the drifter caught fire herself. Macgregor died at the wheel. I was lucky to be with him and to bring her home. The curious thing was, sir, that, as I cleared the area, I sighted a ship steaming fast to the northward. I'm sure she had the same silhouette as the ship who attacked us — a big container job. But the

245

strange thing was…' Otway waited for the line to clear and Brodie was still there.

'She was fully illuminated — the length of her decks.'

Otway held the phone in his hand, his mind racing. He could see those ships now in his imagination, standing off, concealed by their mantle of darkness and secrecy while they blasted innocent men to eternity.

'Brodie — the woman the chopper lifted from *Liberté* — who was she?'

'The girl who was abducted from Innochervie, sir, months ago.'

'Is she all right?'

'Yes, thank God. Sheena Macgregor, my girl.'

'I'm glad. Anything else, Brodie? No? Thanks for your report. I'll be getting in touch.' Otway put down the phone and for an instant reflected upon what he had just learned. He was relieved for Brodie — those two had gone through hell together. Meanwhile, the situation in the North Sea was developing and the Air Chief had asked for the short range display.

The wall map had merged for an instant while the Duty Controller operated the push for the large scale display. The whole of the British Isles and the Norwegian coast, round North Cape to Novaya Zemlya, drifted into focus. The enemy seemed close now, with those red pinpoints glowing where they indicated the positions of his units — submarines, aircraft carrier, cruisers, missile destroyers and fast patrol boats. The quick flashing red lights represented those enemy units with nuclear capability. They made a formidable array, as they slowly converged on the Brent and Cormorant fields. How sparse and thin the blue lights seemed in comparison…

The First Sea Lord was holding his main strike in reserve — some two hundred miles to the north west of the Faroes. Until he knew clearly the Russian intentions, he was not to be drawn. Without a carrier he was hamstrung — every second counted now. The RAF were doing their best, but what *could* they do with no mobile seaborne base from which to operate? Otway leaned across to his Director and spoke quietly of the conversation he had held with Brodie. DNI rose from his desk and walked across the floor to the First Sea Lord's desk.

Otway watched the drama unfolding before his eyes. The complete operational staff paused in what they were doing, waiting to know which way their chief would turn. The Chief of the Defence Staff and his three service chiefs rose from their seats to join him in front of the wall display. They stood for some time conferring together. The Defence Chief then walked across to the Minister of Defence. 'May I talk personally to the Prime Minister, sir?' he asked.

Otway watched as the red light glowed on the PM's direct line. Churchill's ghost was never far absent here, but if Winnie had been around, he would have been sleeping here all night in his siren suit… Ronald Pugh picked up the instrument.

'Sorry to disturb you, PM. We're reaching a showdown here. I think you should speak with the Chief of the Defence Staff.'

The Field Marshal was as polite as a soldier could be, but Otway could sense the steel and the strength of will beneath that calm exterior. He could discern, too, the tension between fighting man and politician: one straightforward, the other, opportunity-seeking, devious, nervous of making a false move — what the hell could this Prime Minister know of these split-hair moments of decision? The man had never in his life picked up a rifle in defence of his country.

'I'm pretty certain we've located the attacking force, sir. Two unidentified ships somewhere north-west of Ireland.'

There was a long pause. 'No, sir, I'm not absolutely sure. We would have to board and search the vessels. Now that we've lost our radar complex in Iceland, we can't cover the whole area... No, sir, I cannot...'

Another long silence, punctuated by several 'buts' and 'yes, but...' from the Field Marshal. Finally, holding the telephone firmly in his hand and speaking directly into the mouthpiece, the Chief of the Defence Staff said briskly: 'You know very well, Prime Minister, why we haven't enough ships. The Navy cannot board a ship without sending sailors across in a boat. If a vessel resists arrest in peacetime, the Navy can use only force to carry out a search.' There was another pause and then Sir Philip said shortly: 'I am responsible to the Sovereign and you, sir. I shall do as I think best for the security of the realm.' He replaced the receiver, turned round and spoke briefly with his three brother officers. They nodded in agreement, then stood back to once again study the map in front of them.

'Peter,' Bill Bowes asked the Air Chief, 'can you spare me two Nimrods to sweep that area north-west of Sulisker?'

The Chief of the Air Staff paused to glance once more at his Air State board. He shook his head. 'It may seem ridiculous, Bill, but I have to ask whether your request includes Nimrod Charlie which is up there already? I just haven't the aircraft. I daren't disperse my reconnaissance coverage any further.' Otway remembered the bitter disputes that raged in the House last winter when, for the third year running, this government had sliced the service estimates. The country was about to pay dearly for this lunacy.

The First Sea Lord smiled ruefully: 'Thank you, Peter. Two Nimrods, please, including Charlie.'

'You can have my last reserve, then.' The two men glanced at each other and Otway could see the resignation on their faces. Even with such a small operational demand as was presenting itself off Sulisker, there were no reserves. Every unit of the Royal Navy was committed to confronting the Russian threat in the North Sea, which was why Britain was forced to pull out of the Mediterranean when it was most needed by NATO and its Western allies…

'Peter,' the First Lord said crisply, 'please despatch the second Nimrod to intercept, interrogate and identify the two ships approaching the north-west of Ireland from the Atlantic. Ask him to report immediately if either ship darkens when she is challenged. I'd like the second Nimrod, Charlie, to carry out a sweep with the same objective on the other two ships steaming westwards from the Butt. If either ship darkens, I must know at once. There's another forty minutes of darkness yet.' He turned again to the wall map.

'If any ship darkens, Peter, the Nimrod is to order her to heave-to until C-in-C Fleet's detached unit arrives from the Faroes area. Whom could the C-in-C spare, Staffie, assuming the situation off Brent deteriorates no further?' The Admiral was thinking out loud, but his Chief of Staff was a jump ahead.

'Would you release either of the two VTO cruisers, sir?'

'No, I need them. The enemy may move closer yet.'

'What about *Fife*, sir? She's on stand-by and the furthest of our destroyers to the westward.'

'How long has she been in State Two?'

'Eight hours, sir.'

'Luckier than most. Suggest to C-in-C, Fleet, that he uses *Fife*. She is to proceed with utmost despatch to the westwards on an interception course with Nimrod Charlie's contact. At least she'll be steaming in the right direction, though she'll take a while to overhaul. Ask C-in-C to send a frigate with her.' He suddenly clapped his fist into the palm of his other hand. 'My God, I know now how Nelson must have felt — always short of frigates. If I had just one carrier...' Otway saw the face harden, the lips compress bitterly.

The First Sea Lord turned to his staff. 'Gentlemen,' he snapped. 'If those two ships steaming to the westward from Sulisker carry out the wartime operation of darkening, they are to be treated as warships. They are to be ordered to heave-to. If they refuse, they are to be disabled or slowed down until *Fife* intercepts. If they then resist our boarding parties, the ships are to be taken by force. If resistance is such that we risk serious casualties, the ships are to be sunk without further orders.'

He turned to his Defence Chief.

'May I proceed, sir?'

The Field Marshal was still scrutinizing the display. He stood rock-like, his hands behind his back.

'Permission granted, Bill,' he said quietly, without turning round. 'For once, the lion's tail is to be twisted no longer. The attacks on *Liberté* and *Sula* have been premeditated and therefore are an act of war, let alone piracy on the high seas. The perpetrators of this attack must take the consequences.' As he glanced at the Minister of Defence for approval, the Air Chief spoke up.

'What if the ships carry on upon their lawful occasions and do NOT darken?'

The Defence Chief remained in thought for a full half minute. He turned slowly to address the Minister of Defence and his subordinate ministers, who so far had remained remarkably silent. 'If these ships are allowed to escape, gentlemen, we shall have to accept defeat. That is the cost of weakness.'

He paused momentarily as he met Pugh's eye. The Defence Chief began walking back to his desk, when the signal monitor started to flicker. The yellow letters streamed across the screen:

MOST IMMEDIATE Enemy Report Nimrod Charlie position 312 Butt of Lewis 32 miles reference container ship in my SITREP TOO 0301 her course now 328 speed 29 knots have interrogated but no reply She immediately turned into the wind and reduced speed while evolution of clearing upper deck took place appears to be ranging one VTO type aircraft on deck she darkened ship with naval precision when I made initial approach Have her on radar and am shadowing TOO 0322 ends.

There was an unseemly buzz about the hall. The implication contained in the Nimrod's report was obvious to every member of the Defence Council and every officer working on the staffs.

The Field Marshal addressed his political chief. 'Request permission,' he asked, 'to stop and arrest these ships?'

The Chairman of the Defence Council shifted uneasily in his chair. 'Permission granted,' he said brusquely. 'Top priority — for Nimrod Charlie's sake.'

The Defence Chief nodded at the First Sea Lord. 'Carry on please, Bill.'

Admiral Sir William Bowes stuffed his hands deep into the pockets of his reefer jacket. Facing his burly Chief of Staff, he spoke distinctly, without hesitation, 'Make the following to

Commander-in-Chief, Fleet: "The two container ships referred to in my previous signal are to be treated as enemy warships. They are to be stopped and searched. If they resist arrest, they are to be sunk.'"

The short silence that followed was broken by the Field Marshal. He was addressing the Minister of Defence. 'You should implement Alert State Purple, sir. The Russians won't like this a bit.'

The two men on whom the country's safety depended, and perhaps that of the world, smiled briefly at each other.

For the first time in many years, the nation was not divided.

A NOTE TO THE READER

Dear Reader,

If you have enjoyed the novel enough to leave a review on **Amazon** and **Goodreads**, then we would be truly grateful.

Sapere Books is an exciting new publisher of brilliant fiction and popular history.

To find out more about our latest releases and our monthly bargain books visit our website:
saperebooks.com

Printed in Great Britain
by Amazon